Penguin Books

• This Freedom •

P9-CCC-681

John Morrison was born in 1904 at Sunderland, England, and migrated to Australia in 1923, earning his living as a bush worker before marrying and settling in Melbourne in 1928. He spent the rest of his working days there as a gardener, with a break of ten years as a wharfie.

His short stories, most of which first appeared in the journals *Meanjin* and *Overland*, made up the collections *Sailors Belong Ships* (1947), *Black Cargo* (1955), *Twenty-Three* (1962: awarded a gold medal by the Australian Literature Society), *Selected Stories* (1972), *Australian By Choice* (1973), *North Wind* (Penguin, 1982) and *Stories of the Waterfront* (Penguin, 1984). His work has been published in ten languages, including Russian, Chinese and Italian, and many of his stories have featured in anthologies.

The award of Commonwealth Literary Fund Fellowships in 1947 and 1949 enabled Morrison to write his two novels *The Creeping City* and *Port of Call*. He now holds an Emeritus Fellowship granted by the Australia Council.

John Morrison

•This Freedom•

Penguin Books

Penguin Books Australia Ltd,
487 Maroondah Highway, P.O. Box 257
Ringwood, Victoria 3134, Australia
Penguin Books Ltd,
Harmondsworth, Middlesex, England
Penguin Books,
40 West 23rd Street, New York, N.Y. 10010, U.S.A.
Penguin Books Canada Ltd,
2801 John Street, Markham, Ontario, Canada L3R 1B4
Penguin Books (N.Z.) Ltd,
182-190 Wairau Road, Auckland 10, New Zealand

First published by Penguin Books Australia, 1985

Typeset in Galliard by Dovatype, South Melbourne
Made and printed in Australia by
The Dominion Press-Hedges & Bell

CIP

Morrison, John, 1904-
This Freedom.

ISBN 0 14 008633 1.

I. Title.
A823'.3

· Contents ·

• Sources of stories •

'The Busting of Rory O'Mahony', *Black Cargo* 1955

'Sailors Belong Ships', *Bulletin*, collected in *Sailors Belong Ships* 1947

'The Children', *Meanjin*, collected in *Selected Stories* 1972

'Lena', *Meanjin*, collected in *Black Cargo* 1955

'The Blind Man's Story', *Overland*, collected in *Australian By Choice* 1973

'Man in the Night', *Black Cargo* 1955

'Christ, the Devil and the Lunatic', *Sailors Belong Ships* 1947 and *Selected Stories* 1972

'The Ticket', *Overland*, collected in *Twenty-three* 1962

'This Freedom', *Meanjin*, collected in *Selected Stories* 1972

'The Man on the 'Bidgee', *Meanjin*, collected in *Twenty-three* 1962

'Black Night in Collingwood', *Bulletin*, collected in *Twenty-three* 1962

'The Fugitive', *Meanjin*, collected in *Black Cargo* 1955

'It Opens Your Eyes', *Meanjin*, collected in *Selected Stories* 1972

'Bushfire', *Overland*, collected in *Coast-to-Coast* 1965

'The Prophet of Pandaloop', *Sailors Belong Ships* 1947 and *Selected Stories* 1972

'Appointment at Princess Gate', the *Sun* (Melbourne)

· The Busting of Rory O'Mahony ·

'Rory' O'Mahony on three hundred and sixty-four days a year; 'Michael Eugene' O'Mahony on the three hundred and sixty-fifth. And he let you know it. On that one day every year he was in just the right humour to let you know it. Don't ever boast you know any particular Irishman until you've seen him on Saint Patrick's day — even a colonial Irishman. O'Mahony was no blue-eyed son of Erin. He told me himself he was born in the Baw Baw ranges of Victoria, 'where the kids are so wild they got to be yarded and roped at bedtime.' I didn't doubt that either.

However, but for his lack of brogue, and the universal accident of birthplace, O'Mahony was an Irishman. He was at some pains to stress the fact when, on the first Saint Patrick's day of our acquaintanceship, I was indiscreet enough to question it. He glowered, holding up two clenched and bony fists. It looked so much a fighting gesture that I backed away, but was reassured as one grubby finger after another disengaged itself and popped up as representative of some light of the Baw Baws O'Mahonys.

'Me father was Daniel Michael O'Mahony. Me mother was born Kathleen Mary McGinty. And there's me brothers Timothy, Desmond, Patrick, and Doolan. And me sisters Kate, Maureen, and Sheila.' In the stunned silence which followed this in-fighting I received the knock-out: 'And if that ain't enough, then let me tell yer me mother's mother was Bridget O'Donnell before ever she seen the colour of Jimmy McGinty's whiskers!'

I'm not likely ever to forget that seventeenth of March.

'And for the love of Heaven see you don't call him Rory when he comes in,' said Mrs O'Mahony.

1

It was about six o'clock in the evening, and she and I — and Maureen, the fifteen-year-old daughter, last of the offspring still at home — were seated in the kitchen awaiting the homecoming of the head of the house. Rory Michael Eugene had been away since mid-morning.

I looked at my landlady in enquiry.

'He'll be Michael Eugene tonight,' she supplemented, 'and don't you forget it.'

'Michael Eugene O'Mahony,' I murmured appreciatively. 'There's music in it!'

She nodded grimly. 'Yes, and he'll set it to music before the night's out. You'll have it all to yourself if you're staying in.'

'Then you're going out, Mrs O'Mahony?'

'I always go out Saint Patrick's night. I'm taking Maureen to the pictures.'

She put such determination and significance into her voice that I wondered if it would not be as well to go out myself, after all.

She must have guessed my thoughts, for she added hastily: 'No violence, mind you, Mr Johnston. He just talks; maybe a song or two.' Her lips curled sardonically. 'He's not really a marrying man, and he lets the whole world know it every Saint Patrick's day.'

Maureen had put down her book and was regarding me with an impish smile. 'He'll tell you what he's going to do to Mr Neville when he gets the rest of his family safely up. That's me.'

Mr Neville was O'Mahony's employer. It is amusing, and perhaps not without significance, that the wild child of the Baw Baws was engaged in what is generally considered the most peaceful of all occupations — gardening.

Mrs O'Mahony was knitting. She pouted, and her needles began to click a little faster. 'As soon as Maureen is able to look after herself he's going to give Mr Neville a punch on the nose and go sundowning for the rest of his life. He's been telling me that every Saint Patrick's day for fifteen years.'

I smiled incredulously. 'A rosy future, Mrs O'Mahony!'

It was a relief to see her honest face break into a smile also, for if there is one thing I detest it is being made the confidant of people's intimate domestic affairs. Moreover, I'd been lodging with the family for some months, and liked them all so well that the mere hint of discord gave me a little pang.

Maureen went up to her room to change. Mrs O'Mahony, after a glance at the clock, asked me if I would like her to serve dinner. I told her I preferred to wait until the family circle was complete.

'I don't take no notice of him now,' she resumed indulgently. 'He's a good man, only he gets notions like the rest of us. I used to worry about him once, because he knocked about a lot before he was married and it took him a long time to settle down. Every time we had a bit of a tiff he used to threaten to go back to the bush or off to sea again. But it never came to nothing. Now he only breaks out once a year, and I just lets it go in one ear and out the other. He knows where he's well off.'

In justice, no less than courtesy, I nodded approval of the last statement, for Mrs O'Mahony certainly ran a model home. At the same time I was beginning to suspect the existence of impulses a little beyond her comprehension.

'So he's been to sea, Mrs O'Mahony?' I suggested encouragingly.

'H'm, the quickest way for Rory to tell you where he *has* been is to tell you where he *hasn't* been! Ask him that tonight and you'll be in bed all the quicker. Some day he's going to bust — like that,' she flung out her arms in an explosive gesture, 'and start the good old days all over again. He doesn't seem to realize he's getting up in years. Imagine him going on the wallaby at his time of life, and after what he's been accustomed to.'

'The fighting Irish!' I chuckled.

Mrs O'Mahony's needles clicked, the clock ticked, on the stove the pots bubbled and hissed. It was all very prosaic and peaceful. In my imagination, though, the absent Rory was gradually taking on colours and tones. It was amusing trying to reconcile the smouldering spirit of Mrs O'Mahony's description with the drab and humdrum creature I'd seen coming home at five-thirty every evening, washing, changing into slippers and clean clothes, bowing over the serviette tucked under his chin while Maureen said grace, then sitting quietly at the fireside reading his newspaper until it was time to go to bed. For that, indeed, was the O'Mahony I knew. I had visions now of a stocky bow-legged figure groping an erratic homeward course along the darkening streets, and felt that tonight for once there would be an element of drama in his arrival.

Mrs O'Mahony also was still thinking of him. 'I sometimes believe he would be happier if we could get to the country to live,' she said wistfully. 'I always had a bit of a hankering after it too, but where there's kids to consider you've got to stay where your bread and butter happens to be. Maybe we'll be able to manage it when Maureen gets away.'

I was aware that three sons and a daughter had already left home; Des and Jim in search of the big wages on the Queensland canefields, Joe married and farming somewhere in the Mallee, and Kathleen, also married, and living at Nar-nar-goon.

Just as Mrs O'Mahony finished speaking the wanderer returned. Looking back on it now, I recall his arrival as one of the little thrills of my life. O'Mahony had gone out a dwarf; he came home a giant. Not in physical dimensions, for he was barely five foot eight inches high. It was all in his bearing, in the forward thrust of his scowling face, the brace of his shoulders, the belligerent flash of his dark eyes. He stood for a moment steadying himself with one hand on the door-jamb, and there was something of the eagle in the glance with which he swept the room.

Yes, I was thrilled. I hadn't believed that a few whiskies and a saint's day could so transform any man. Even his moustache was different. It was of the drooping variety, and, ordinarily, added a final artistic touch to one of the sourest faces I have ever seen, a face in which every line was turned downwards. Tonight, however, the moustache was still in noble harmony with the transfigured features. Rory, or some other with a nice sense of the appropriate, had given the points an oiled and villainous twist. He looked like a Mexican bandit.

'How are you, Rory?' I sang out, forgetting Mrs O'Mahony's warning.

'My name's Eugene — Michael Eugene O'Mahony!' he bellowed, and lurched into the room.

Mrs O'Mahony rose to serve dinner, giving me a rich grin

as she passed. She couldn't but have been gratified at such swift and complete vindication.

'Well, and where did you get to?' she enquired breezily as she returned to the table with a big pot of stew.

'Where did I get to?' His voice, usually a morose mutter, had the resonant clang of a bell. It shook the room. He flung his head backwards so suddenly that his hat fell off. 'I've been with that grand old bugger, Patsy Whelan!'

We dined. Mrs O'Mahony, Rory, Maureen and myself. Afterwards mother and daughter went out, and I was left alone with Michael Eugene. He had two bottles of whisky and a pocketful of cigars that looked as if they had been steeped in molasses. He put them all on the table a minute after the front door banged behind his departing family.

'Good riddance!' he grunted, flinging a mallee root on to a fire which was already giving off an intolerable heat. 'Pull your chair up, Jim. I got a drink for you.'

He certainly had. I've always prided myself on an ability to carry whisky, but in the company of Michael Eugene O'Mahony I was a novice. Heaven only knows what he had already swallowed that day. The impressive fact is that he was half drunk when we started on those two bottles, and still only half drunk when I was dizzily squinting at his wavering and distorted image across the fireplace. It is by drinks that I can fix the successive stages in his indictment. He wasn't long getting down to tin-tacks, my first drink being offered with the scurrilous comment: 'Real Johnny Walker that, the only decent thing that ever come out o' Scotland.'

'Good luck, Rory,' I said.

'Good luck.' Wiping his mouth on his sleeve, he dropped into a chair and bit the end off a cigar as if he were taking a bite off a sandwich. 'Funny how blokes like them can make such good whisky,' he bawled. 'Have a cigar?'

I lit one, finding it not nearly as dangerous as it looked.

O'Mahony reached his grievance in three jumps: whisky to Scotland, Scotland to his wife, his wife to married life in general.

'The wife's half Scotch,' he said with infinite contempt. 'You can tell it by the look of her. She's a Gilmour — laced straight up the back, buttoned in front, and tied at the neck. Stiff as a corpse. I know them.'

'She's a toiler, Rory.'

'Toiler be damned! Who said we was to toil? I was born a free man. Me old man couldn't tame me with a stockwhip. I'm Irish — she's Scotch. She likes toil — I don't. She — look here, I want to tell you something. Wait —'

I waited while he poured the second whisky.

'Good luck, Rory.'

'Good luck. Now listen to me — I'm a nice, quiet, homely family man, ain't I?'

'Better ask me that tomorrow, mate!'

He glared. 'Now, fair dinkum, I'm talking sense. Have you ever seen me shicker?'

'Not until tonight!'

'Do I back horses?'

'No.'

'Do I run after other women?'

'Not that I know of —'

'I chop the wood for the missus?'

'You do.'

'I mow the lawn of a Sunday morning?'

'You do.'

'And oil the locks when they squeak?'

'You do.'

'And put the cat and the billy out every night before I go to bed?'

'You do.'

His expression was satanic.

'Then I'm what you'd call a good family man, ain't I?'

'On the strength of all that, Rory, you are.'

'And I got a model wife, ain't I?'

'She's a good one.'

'Ye — es.' He used a whole breath on the one word. 'A model wife. Makes me bed, darns me socks, cooks me dinner, cuts me lunches, washes me shirts, lays out me wages. Ye — es, a great — little — woman. I ought to know it. I been told often enough. I ought to be happy. I got everything I want, eh? Look at it!' He flung out his arms in a gesture that embraced the entire room. 'A nice shiny fireside, a cosy chair, me slippers warmed up, me dinner all ready to sit down to. Every bloody night for twenty-six bloody years!' He groaned, and flopped backwards. 'Twenty-six years, and I hardly ever set foot outside of Melbourne!'

I understood, of course, but wasn't supposed to.

'What's the trouble, Rory?'

'Trouble? — I got no troubles. Ain't I just told you? I got everything a man wants — except a bit of freedom.'

I nodded patiently, and waited.

'They're so blasted stupid,' he said despondently.

'Who?'

'Women, of course. Who else? They got no dash, no go, no fireworks, no —,' he waved his hands, shook his head, and gave up in disgust. 'I dunno, there's something about them that gets me down. Something stiff — they bog a man down like treacle. They don't see nothing, they don't want to see nothing. By cripes, it was a great idea to make a man stick to one woman. They knew what they was doing, the blokes that made them laws. They fixed us good and proper. Where would capitalism be today if it wasn't for the marriage laws? No wonder they talk to us about the sanctity of home life! They get you all nicely tied up to a woman and kids, then they go to work on us. No more telling the boss to go to hell. No more bunging a job in at a minute's notice and walking off with a billy can and a roll of blankets, as independent as Tyson. Where d'you think I'd have been these last twenty-six years if it hadn't been for the wife and kids?'

'Where wouldn't you have been!'

He pointed a horny forefinger at me. 'If I'd have been a single man I'd have given Neville a kick in the teeth the very first morning I worked for him.'

'I've heard he's no chop, Rory.'

'No chop? — he's a bastard. And I've toiled for him twenty years. I've let him wipe his dirty feet on me for twenty years. And why? — because of a wife and kids. I'd only been with him two days when he up and asks me how many kids I had. I told him I was expecting the third any time. And d'you know what he told me? "H'm," he says, "you'll have to take care of your billet." Just like that. Get the idea? Me weights was up. He was getting me by the nose-ring. I had to be a good boy, and work hard, and not give any backchat, or I wouldn't be able to feed me kids. I took it, too. I suppose he knew he'd got a bloke with a sense of duty.'

O'Mahony rose, spitting out a curse that made me shudder. His arms swept upwards, his voice was a roar. 'But some day I'll bust! The lid'll blow right off — like that! I got it all bottled up. Just let me get this last kid off me hands — he'll see then. He'll find out what he's been monkeying with all these years. I'll call it a day then, b'the living God I will!'

He poured the third drink.

'Good luck, Rory.'

'Good luck — and to hell with Neville!' He sat down again. 'Twenty-six years in one house and twenty years in one job — and I used to boast the job wasn't made that could hold me down six months!'

Draining my glass, I stretched my feet lazily towards the fire. I'd had a lot of experience of drunks, and I knew my work — drink, smoke, and be agreeable. In the following hour or two half the world rolled in magnificent panorama past my gradually fuddling senses. Half-canned though he was, O'Mahony was easy to listen to. He seemed to have been everywhere, tried his hand at every calling. Beginning his rambling narrative in Victoria, in the wild Baw Baws, he carried me with him in a succession of entertaining anecdotes north to the Riverina, to Sydney, to the gulf country of Queensland. With the fifth whisky we were bore-sinking out from Cloncurry, then overlanding cattle to Adelaide, thence train-jumping to Port Augusta and across the Nullarbor to Kalgoorlie. Six months in the gold-mines was followed by a hectic venture into pearl fishing up on the tropical north-west coast. Then, by deep waters, and in the stokehold of a tramp, to South America. I lorded it as a foreman stevedore in Valparaiso, smuggled rifles for both sides in a Bolivian revolution, hunted rubber up the Amazon, shot a petty government official at Manaos, and shipped to Europe out of Pernambuco with the police of two countries hard on my heels. Liverpool — South Africa — the Rand — diamonds — Kaffirs. I myself have travelled little, but O'Mahony, skin-full of whisky though he was, made me see and feel and hear. Sitting against the table, with one hand hovering in magical gesture over the faded green cloth, he called up more wonders and beauties and thrills than I had ever dreamed of.

Now and then, in the least colourful moments, I fell to musing on the man himself, on Mrs O'Mahony, and on the grim humour of the gods who had united them. Above all I marvelled at the fellow's extraordinary discipline, at the immense self-control and sense of duty which had kept his nose faithfully to the domestic grindstone all these long years. And at the same time I pitied him. I kept thinking: you're too late, Rory, my boy, too late! All this is your youth, and it's gone, gone forever! You're nearing sixty, and you can kick and splutter and fume as much as you like, but it's Melbourne and Neville and Mrs O'Mahony for you now to the very end of your days.

I did not, of course, say anything like this. No good purpose would have been served. O'Mahony was the victim of a fixed idea; once during the evening he crystallized it in words that made my blood tingle.

'Look, you,' he yelled, 'you know Dandenong Road?'

'I know it, Rory.'

'Well, that's the Princes Highway. It runs just through there, a few streets away. D'you know how far that road goes?'

'I've covered it to Bairnsdale.'

'Bairnsdale!' He snorted with infinite contempt. 'That's just the first short leg. You could go on from there right up the east coast of Australia, starting at Caulfield. There's a sign there what says: "Two thousand six hundred and fourteen miles to Cairns." Two thousand six hundred and fourteen miles — get your teeth into that! Jim, I've stood looking at that sign till me bloody eyes nearly dropped out. And Murrumbeena's as far as I've been along that road in twenty years.' He paused, and added with vicious finality, 'Some day I'll get on it and just keep sticking one foot in front of the other till I drop. Let's have a drink.'

He opened the second bottle.

'Good luck, Rory.'

'Good luck, Jim.'

So the night wore away. I got pretty drunk, and the last thing I remember is Rory suddenly leaning forward and shouting 'Pop — pop — pop —' at me at the top of his voice. I got it

out of him next morning that he was trying to tell me something about Popocatapetl, a mountain in Mexico, but as I can't
pronounce the name when I'm sober I could hardly expect
O'Mahony to pronounce it in drink.

I lived with him for two years after that. Two quiet years, the
only purple patches being the two Saint Patrick days. On one
I went out with Rory, saw the procession, and finished up with
a hilarious night at the home of 'that grand old bugger' Patsy
Whelan. On the other I had to go and bail Rory out of the city
watchhouse, where he'd been lodged on a charge of being
drunk and disorderly. This latter adventure struck me as rather
shocking in a man who could remain strictly sober for three
hundred and sixty-four days every year, but Mrs O'Mahony was
quite unmoved. The annual spree had long ago become part
of the domestic routine.

'He'll be all right now until next Saint Patrick's day,' she
assured me complacently the morning afterwards. She seemed
to find it quite easy to condone this kicking-over-the-traces
once a year. 'It's not like as if he did it every Friday night, like
some of them.' He was a good husband — and she was a good
wife. Her imagination just couldn't reach beyond creature
comforts. 'There's not many men looked after as well as he is.
He's never gone out with a hole in his socks since the day he
was married. He's never had to wait a minute for his dinner
of a night. And he's never known what it is to have a bill pushed
into the letter-box that he didn't know all about.'

She had my sympathy, for she really was a splendid manager.
The simple fact was that she had married the wrong man and
hadn't realized it yet, even after twenty-six years. The position
interested me, for after that first Saint Patrick's day it was
impossible to underestimate the depth of his grievance. Listening to Mrs O'Mahony I reflected: my good woman, you're sitting on a live bomb, and one of these days it will go off —
whoof!

Saint's days apart, it was amazing how the man could hide
his terrific yearnings. Mrs O'Mahony was above all things a
creature of routine, and she it was who dominated the entire
household. In all the time I lived there I don't remember her
once having to call Rory to order. Through the years he also
had fallen a victim to drilled habits. Every evening he arrived

home at precisely five-thirty. Every evening he laid his lunch-bag on the cover of the sewing-machine, hung his hat and jacket behind the kitchen door, and went into the bathroom to change and wash. Every Monday, Tuesday, and Wednesday night he read the newspaper sitting in the same chair, fell asleep, and was awakened by Mrs O'Mahony at nine-thirty for a cup of coffee. Every Thursday night he took the family to the pictures. Every Friday night he went shopping with his wife. Every Saturday afternoon he went to a cricket or football match, and every Saturday evening to a men's club for a game of billiards. Every Sunday morning he tidied up the garden, chopped wood, and mended boots. Every Sunday afternoon he went to bed, and every Sunday evening he either had visitors or went visiting. Mrs O'Mahony herself had no outside interests beyond Sunday morning church and the meetings of a mothers' club every Tuesday night. Many men would, I suppose, envy O'Mahony, but the fixed scowl on his face, the sly glances of exasperation I often caught him flashing at his wife, and his general air of depressed boredom, showed me full well in what a stifled little hell he was living.

I remember an occasion on which secret longings bubbled up rather pathetically. It was in my third year there, and shortly after the departure of Maureen into domestic service at Toorak. We were sitting on the back verandah one mild spring evening, Mrs O'Mahony, Rory, and myself. The first-named was contentedly knitting, while Rory and I watched the clean black silhouette of the Dandenong Ranges some twenty-five miles away. We'd been chatting desultorily about the previous Saturday afternoon's football and had gradually fallen silent. I wasn't thinking of the hills, my gaze having come to rest on them merely because they happened to be straight before me. Not so with Rory. Glancing at him, I observed in his eyes the wistful and hungry intensity of a starving man watching a feast spread out beyond his reach.

'We'll get rain soon, Rory,' I observed.

He started. 'What?'

'I said we'll get rain soon.'

'Because the hills look near?' He nodded gloomily. 'Yes, it ain't a bad sign. We used to say something the same up there.

We could pick out trees and houses at Westernport just before a change.'

'You lived up there, then?'

'I've lived everywhere,' he replied brusquely, and spat.

'What were you doing?'

'Woodcutting mostly. Possums on the side. There was money about then. I had some of the best times of my life in them ranges.'

Mrs O'Mahony began to roll up her knitting. 'Cheer up, Rory, me boy. We might be able to get out of Melbourne now we've only got ourselves to think of.'

'We might!' he muttered. He knew she didn't mean it.

She went into the house, apparently quite unconscious of the scorn with which his last words had been invested. Rory and I remained, sitting in silence while the distant hills lost themselves in the darkening sky. Now and then one of us would slap his face or ankles where a mosquito was biting, but there was one time when I thought my companion seemed to be *wiping* his face. Immediately afterwards he sniffed, and I wondered if the wild child of the Baw Baws had actually shed a tear.

It was out of those same hills that, only a few weeks later, relief came to him at last. He was a few minutes late arriving home one night, and, encountering him in the doorway, I knew on the instant that he had been drinking. He smelled of whisky, and the light of Saint Patrick's day was in his eyes. Mrs O'Mahony, noticing none of these things, merely remarked that he was a bit late.

'I been talking to the boss,' he informed her with quiet deliberation. 'I got a bit of news for you after I'm washed.'

She looked at him hopefully, but without another word he put bag, hat, and jacket where he put them every night and went through to the bathroom. Not until we were seated at dinner did he re-open the subject. I knew before he spoke that the news was good, for I'd never seen him so calmly cheerful.

'I got a new job,' he announced suddenly.

'What?' ejaculated Mrs O'Mahony.

'I got a new job. How'd you like to go bush?'

'Where, Rory? What happened?'

He waved his fork irritably. 'Where? — why? — whaffor? Can't you say yes or no? We've always talked about going bush, ain't we?'

I thought this rather unfair, but realized that we were dealing tonight with Michael Eugene.

'You've got a job in the bush, Rory?' I interposed pacifically.

'Neville's bought a week-end house in the Dandenongs and wants me to go up and look after it. I grabbed at it.' He cast a threatening stare at his wife. 'We got to move up in two weeks.'

Mrs O'Mahony's face had become a study in shocked dismay. I doubt if she had ever, despite all her talk, seriously anticipated anything like this. Nearly all their married life had been passed in one house and one job. The impending upheaval must have assumed for her the dimensions of an earthquake.

'In two weeks?' she murmured.

'In two weeks.' He pushed his plate over to her for a second helping; even his appetite was improved. 'I've got to go up for a week on me own first to get things in order. He says the place is as rough as bags.'

'When are you going?'

'Monday morning. He's going to run me up in the car to show me round. I'll be there for a week, then I come back for a week, then we both go up — bag and baggage.'

'But —'

'You don't seem too pleased about it?'

'You needn't get snotty about it, Rory. You haven't told me anything yet. Where is it? What money are you going to get? What sort of a house will we have? I suppose there's no gas or electric light —'

Very deliberately he laid down his knife and fork and cleared his mouth. Heaven only knows what he would have said had I not rushed to the rescue. Mrs O'Mahony hadn't yet grasped that this was a special edition of the Saint Patrick's day Michael Eugene.

'Whereabouts in the ranges is it, Rory?' I asked.

'Up on One Tree Hill, not far out of Ferny Creek.'

'Then there should be electricity. The line goes right through to Olinda now. What's the pay?'

'Same as I'm getting now, less ten bob for the house. All me milk, vegetables, eggs and firewood thrown in. Anything wrong with that?'

'It sounds good if the house is all right.'

'Well, I ain't seen it yet, but according to Neville it ain't been up ten years. Four rooms and a kind of laundry place with a bath in it. God's truth, the two of us don't want no more than that.'

These details had some effect on Mrs O'Mahony. No doubt she'd been visualizing a shack in the primeval forest. She asked me what kind of a township Ferny Creek was, and I told her — a good general store, a greengrocer and a butcher. She sighed.

'I suppose them's the main things,' she said philosophically.

'What more d'you want?' demanded Rory. 'You can have a day's shopping in town whenever you like. It's only ten bob return by service car.'

She began to smile, but I suspected it was more to please Rory than because she was pleased herself. I caught her throwing a stealthy and apprehensive glance around the comfortable room, and couldn't help feeling sorry for her. No doubt, in her earthy woman's way, she was already suffering the pangs of amputation, the dragging out of furniture, the tearing up of linoleums, the taking down of all the ancient family portraits, the uprooting of cherished bulbs and herbs from the pocket handkerchief of a back garden. Admittedly it was a fearsome prospect for a woman of her type and age. She tried to put a brave face on it, but it was plain to me that the whole thing simply awed her.

'I suppose you're satisfied now?' she remarked to Rory with a watery smile.

'Satisfied?' His grin stretched from ear to ear. 'I could have kissed the lousy old bastard when he told me. I got a little drink to christen it with as soon as the missus goes out, Jim.'

It was Tuesday night, and when Mrs O'Mahony had left for her meeting Rory and I went out and lay on the back lawn. There was only a small bottle of whisky, enough to mellow our humour of pleasant contentment. Darkness had fallen, but I observed that Rory deliberately composed himself so that his face was turned towards the invisible hills.

I was thinking of an old Jewish saying 'If you can't get what you like, like what you've got.' I had a doubt, but it would have been beyond Rory's comprehension, so I merely remarked, 'Well, you won't need to bust now, mate!'

He chuckled. 'No, I'll see it off now, Jim. We'll be all right up there, the old woman and me. Neville'll only be up at weekends and holidays. The wife don't have to do anything. It's a big house he's got, but he says he'll fetch maids with him when he comes. He'll have a lot less to be fussy about, too. He says he wants a nice wild bush garden.' Another chuckle. 'By the living Harry, I'll give him a wild bush garden!'

We had a drink, and lay peacefully smoking and yarning. By and by he got round to telling me what the ranges were like when he lived in them thirty years ago.

'No guest houses and weekend joints then. Only a few acres here and there settled at all — berry farming and woodcutting. Everything rough as bags. They had the best poker school up at Sassafras I ever played in. We used to go at it every night and all day Sundays. Plenty booze, too. Down at the Gully, mind, but you could get it any time day or night. I've seen us run short and ride down to finish up at the pub at three in the morning.'

When, heaving a tremendous sigh, he wondered if any of the old-timers were left, I hoped for Mrs O'Mahony's sake that there weren't.

Monday morning came, with Mrs O'Mahony thoroughly downcast. This was to be the first time in all their married life that they had been separated. Rory radiated the joyous irresponsibility of a schoolboy setting out on holidays. Given his own way he would have gone off quite cheerfully in his workaday clothes, with a change of shirt and trousers wrapped up in a newspaper and tucked under his arm. As it was he sat down to breakfast in his best suit, and with a well-packed kit bag all ready to carry out. More than once in the past few days I'd wondered if he was worth it all. I understood, and sympathized with, his secret yearnings, but there was something to be said for the woman also. She was so smoothly and dependably efficient. And so pathetically devoted.

A belated realization of this must have come to Rory also during that last meal, for he was considerably more civil than usual. Once he even clapped her on the bottom as she passed him.

'Cheer up, old girl! It's only for a week.'

It was the first time I'd ever heard him address her that way, and she smiled down on him with a very real affection.

'You're perky enough about it, anyway!'

'Too right I am. You wait till I get you up there. You got no idea what a lousy hole Melbourne is till you get out of it.'

He went on in this strain all through breakfast, telling us how fine it would be to wake up of a morning and hear magpies singing, to step straight off the verandah on to his job, to smell burning gumleaves again, and to hear cowbells and the screeching of black cockatoos in the forest.

'We'll have our own cow and chooks. That'll be a job for you, mum — feeding the chooks. I'll make a fair dinkum woop woop out of you in no time.'

I'd been anticipating Monday morning with some uneasiness, but everything passed off smoothly. Rory's seriousness over the adventure pleased and relieved me, for I'd had a suspicion that this might be the long-promised 'bust' in disguise. There was no doubt that he really did think he was on the threshold of a new life, and in the half hour at breakfast managed to impart a little of his enthusiasm to his wife. I shook hands with him in the kitchen, wished him good luck, and watched the two of them go down the passage with their arms round each other's waists. It was all rather touching, and I hoped from the bottom of my heart that Neville and the gods would treat them kindly. I recollect that Mrs O'Mahony turned into the bedroom before coming through to the kitchen. Her face was flushed and I knew she had been weeping.

All through the following week I made it my business to fortify her against the coming dissolution by praising the absent Rory and pointing out the advantages of rural over urban life. She'd never lived outside of Melbourne and had but the haziest ideas of what life was like in the bush. She imagined that no water was laid on to the houses, that all tank water was 'crawling with vermin', that the women did their cooking in open fireplaces, that scorpions and ants and tarantulas swarmed like flies, and that bushfires were an everyday hazard.

Having myself lived for many years in Kallista I was well

equipped to describe precisely what she might expect. I told her that the only things she was likely to miss were gas, pavements, and the clamour of passing traffic.

She shook her head dubiously. 'There's more than that I'll miss, Mr Johnston.'

'You'll soon make fresh friends, Mrs O'Mahony. Bush people are very quick in that respect.'

That, I well knew, was the real rub — the severing of familiar human associations. As a girl she had gone to school in Malvern; as a woman had spent Rory's wages in Glenferrie Road on a thousand Friday nights. The daily chat with butcher, greengrocer, and baker; the petty gossip about ailments and commodity prices with kindred spirits met on the street; the weekly trip to the pictures; the Sunday morning church — these were the things which constituted Life to Mrs O'Mahony. Through them she had found happiness, and it would have been a presumption for me to belittle them.

I struck, therefore, a note of gentle insinuating flattery, beginning by pointing out that Rory had never been really content in the city but had remained in it for the sake of his family. I remarked that the change would act on him as a tonic, probably prolong his life, and — this with my tongue in my cheek — make him easier to live with.

'It involves a sacrifice on your part, Mrs O'Mahony,' I concluded. 'But you'll get used to it after a while, and you'll be better off in the long run. He was — a bit difficult here at times, wasn't he?'

She pulled a wry face. 'He was. He'll have to stop his Saint Patrick's day shenanigans if I go up there. I suppose he won't be able to get it so easily in the bush, anyhow.'

I understood she was referring to whisky, and deemed it wisest not to disillusion her. 'Not too easily. There's no hotel at Ferny Creek. You'll find life very quiet and restful.'

She sniffed. 'H'm, that'll suit Rory!'

Nevertheless, by the time the weekend came I considered I had done good work. Though not yet enthusiastic over the enterprise, she was at least calmly reconciled to it. She was also pathetically anxious for Rory to come back. A score of times during the week she told me she felt lost without him, that it was funny having no lunch to cut of a night, that the kitchen door looked horribly bare without his old hat and coat, and that every evening she kept listening for his footsteps coming along the side path. I asked her once if he would write, and she chuckled.

'Him write? He never wrote a letter in his life. We won't know nothing till he marches in at that door.'

She never said a truer word.

He came back on the Saturday, a day earlier than he was expected.

I'd been away since early morning, and got back just before midnight to find Rory the sole occupant of the kitchen. He was lying on the sofa, but immediately rolled his legs off and sat up.

'Hello, Rory.'

'How are you, Jim?' He eyed me quizzically, as if trying to estimate my surprise at seeing him. 'I — got back.'

'I thought you weren't coming till tomorrow.'

'So did I.'

I sensed there was some special significance in this early return, for his voice trembled with suppressed excitement and there was the very devil of a twinkle in his eyes.

'Well, how did you find things in the hills?'

He hesitated, looked sheepish for a moment, then grinned the most wicked and spontaneous grin I have ever seen.

'Good — I did the job in!'

'You what?'

'I did the job in. Very nearly did Neville in, too!'

I sat down facing him. 'No kidding, Rory.'

'It's dinkum all right. He came up asking for it, and this time he got it. Just a back-hander, but good enough for a sore jaw and a split lip.'

I could only stare at him; this was something I certainly had not expected. What puzzled me most was the fact that he was so obviously pleased about it. Although by then he must have fully realized the consequences, he was simply brimming over with satisfaction.

'Does Mrs O'Mahony know?' I asked.

He nodded ruefully. 'Yes, she knows. We had the very hell of a row and she beat it off to bed.'

'But what in creation did you do it for?'

'He come the bounce, I tell you. And I bounced him. He got snotty about a job I done what didn't quite please him —'

'And you came to blows?'

'You can put it that way. He couldn't knock the skin off a rice pudding. Good thing for him I didn't use me fist, it would have took his bloody head off.'

'Was anyone else there?'

'Only his missus and son-in-law.'

'What did they do?'

'Hollered for help and dragged the bastard inside. Cripes, you should have seen him spitting blood all the way across his nice lawn!'

We fell silent. O'Mahony seemed so utterly unconcerned about consequences that I began to wonder if this was, after all, an elaborate scheme.

'When did it happen?' I asked next.

'About six o'clock. I took the first car back to the city.'

'Neville only came up today?'

'Yes, first time I've seen him since last Monday.'

'You're a fool, Rory,' I said bluntly.

For the first time the grin left his face. He rose, hitching up his trousers. 'Yes, and I've been well told about it since I got back. But it's no use talking. I done it, and that's all there is to it.'

'You ramping savage! Couldn't you control yourself once a week after having him every day for twenty years?'

'This was different.' He sat down again, laying a hand on my knee. 'Jim, you ain't knocked about the world like I have. There's a lot of things you don't know nothing about yet. And this is one of them. I been thinking it over since I got back, and I got it all nutted out. I know now what did it. It was like putting a tamed lion back into the jungle again. I had a whole week on me own. No boss standing over me and no women fussing about. I heard old Bob Bruce was still living down near Perrin's Creek, and most nights I used to go down and yarn with him. Jim, I could sit here and talk till I was black in the face, and you still wouldn't know how I felt about that. Bob and me was cobbers. We was pinched together one day after a football match at the Gully. We used to go fishing over at

Paradise and get so drunk on the way we couldn't see to bait a hook when we got there. This last week we got talking about it all. He's got a bit of a shack and some berry fruit just down off the Monbulk Road; no missus, no kids, no boss. And he's been there all the time, all these twenty years I been making a chopping block for Neville. It wasn't only that, either — it was everything else. Things ain't changed such a lot up there. There's still plenty of trees left, and of a night I used to lie listening to the wind in them. I'm no sissy — you ought to know that — but I used to get all stewed up. I used to come out of a morning, and there was all the smoky blue ranges just like they was thirty years ago. I reckon it made a new man of me, and it was Neville got the good of it!'

Rory stopped, and savagely knocked out his pipe on the hearth. Poor devil, he did me an injustice when he said I didn't understand. I understood so well that I felt like kissing him.

'The call of the wild, eh?'

He looked at me suspiciously, but, seeing that I was quite sympathetic, began again. He was desperately anxious to vindicate himself.

'I was on the level, Jim, fair dinkum I was. All the week I kept thinking to myself how lucky I was, and what a fine time the old woman and me would have when I got her up there. Yes, you've heard me run her down, but I'd forgot all about that. I know a good thing when I see it, and that job was right into my barrer. I worked like a son of a gun, harder than ever I worked at Neville's city joint. It was like making me own home, and I bogged into it. I got thinking out all sorts of ideas and improvements. I even spent seven bob of me own money on kalsomine and did two rooms out so the missus would have a start when she got up. You know how she is — all spit and polish. And there you are — that lousy cow Neville had to come up and chip me over a couple of shrubs I'd shifted where he didn't want them.'

'You should have stuck it, Rory,' I murmured sadly.

'I know I should, but it's too late now. I tried to take it, so help me God I did. But something boiled up in me and I answered him back — the first time in twenty years. And he looks at me with his eyes nearly popping out of his head. 'I don't want no insolence, O'Mahony!' he says. And I just hauled off and lobbed a beaut fair in his moosh. "Then cop that!" I said.'

Rory fell silent, staring gloomily at the floor between his feet. I looked down on his unruly grey hair with mingled pity and admiration. He'd been foolish, but in a way that made my blood leap. The serious aspect was that he was an ageing man and work was not easy to get. But for this his deed would have been almost commendable. It was thrilling to picture Neville leaving the humble Rory up in the hills one day and going back a week later to find the inspired Michael Eugene. For that's what it all amounted to. Only this time neither saint's day nor whisky had anything to do with it. Instead, it was a matter of far-flung horizons and awakened memories, a whiff of gum leaves and cow dung, and a bird or two singing in the morning. That modest little freedom which, all unbidden, had come quietly to his side.

Reproaches and condolences would have served no useful purpose, so I prepared to go to bed.

'So you bust after all, Rory!'

He raised his head, and I was glad to see again the familiar wicked grin. In spite of everything he was still enjoying his vengeance. I clapped him on the shoulder.

'Take my advice and don't think about it any more tonight. Turn in and cuddle the wife. Make it up with her and talk it all over in the morning. You weren't dependent on Neville for a living.'

He gave a smothered curse. I left him sitting there.

In the small hours of the morning Mrs O'Mahony awakened me from a sound sleep to tell me he had gone. She had lain awake waiting for him until, no longer able to contain her anxiety, she had gone through to the kitchen. She showed me a note he had left on the table. It ran:

I'm beating it for keeps Mag. You're a good sort, but I can't stick it no longer. Go and live with Kathie.

She was, naturally, in a frightful state, and wanted me to follow him. But I assured her there was no knowing which way he had gone. There was simply nothing to be done about it. Michael Eugene O'Mahony had called it a day, and gone off on the wind that tramps the world.

• Sailors Belong Ships •

I got an address in King Street and went along and found a crowd of men staring at a lot of pieces of paper pasted on a shop window. All kinds of jobs: station hands, shearers, boundary riders, butchers, labourers.

I expected to find the place packed inside, but it wasn't. A few men sitting on a bench against the wall, waiting, and a woman at a desk. I took off my hat and went over to her. I couldn't milk, I couldn't put the winkers on a horse, and I couldn't kill a sheep — not so it would be fit to eat afterwards anyway. So I asked her about the labouring.

'It's out of town,' she said with an apologetic look.

'Where?' I asked her, as if it mattered.

'Near Ferntree Gully, It'll be a long job.'

'What's the pay?'

'Award rates — four pounds six and keep yourself. There's a tent, and a store not far away.'

'Who do I have to see about it?'

She smiled. 'Just me, if you want it. I can engage you.'

'I'll give it a go.'

'Very good. Five shillings is the fee, please. What's your name?'

'Burnie. Robert Burnie.'

'Sign here, please, will you?'

Sign here, please. That was all. Easy, like a dream. She told me to take the six-thirty train for Ferntree Gully and get out at Boronia. A buggy or something of the sort would meet me and take me out to the job.

I came out on to the footpath folding up the piece of paper and feeling as if I'd just bought a half share in Australia. I belonged. All I had to do now was kill five hours, get my gear off the ship, and keep clear of any of the crew who might be ashore. The six-thirty train was handy, because it would be dark by five-thirty. I could hire a taxi then, run down to the berth, and get my gear off by climbing down the shore net of one of the for'ard hatches. Lou was aboard and might give me a hand, although he'd be sore over losing his wager.

'Sailors belong ships,' he'd said that morning.

'Sailors belong nowhere,' I'd replied, 'not even ships.'

'Every port you say ... no more! You and your shore job, you make me sick. Vancouver, Seattle, Wellington, Sydney ...'

'I'd have made it in Sydney if I hadn't met the crowd and got drunk.'

'I know. And today you meet the crowd again and get drunk.'

'You'll see. They tell me you can always pick up a job in Melbourne.'

'Give me your ukulele if you come back drunk?'

'Give me your grey strides if I come back sober?'

'It's a deal!'

Funny how different everything appeared with that job in my pocket. I wanted to talk to somebody right away, to see what it felt like being one of the crowd. I was a bit frightened for myself, too, and wanted to get tangled up with somebody who'd keep me out of trouble until half-past five. I picked a steady looking fellow about my own age.

'How far out is this Boronia?'

'Twenty miles. You took a job there?'

'Yes, I've got to go out tonight. Where's the railway station?'

'Up Flinders Street.' He jerked his head. 'Anybody'll tell you.'

'Thanks. I'm a bit new here.'

'You're American, aren't you?'

'Canadian.'

'I took you for a Yank. When did you leave your ship?'

'What makes you think I've left a ship?'

He smiled. 'I can pick a seaman. I've been around myself.'

'All right, I came ashore an hour ago. I'm through. I've been trying to turn it up for years.'

He nodded sympathetically. I forget what else was said just then, but we stood talking for some minutes. And all the time I was getting more and more at ease with him. By and by he

looked at his watch and said he felt like some dinner. He said
it like an invitation, so I nodded, and walked along with him.
And when he suggested a drink would go all right I said I'd
be in that too.

Well, we had four drinks, then moved on and ordered steak
and eggs in a restaurant in the same street. He got to telling
me all sorts of things about Australia, about different kinds of
jobs, and the good wages that were to be made. And the more
he told me the better I felt. The beer had given me an appetite,
and when the steak was gone I had a helping of ham and eggs.
The waitress smiled when she set it up, and said I must be
hungry. That made me feel good, too. She was a pretty kid, and
I got a great kick thinking I'd be able to ask a girl out any time
now once I got settled in and had a few shillings in my pocket.

My mate told me his name was Gil. He asked me what I kept
grinning for.

'You ought to know,' I said. 'Not having to go back to that
damned ship. I feel as if I'd just bought Melbourne town.'

We sat talking and smoking for a long time. Then, without
any plans at all, we came out and walked along a street all pubs
and theatres and shops — big shops. Just strolled along in the
sunshine, looking in the shop windows and telling each other
what a rotten life the sea was. I was checking up on all the
things I was going to buy when I got the money. I decided I'd
look for a better job soon, perhaps in the city, where I could
have a nice room, get a few things together, look after my
clothes, and dress up any night and go out like a Christian. The
sunshine was lovely, and it was fine rubbing shoulders with
people in a place where I was going to stay put. But I was
impatient, too. I wanted the night to come. I was in a hurry
to get that taxi, go down to the ship, and get my gear off. I felt
like a fly battling out of a spider's web, with only one leg still
caught. But it was only half-past two, and when Gil mentioned
another drink I thought it was a good idea.

We talked about all kinds of things, and I don't remember
feeling any anxiety till he put his hand on my shoulder and
said, 'Bob, stop blowing about Ferntree Gully. You ain't going
there.'

'Who says I'm not?'

'I do. You're coming with me.'

'Where to?'

'Deniliquin. Listen to me ...' I noticed his voice had got thick, and there was that sleepy look in his eyes that said he was having too much. I took stock of myself then, and decided I was going all right. I began to regret meeting him, though, because I knew how these things end up, and how all my dreams would go bang again if I didn't watch out. I could hear Lou's voice whispering, 'You and your shore job — you make me sick. Vancouver, Seattle ...'

'Listen to me ... I took a fancy to you. We're sailors, see? Two sailors. We got the game by the throat. I know a job in the Riverina worth a hundred quid. We'd chop it out in a month.'

'Fencing? I've never done any in my life.'

'Spare me days! ... you could punch a post-hole, couldn't you?'

'Look, Gil, I've got a job ...'

'Job!' He rolled his eyes. 'Pick and shovel! That ain't a job. That's only ... here, give us another drink. I'm going to talk sense to you ...'

I ordered more drinks, but they weren't beers. He called the barman back and made them both whiskies. I was still stone sober myself, but ... well, there was a familiar feeling coming over me. I was getting all hot and tired. I wanted to sit down, like we do in Vancouver. They drink rough in Australia ...

I said to Gil, 'Isn't there somewhere we can sit?'

'Whaffor?' he guffawed. 'You ain't feeling squiffy, are you?'

'No, but you can drink sitting down, can't you?'

He laughed again, and patted me on the arm. 'Bob, my boy, I knew it had to come. You wouldn't be a Canadian if you didn't blow.'

'I'm not blowing ...'

'No, you were just going to, weren't you? Vancouver, where they drink sitting down. I told you I'd been around. I been tossed out of every pub in Granville Street. But you're in Australia now, lad, and when in Australia you do as ... hup ... Rome does. Aussies don't care ...'

He'd raised his voice, and a few of the men in the bar were watching me in a way I didn't like. I began to be real sorry I'd met him. But the whisky was starting to tell on me, and I didn't feel sore against him. I felt all soft and confiding. And I got telling him some of the little secret thoughts a sober man usually keeps to himself. About how I was sick of the forecastle because there was no privacy there. Sick of being isolated from society the way sailors are.

And all the time I talked he kept watching me with a funny sort of smile and his eyes half-closed. And every now and then he'd call for more drinks, and I'd keep sinking them and saying 'Good luck!' without really meaning it. And I got sillier and sillier, like he did.

I remember him leaning on me and telling me I was just a kid, and what I needed was a bloke to take me under his wing and show me round and keep the sharks off. But although I still wasn't sore on him I didn't like that. I kept putting two fingers into my vest pocket and feeling the bit of paper. And I told myself over and over again that nothing was going to prise me off it this time.

I was getting frightened, though, because things had gone like this before. I kept hearing Lou croaking, 'Sailors belong ships!' and seeing pictures of the *Chippewa Star* lying down at the timber berth. And they weren't like a picture I'd had earlier in the day, when I came out of that registry office. The *Chippewa* had seemed a little ship then, little and innocent, and I'd felt a superior kind of detachment toward it, like a moth looking at a chrysalis case it has just crept out of.

But it wasn't like that now. It was big again, like it was in all the other ports. Big and dark like a gaol, and there was a knowing grin in the lines of its rusty hull. A big spider, and I was a fly, and it had me by one leg, and I was being . . .

'What are you talking about?' bellowed Gil.

'I want to fly . . .'

'You're drunk . . .'

Yes, I'm drunk. And if I don't watch out . . .

All of a sudden a voice rose above the tipsy babble, 'All right, boys, give us a go! Six o'clock!'

For the first time I noticed the lights had been turned on and that it was black dark outside. Everybody started jostling.

'Gil,' I shouted, 'I've got to get a taxi! I've got to get my gear off!'

'Whaffor? You got plenty time. Tomorrow . . .'

'No, I'm going to that job . . .'

'Job? . . . there's millions of jobs . . .'

'But you don't know me. I've got to go . . .'

'Got to? There ain't no got to in this country!' He began to sing in a cracked voice, 'Aussies don't care . . .'

'Gil,' I pleaded, 'you're a swell guy . . .' I grabbed hold of him and started for the door, but a big bloke with a full pot of beer in his hand brought me up with a jerk.

'Who d'you think you're pushing, Yank?'

'I'm not a Yank!' I flared.

'Then stop talking like one. You're not at home now.'

I let fly, and he staggered backwards, carrying a couple of other fellows with him. Gil got stuck into it, too, yelling like a Red Indian. But something crashed into the side of my head, and I went down like a pole-axed bullock.

When I came to I was outside in the night air, sitting against the wall with Gil and a policeman bending over me. A lot of other men were standing around, and I saw a taxi pull in to the kerb.

'Here it is,' said the policeman. 'Now get him away quick and lively, or I'll take him in.'

'What's your ship, cobber?' asked Gil.

'What time is it?' My head was spinning like anything, and there was a taste of blood in my mouth.

'Twenty-past six. Come on, what's your ship?'

Chippewa Star. Berth seventeen south.'

They helped me up. Gil was about as steady as I was. I slipped a finger into my vest pocket and felt the piece of paper, but it didn't mean anything any more now. The little waitress in the restaurant was smiling a long way off. The forecastle of the *Chippewa* was a lot nearer.

'What's that you said?' asked Gil.

'Sailors belong ships . . .'

'You're drunk. You don't know what you're saying.'

Yes, Gil, I'm drunk. But I know what I'm saying.

· The Children ·

He was almost ready to go when I found him. He was, to be exact, engaged in putting the final lashings onto his big truck. Blackened and blistered, and loaded up with all his worldly possessions, it was backed right up to a dry old verandah littered with dead leaves and odds and ends of rubbish. He turned to me as I got near, his bloodshot eyes squinting at me with frank hostility.

'Another newshawk.'

'The *Weekly*, Mr Allen.'

His expression softened a little. 'I've got nothing against the *Weekly*.'

'We thought there might be something more to it,' I said gently. 'We know the dailies never tell a straight story.'

'They did this time,' he replied. 'I'm not making excuses.'

With the dexterity of a man who did it every day, he tied a sheepshank, ran the end of the rope through a ring under the decking, up through the eye of the knot, and back to the ring.

'I've got something to answer for all right,' he said with tight lips. 'But nobody need worry, I'll pay! I'll pay for it all the rest of my life. I'm that way now I can't bear the sight of my own kids.'

I kept silent for a moment. 'We understand that, Mr Allen. We just thought there might be something that hasn't come out yet.'

'No, I wouldn't say there's anything that hasn't come out. It's just that — well, people don't think enough, they don't think, that's all.'

He was facing me now, and looking very much, in his immobility, a part of the great background of desolation. The marks of fire were all over him. Charred boots, burned patches on his clothes, singed eyebrows, blistered face and hands, little crusts all over his hat where sparks had fallen. Over his shoulder the sun was just rising between Hunter and Mabooda Hills, a monstrous ball of copper glowing and fading behind the waves of smoke still drifting up from the valley. Fifty yards away the dusty track marked the western limit of destruction. The ground on this side of it was the first brown earth I had seen since leaving Burt's Creek; Allen's house the first survivor after a tragic procession of stark chimney stacks and overturned water tanks.

'It must have been hell!' I said.

'That?' He made a gesture of indifference. 'That's nothing. It'll come good again. It's the children.'

'I know.'

The door of the house opened. I saw a woman with children at her skirts. She jumped as she caught sight of me, and in an instant the door banged, leaving me with an impression of whirling skirts and large frightened eyes.

'The wife's worse than me,' said Allen, 'she can't face anybody.'

He was looking away from me now, frowning and withdrawn, in the way of a man living something all over again, something he can't leave alone. I could think of nothing to say which wouldn't sound offensively platitudinous. It was the most unhappy assignment I had ever been given. I couldn't get out of my mind the hatred in the faces of some men down on the main road when I'd asked to be directed to the Allen home.

I took out my cigarettes, and was pleased when he accepted one. A man won't do that if he has decided not to talk to you.

'How did it come to be you?' I asked. 'Did Vince order you to go, or did you volunteer?' Vince was the foreman ranger in that part of the Dandenongs.

'I didn't ask him, if that's what you mean. I don't work for the Commission. The truck's my living, I'm a carrier. But everybody's in on a fire, and Vince is in charge.'

'Vince picked you . . .'

'He picked me because I had the truck with me. I'd been down to the Gully to bring up more men, and it was parked on the break.'

'Then it isn't true . . .'

'That I looked for the job because of my own kids? No! That's a damned lie. I didn't even have cause to be worried about my own kids just then. I'm not trying to get out of it, but there's plenty to blame besides me: the Forestry Commission, the Education Department, and everybody in Burt's Creek and Yileena if it comes to that. Those children should never have been there to begin with. They should have been sent down to the Gully on Friday or kept in their homes. The fire was on this side of the reserve right up to noon.'

He wheeled, pointing towards the distant top of Wanga Hill. Through the drifting haze of smoke we could make out the little heap of ruins closely ringed by black and naked spars that had been trees. Here and there along the very crest, where the road ran, the sun glinted now and then on the windscreens of standing cars, morbid sightseers from the city.

'Just look at it!' he said vehemently. 'Timber right up to the fence-lines! A school in a half-acre paddock — in country like this!'

His arm fell. 'But what's the use of talking? I was told to go and get the kids out, and I didn't do it. I got my own. Nothing else matters now.'

'You thought there was time to pick up your own children first, and then go on to the school, Mr Allen?'

'That's about the size of it,' he assented gloomily.

I'd felt all along that he did want to talk to somebody about it. It came now with a rush.

'Nut it out for yourself,' he appealed. 'What your paper says isn't going to make anybody think any different now. But I'll tell you this: there isn't another bloke in the world would have done anything else. I should be shot — I wish to God they would shoot me! — but I'm still no worse than anybody else. I was the one it happened to, that's all. Them people who lost kids have got a perfect right to hate my guts, but supposing it had been one of them? Supposing it had been you ... what would you have done?'

I just looked at him.

'You know, don't you? In your own heart you know?'

'Yes, I know.'

'The way it worked out you'd think somebody had laid a trap

for me. Vince had got word that the fire had jumped the main road and was working up the far side of Wanga. And he told me to take the truck and make sure the kids had been got away from the school. All right — now follow me. I get started. I come along the low road there. I get the idea right away that I'll pick up my own wife and kids afterwards. But when I reach that bit of open country near Hagen's bridge when you can see Wanga, I look up. And, so help me God! there's smoke. Now that can mean only one thing: that the Burt's Creek leg of the fire has jumped the Government break and is heading this way. Think that one over. I can see the very roof of my house, and there's smoke showing at the back of it. I know there's scrub right up to the fences, and I've got a wife and kids there. The other way there's twenty kids, but there's no smoke showing yet. And the wind's in the north-east. And I'm in a good truck. And there's a fair track right through from my place to the school. What would you expect me to do?'

He would see the answer in my face.

'There was the choice,' he said with dignified finality. 'One way, my own two kids. The other way, twenty kids that weren't mine. That's how everybody sees it, just as simple as that.'

'When did you first realize you were too late for the school?'

'As soon as I pulled up here. My wife had seen me coming and was outside with the kids and a couple of bundles. She ran up to the truck as I stopped, shouting and pointing behind me.' He closed his eyes and shivered. 'When I put my head out at the side and looked back I couldn't see the school. A bloke just above the creek had a lot of fern and blackberry cut, all ready for burning off. The fire had got into that and was right across the bottom of Wanga in the time it took me to get to my place from the road. The school never had a hope. Some of the kids got up as far as the road, but it's not very wide and there was heavy fern right out to the metal.'

I waited, while he closed his eyes and shook his head slowly from side to side.

'I'd have gone through, though, just the same, if it hadn't been for the wife. She'll tell you. We had a fight down there where the tracks branch. I had the truck flat out and headed for Wanga. I knew what it meant, but I'd have done it. I got it into my head there was nothing else to do but cremate the lot, truck and everything in it. But the wife grabbed the wheel. It's a wonder we didn't leave the road.'

'You turned back . . .'

'Yes, damn my soul! I turned back. There was fire everywhere. Look at the truck. The road was alight both sides all the way back to Hagen's. Just the same, it would have been better if we'd gone on.'

That, I felt, was the simple truth, his own two innocents notwithstanding. I had an impulse to ask him what happened when he reached Burt's Creek, but restrained myself. His shame was painful to witness.

A minute or two later I said goodbye. He was reluctant to take my hand.

'I kept trying to tell myself somebody else might have got the kids out,' he whispered. 'But nobody did. Word had got around somehow that the school had been evacuated. Only the teacher — they found her with a bunch of them half a mile downs the road. And to top it all off my own place got missed! That bit of cultivation down there — you wouldn't read about it, would you?'

No, you wouldn't read about it.

In the afternoon, at the Gully, standing near the ruins of the hotel, I saw him passing. A big fire-scarred truck rolling slowly down the debris-littered road. Behind the dirty windscreen one could just discern the hunted faces of a man and woman. Two children peeped out of a torn side-curtain. Here and there people searching the ashes of their homes stood upright and watched with hard and bitter faces.

· Lena ·

'Tins, Joe!'

Half-past three, and the usual note of irritation has crept into Lena's voice. Without getting up from my knees, I reach backwards, seize a couple of buckets, and push them through under the drooping leaves of the vines. Before I can release them they are grabbed and pulled violently away from me. Between the top leaves, and only fifteen inches away, I get a glimpse of a freckled little face, keen eyes leaping from bunch to bunch of the clustering grapes, always a split second in front of the darting fingers and slashing knife. I hear the thump of tumbling fruit, and get up wearily. No use trying to feed her with tins as we go — she's too quick, too experienced, too enthusiastic. Or is it just that I am too old and too slow?

Empty tins are thrown only into alternate rows, leaving the other rows clear for the passing of the tractor that takes away the gathered fruit. Right from the start of the picking it has fallen to me, no doubt as gentleman's privilege, to work that side of the vines where the empties are. As Lena and I make equal division of the day's earnings, I try to keep up with her, but every now and then forget to keep her supplied with tins.

'You should let me know before you cut right out, Lena,' I say gently as I push the first ones through just ahead of her.

She doesn't answer, which means that she's lost patience with me. I, too, am irritated. Irritated by this tally anxiety that seizes her every day about this time. But I remind myself that at tea tonight, with the day's work over, she will forget everything, wait on me like a devoted daughter, chatter brightly about the circus we're all going to in Redcliffs, ask me if I have anything for the wash tomorrow. So I go about twenty yards down the row, pushing through a couple of tins every few feet, and say nothing until I get back.

It is a relief to bend my aching legs again, to press my knees into the warm red earth, to get my head out of the sun and stare into the cool recesses of the vine leaves. Off the first bunch of grapes I pull a handful, stuff it into my mouth, swallow the juice, and spit out the residue. While I was away Lena has conscientiously picked right through to my side, leaving only one or two clusters she couldn't reach, so that in only a few minutes I'm up with her again. I can't see her, but the violence with which she is banging the buckets tells me that she is still sulking.

'Angry with me?' I ask.

No answer. I wait a few seconds, then bang a bucket myself just to let her see that I too can be provoked.

'You never have much to say this time of day, do you?' I venture.

'You can't talk and work.'

'You can in the mornings. You were telling me all about your dad before lunch.'

'That's why we're behind. We only got two hundred and ten buckets this morning.'

'Only! Isn't that good?'

'We should have got two hundred and fifty. We'll be going flat out to get four hundred and fifty today.'

'Do we *have* to get four hundred and fifty?'

'Yes!' Very emphatically.

To that I give no reply. Everything I could say has already been said, more than once. I can, at the moment, think of no new lead in an argument which has become wearisome. To Lena, piece-work is the road to riches — 'the harder you work, the more you get.' She's too young to know anything of the days when armies of unemployed converged on the irrigation belt to struggle for a chance to pick grapes at 5 shillings per hundred tins. We're due for a visit from a union organizer; I keep wondering what she'll say when he asks her to take a ticket.

I'm working on, not saying a word, but she takes my silence as a sign of weakness and presses the attack herself.

'It's all right for you. I need the money.'

'We all need money, Lena.'

'You'll get plenty when you get back to the wharves. And get it easier too, I bet!'

'Sometimes. It depends on what the cargo is. But we never get paid by the ton!'

'Wharfies wouldn't work, anyway.'

Hitting below the belt. She must be quite upset to say a thing like that. I let it go, though, because it would be a preposterous thing to fall out with her. We're both Australians, but in a way that has nothing to do with geography I know that we come from different countries. She's a big, lovable child, inherently forthright and generous, and usually quite merry, but her philosophy is a bit frightening to a man brought up on the waterfront of a great city. She comes from a poor little grazing property deep in the mallee scrub over the New South Wales border. One of a family of eleven. For forty-six weeks in the year she works sheep and helps to bring up nine younger brothers and sisters. The six weeks' grape-picking is the annual light of her drab little life: money of her own, appetizing food, the companionship of other people's sons and daughters, above all the fabulous Saturday morning shopping excursions into Mildura. After the picture of home that she painted for me this morning I can understand all this, but I'd give something to open her innocent young eyes to the world I know. Her conception of fighting for one's rights extends no further than keeping a wary eye on the number of filled buckets. 'You've got to watch these blockies,' she tells me every day. It would never occur to her that there are robbers higher up, that hard-working Bill McSeveney also may not be getting what he deserves. That is why at night-time here, looking out through the fly-wired window of the men's hut, I'm conscious of a darkness deeper than the heavy shadows that lie between the long drying-racks and over the garden of the sleeping house.

And it seems to me that this obsession of Lena with piece-work is where the darkness begins. There was the twilight of it just a minute ago when she passed that unpleasant remark about wharfies.

We pick on in silence for perhaps a quarter of an hour.

I'd always imagined that there was a fair amount of noise associated with grape-picking. Perhaps there is on some blocks.

On this one it is always quiet. The rows are unusually long, and between the visits of the tractor to replenish the supply of empty tins and take away the full ones, we hear nothing except the occasional voices of the two boys picking several rows away, and the carolling of magpies in the belars along the road. The sun is beginning to go down at last, but it's been a particularly hot day — a hundred and ten in the shade at noon — and I'll be glad when five o'clock comes, whatever the tally. That is always the best part of the day, when we trudge up to the house and throw ourselves on to the cool buffalo grass under the jacarandas, and Bill, the boss, cuts up a big sugar-melon, and hands out pink juicy slices that we can hardly open our jaws on. It would be better still, though, if they would talk of something else then besides the day's work. Smoky, the house cat, usually joins us, and I can never contemplate his great lazy blue hide without reflecting, O, You wise old brute! Even as I went out to work this morning you were lying in the coolest spot under the water tank, and every hour of the day you've followed the shifting shadows. While I —

The hum of the approaching tractor gives promise of some relief, and as the crash of falling buckets sounds far off down the row I say to Lena, 'Here they come. How many have we got?'

'If you were such a good union man you'd be counting them yourself.'

True, no doubt, but coming from Lena it's quite meaning-less. She doesn't know what a trade union is. Instinctively I cast a glance up the row to see if our long-expected visitor, the 'Rep' is coming.

'Aren't you going to tell me the tally?'

'All I know is we're behind. We only had three hundred and thirty at smoko, and this is the shortest run.'

'That patch of mildew kept us back early in the afternoon.'

'It wasn't that.'

'Was it through me not keeping you up in buckets?'

She doesn't answer that. Whether she knows it or not, she's angry with me not for what I do or don't do, but for the things I say. I work hard, but I've said some harsh things about piece-work, ridiculed her persistent argument that 'the only way to

get money is to work for it.' It would be a good world indeed
if that were true. She knows I don't approve of competing with
the boys for big tallies, but she can't see that, out of principle,
I must try to keep up with her because I get half of our combined earnings.

The tractor pulls up, and I crawl through to Lena's side and
go for the water bag hanging from the canopy. The grimy faces
of Bill McSeveney and Peter, the rackman, smile down at me.
They call me 'Sponge-guts' because of the vast amount of water
I drink without getting pains.

'How's your mate, Joe?' asks Peter.

'She's got the sulks again. She thinks I'm sitting up on her.'

Bill, in the driving-seat, gives Lena a friendly wink. Naturally
— they're his grapes. He's a good employer, even as employers
go these days, but I'd be interested to see his form if pickers
were easier to get. He and his wife think the world of Lena.
She's an expert picker, but she's also a nice change in the home
of a couple who've raised three sons and no daughters.

He's observing her now with all the detached benevolence
of a bachelor uncle.

'Get your five hundred today, kid?'

She steals a cautious sidelong glance at me, pouts, and
shakes her head. She makes a charming picture of bush youth,
standing stiff and straight in the narrow space between the tractor wheel and the vines. She wears old canvas shoes, a pair of
jodhpurs several sizes too big for her, a man's work-shirt with
the sleeves cut off, and a limp-brimmed sun-bonnet that
throws a shadow over half of her cherubic face. The fingers
of the hand nearest me fidget ceaselessly with the knife. Usually she's full of talk, particularly with Bill, but at the moment
she only wants to work. And she can't even kneel down with
the tractor standing where it is. Her restless eyes leap from me
to Peter, and from Peter to Bill.

'Come on,' she says, 'load up. We've got over a hundred
buckets to pick yet.'

'All right, Boss!' Bill releases the clutch, and as the tractor
moves on I swing the first bucketful up to Peter.

Slowly we move along the row. Sixty full buckets, about
twenty pounds of fruit to the bucket — 'fill 'em up to water-

level!' They get heavy towards the end; one has to work fast to keep up even with the snail-crawl of the tractor. I come back to Lena sweating afresh, and blowing a bit.

She hears me, and without stopping, or looking at me, demands peremptorily, 'How many?'

'Sixty on the load, and twenty-five left.'

'That makes three hundred and ninety. We've got fifty minutes to get sixty more.'

'Who says so?'

'I do.'

'Suppose we don't get them?'

'We've got to get them.'

It's on again, but before the usual evening dispute can get properly started a man I haven't seen before ducks through from the next row and confronts me. I give him good-day. Lena takes a long curious look at him, then goes on working. Middle-aged, and wearing a blue suit with an open-necked sports-shirt, he carries a couple of small books in one hand, and in the other a handkerchief with which he wipes his moist forehead. He'd have made a better first impression if he'd kept those books in his pocket a few minutes longer.

'Sorry I've been so long getting around,' he says affably. 'I'm the union rep Australian Workers' Union.'

'I'm glad to see you.'

We've been picking here for four weeks, and the A.W.U. is the wealthiest trade union in Australia. Something of what I'm thinking must be showing in my face, for his manner becomes a trifle apologetic.

'I've been going flat out like a lizard since eight o'clock this morning. My God, it's hot, ain't it? How're you for tickets here?' He just can't get to the point soon enough. 'I've seen the boys through there; they're all right.'

'I've been waiting for you,' I tell him, bringing out a ten shilling note.

He opens one of the little books, takes a pencil from his breast pocket. 'Good on you, mate! How about the girl?'

'I'm one of the family,' replies Lena, with a promptness that shows not only that she has been listening, but that she has been well-schooled. McSeveney has no time for trade unions.

The organizer gives me a conspiratorial smile, which I do not return.

'You could still join if you wanted to, girlie.'

Lena doesn't answer that. She hasn't stopped picking for an instant. She's already a few feet away along the row, slashing and bucket-banging in a way that tells both of us not to be too long about it.

I watch him write in the date.

'I wish they'd all come in as quick as you,' he says in a lowered voice. 'You've got no idea the song some of the bastards make about it. I can give you a full ticket if you like? Cost you thirty bob.'

My gorge rises. What does he think he's selling? The great Australian trade unions weren't built by men like him.

'No thanks — just a season ticket. I'm already in a union. You don't cover me in my usual job.'

He begins to write. 'Okay. What are you in?' Just making conversation; he doesn't really care.

'Waterside Workers' Federation.' And for the life of me I can't keep a note of superiority out of my voice. I get the very devil of a kick out of it.

He goes on writing, without looking at me, but I can fairly see the guard coming up. 'That's a pretty good union. You'd make better money on the wharf than up here, wouldn't you?'

'Yes. We're well organized.'

A deliberate challenge, but he pretends not to see it.

'Up here for a bit of a change?'

'I was ill. Told to get out of Melbourne for a few weeks. A family man has to keep working, though.' I wouldn't tell him even that much, only I don't want him to think I came here for the 'big money.' Seventeen and six per hundred tins! — and fill 'em up to water level . . .

I'm tempted to ask him if he's been to the next block, where the pickers are working all hours and living like animals, but he's too easy to read. He isn't an organizer; he's a collector. If he were doing his job he would talk to Lena, as I've talked to her. I watch him tramp away through the dust quite pleased with himself. He's got my ten shillings. He didn't ask if I am getting the prescribed wages, where I sleep at night, what hours I work, or what the food is like here.

It's a relief to get back to Lena. At least she's honest. She'd fight all right if she thought anybody was trying to put something over her. She just doesn't understand, that's all.

For minutes after I catch up with her we work without speaking. She's picking furiously, savagely, and by and by I find that I, too, am clapping on the pace. I've seen it elsewhere, the instinct to do one's bit, to keep up with one's mate. Piece-work isn't an incentive, it's a device. But there's something else fermenting in me. A longing to please her, to win her respect, to get her to listen to me, to chase out of her eager young head some of the lies and nonsense that have been stuffed into it. Only last night I put in a hectic hour at the dining-table trying to explain to her — and others — that it isn't wharfies and railwaymen who gum up the works on the man on the land. Not wharfies and railwaymen . . .

The falling bunches go plump-plump into the buckets. I know that she, too, is thinking. She wants to say something. Every time I catch sight of her bobbing head through the leaves I observe that she is peeping, as if trying to gauge what kind of humour I'm in.

By and by it comes, a non-committal, uncompromising little voice that nevertheless sends a thrill through me:

'Joe.'

'Hullo there.'

'What *is* a trade union, anyway?'

Lena, Lena, where am I to begin . . .?

• The Blind Man's Story •

I have always thought that the ending of Alphonse Daudet's novel *Sappho* is one of the most moving in all creative literature.

The long story of enchantment and degradation has been told. At the hotel in Marseilles Jean Gaussin awaits the coming of Fanny Legrand. Down at the quay a ship is ready to sail, the ship which is to bear mistress and man away to a far country, a final despairing effort by Jean to build something on the wreckage of his life. But at the last minute the fateful letter is put into his hands by a waiter:

'Oh well, I am not going.'

She writes that she is turning back to an old love, the engraver-forger Flamant: 'I am in need of love and admiration and soothing in my turn. He will kneel before me, and he will never see my wrinkles and grey hairs.'

I can never read it without thinking of a man I once knew who really was blind, and who, in his own grimly ironic way, *was* kneeling before a woman without seeing her wrinkles and grey hairs.

His name was David Laidlaw. He had lost his sight in an industrial accident while in the prime of life, but, under the terms of the compensation settlement, had been kept on by his employer as some kind of storeman.

He was about sixty when I first met him but still a fine-looking man, only a little more than medium height, but perfectly proportioned and upright as a rush.

I came across him one evening groping his way with a white stick along the smelly subway of the old Richmond railway station. It turned out that we had both come in on the Box Hill line and were both making for the Frankston line platform. He

41

had no regular guide just then, so I more or less adopted him, and for nearly two years thereafter used to pick him up for the Richmond change-over. He would just stand still where he got off the first train, politely declining all offers of help until I got to him. He told me he found the public very good, and only rarely went unassisted in the peak-hour rush. Our Frankston train was always full, but invariably someone got up to give him a seat. He was fit enough to stand, but he never protested, even if it was a woman. He had a way of accepting that made everybody in the compartment feel good: 'Most kind of you, most kind of you. Thank you.'

He was a happy man. Sometimes as the train began to empty out I got a seat opposite him, and could study him at leisure. There were times when I almost envied him, he looked so serene and self-sufficient. Perhaps even blindness has its consolations. Edith Sitwell's well-known observation that she liked listening to music and silence is quite intelligible to many of us with good hearing who have often wished we were deaf.

My blind man never relaxed against the cushions, but sat bolt upright, hands resting on top of the white stick held between his knees. Occasionally, for a minute or so, his eyelids would close, but he never slept. It took me some time to get used to the fact that the whitened and distorted pupils were telling him nothing.

He always had the air of a man who has no great worry, who has had a pleasant day, who is enjoying present company, and who is going back to a comfortable home and a good wife. Sometimes I wondered how much of the serenity of his expression was sheer discipline, a defence against the knowledge that someone could always be watching him. The blind can never quite relax, never take a chance, never do things in secret. I, for one, got to know every detail of David Laidlaw's face, right down to the little tufts of hairs that grew within his nostrils, a tiny white scar on his upper lip, the single fine furrow that ran across an otherwise smooth forehead.

All the same, there was nothing strained about his alertness. It was, rather, convivial, the alertness of a man who didn't want to be left out of anything. He missed nothing of what went on in the compartment, but drew a nice line between what was for general consumption and what was private. He could overhear a conversation right alongside him without batting an eyelid, but an amusing remark obviously addressed to the company at large would bring an instant smile, even an appreciative turn of the well-poised head. He was like a good guest, with us all the time but never intruding.

My vision of a devoted woman watching over him began to build up from the very first. It showed not only in his abiding air of pleasant anticipation, but in the way he was kept. No doubt he changed on the job, but there was always a crease in his trousers, his shoes were always polished, his shirt well laundered, and he could always pull out a clean handkerchief. It showed also in his conversation, in the little references that inevitably crop up when two married men get together. Casual allusions that can tack themselves on to almost anything. I learned that he had only his wife for family, that there was a daughter who had died in infancy, that his wife was unable to bear another child, that she was in good general health, that she used to go out a lot before his accident but now stayed at home, that she was fond of gardening, and that she was a very good cook.

All this, however, came out without him really talking about his domestic affairs. It was more in response to my own innocent promptings, and as soon as I realized this I stopped prompting. I became aware of a certain wariness in his answers, a reluctance to enlarge, to confide. It struck me as odd, because it was consistent with nothing else about him and because along with it there went a vague air of smug self-assurance. I felt that he knew I was becoming curious and was enjoying teasing me. That he was deliberately letting me smell a secret, but had no intention of letting me in on it. Sometimes, when the conversation led me to say something about my own family, I would glance at him expectantly and catch him with a faint smile, a smile which was not only smug, but scornful, as if I were touching on something about which he was informed far beyond my comprehension.

He didn't in the least mind talking about his blindness, took quite a pride in telling me how he had conditioned himself to it, enjoyed my expressions of surprise at the things he was able to do.

'You must remember, though,' he said one evening, 'that I

was once a sighted man. I've been blind for only ten years. I
grew up with eyes. I know what the world is like. I have my
dimensions right — sizes and distances. I move in a home
where I know where everything is. That's the great secret of getting along with blind people. Don't spring surprises on them,
don't move things about. My wife understands all this. I get
along fine.' He fell silent, and I was about to ask another question when, glancing at him, I saw that he was wearing the familiar little smile. And before I could speak again there came
from him something so incredible, and in such a low voice,
that I couldn't believe I'd heard him correctly.

'I beg your pardon?' I said.

'Nothing that really matters,' he replied, with a shrug of his
shoulders.

I was fairly sure that what he had said was: 'It was the best
thing that ever happened to me,' and the evasion served only
to quicken my curiosity about his private life. There and then,
however, I had no choice but to let the matter drop, and when
we began talking again it was about books, our latest reading.

Indeed most of our conversation was about books. We used
to talk with our heads close together, our voices rising and falling with the noise of the train and the murmur of fellow passengers. He'd been a wide reader, and our likes and dislikes gave
us some fine discussions. He often lamented the limitations
placed on him by braille: 'So little of it, so little that's recent.'
His great joy was the radio. He listened to all the news, all book
reviews, all kinds of educational sessions. He had a fine memory for what he had absorbed in his sighted years. He mentioned Sophocles one day, but courteously dropped the whole
subject of the ancients when he realized I hadn't even dabbled.
He admired English literature, but got no response from me
when he spoke of Smollett, Swift, Fielding, and Goldsmith.
Only on the great writers of France and Russia did we find
common ground, with just enough differences to give bite to
our exchange of views. Unlike me, he preferred Turgenev to
Gorki, Flaubert to Balzac. Yet it was through Balzac that he was
finally tempted to let me in on his secret. That, and perhaps
the fact that a time had come when our paths were soon to
part. I'd moved from Frankston to Hawthorn in order to be

nearer my work, and in a few days would not be going on to Richmond.

We'd been comparing the varying degrees of competence with which great writers handled their women, and he had remarked that all the most conspicuous literary successes in this field had been scored with women who were morally weak.

'By the very nature of things,' I suggested carelessly, and he picked me up in a flash.

'What things?' He had turned his head towards me, as if he wanted to look me in the eyes, and for once I was glad that he couldn't. 'It doesn't do us much credit, does it? Madame Bovary, Fanny Legrand, Manon Lescaut, Anna Karenina, Carmen —'

'You have two kinds of women there,' I pointed out in an effort to recover lost ground.

'Of course. But Tolstoy also intended to be censorious. Flaubert too, though not quite so self-righteously. All the same, none of those women was without compassion. Few women are.' He paused for a moment. Then, in the way of a man getting back to the point at issue, and with his mouth close to my ear, said, 'The great bitches of real life, my friend, are all women of impeccable conventional virtue. Male selfishness and arrogance has led us into getting our values all mixed up. When we speak of a bad man we can mean any one of several kinds of viciousness. When we speak of a bad woman we mean only one thing. Which is absurd. We were speaking of Anatole France the other day — *The Crime of Sylvestre Bonnard* — remember where the dear old man is insulted by Mademoiselle Prefere? I can quote you his very words: "Come, my poor old Bonnard, you had to live as long as this in order to learn for the first time exactly what a wicked woman is." And we are not asked to doubt that Mademoiselle Prefere was a virgin.'

I murmured my agreement and waited, not because there was nothing to say, but because I felt he was deliberately approaching something important, and I didn't want to stop him. A moment later he was referring me to Balzac.

'Balzac was another who said it. You've read *Père Goriot*?'

'Yes, but many years ago. I would have to go back to it.'

'You have a copy?'

'Yes.'

'Go back to it tonight. You'll see what I mean. Remember Madame Vauquier?'

'Yes.'

'Well, not so much Madame Vauquier as a generalization when she is being introduced. Chapter three — yes, I know exactly where it is, it was one of my little literary discoveries. It helped to clarify something which had been tormenting me for a long time. That is what makes great writers, you know: they reveal. Look it up tonight, then I might tell you something more. It's just a little piece, about people who seek in strangers what they can no longer find in their intimates.'

Needless to say, as soon as I got home I looked up the passage indicated. I found it without any trouble, but had to read it several times before I isolated the point which my friend wished to make. I give it now for the sake of continuity. It runs:

Some people, it may be, have no more to look for from those with whom they live; they have displayed the innermost recesses of their hearts to their neighbours, and these are left void and empty; they are conscious that they stand secretly condemned, and with merited severity. But they feel an uncontrollable need for flattery, which none offers them, or they are consumed with anxiety to seem to possess qualities which are not really theirs; and so they hope to surprise the regard or the love of strangers, in spite of the wish of losing it sooner or later.

I can't say, like my friend, that I found it a literary discovery. I wasn't particularly impressed, no doubt because it was relevant to nothing in my own personal experience. Be that as it may, my only thought at the time was to fit the passage into the pattern of my blind friend's life, where it obviously belonged. I felt sure that there was a deep human story behind his references to Balzac and Anatole France, a story which tied in with his abiding air of smug contentment, his caginess about his private affairs. There was also his remark: 'I might tell you something more.'

Several days passed before the subject was raised between us. It wasn't often that we got seats together early in the journey. The train never really began to lighten before it got to Moorabbin, and in the few days following the talk I have recorded there was little opportunity to get back to it. Each evening, however, we managed to sit together for a few minutes, and I thought it significant that he didn't ask me if I had looked up the quotation. I concluded that he was biding his time until we could be sure of twenty or thirty minutes' unbroken conversation, as indeed I was myself.

When the opportunity did come, on our last evening but one, he seized it with almost indecent haste. He had been seated since Richmond. At Hawksburn a man sitting next to him got out and I immediately dropped into the empty place.

I put my hand on his knee and spoke to him, just to let him know who was there, and he sat in silence for a minute or so. Then, not bothering with any preliminaries, and putting his lips close to my ear, he said, in a voice that told me he was smiling, 'Well, did you look that up — Balzac?'

'Yes, I found it.'

'What did you think of it?'

'It rang true, but it was a bit beyond me. I've never met a woman like that.'

'Woman? He uses the word people. There are men like that too, you know.'

'You've met them?'

'As it happens, no. Only a woman. I married her.'

There was a slight tremor in his voice, something new to me. I observed that he was indeed smiling, and holding his lips tightly closed. To control a trembling there also? Some of the excitement he was labouring under was coming to me through his whole body, for we were jammed tightly together.

'You surprise me,' I said cautiously. 'I always had an impression that you were happily married.'

'So I am — now!'

'A second marriage?'

'No, the same woman. She changed. She changed when I became blind. Can you understand that?'

'I think so. You said yourself there is compassion in all women.'

'So there is, but it wasn't as simple as that in this case. I was married to her for twenty years before my accident, and in all that time I lived in a domestic strait-jacket. You must find this a bit embarrassing, listening to a man run his wife down?'

'I do not. What you really want to tell me is that she's changed.'

That seemed to please him. He gave my arm a friendly squeeze. 'Yes, that's what I want to tell you. But first I want you to understand what kind of a woman she was. You know, I'm breaking the precept of a lifetime. Are you happily married?'

'Yes, I was fortunate.'

'I've always maintained that a man who is unhappily married should never confide in a man who has done well for himself. He's never really understood, only scorned. A happily married man likes to take the credit himself. If another man complains, it's because he's a bad husband and won't see it, or because he doesn't know how to manage a woman. Follow me?'

'Yes, I'm with you.'

'Ten years ago I wouldn't have talked to you like this. I'd learned to keep my mouth shut. She was too clever for me. Out-manoeuvring me and building up her own stocks was a science with her. She fooled nearly everybody, even most of my closest friends —'

'One woman to her husband, and quite another one to outsiders,' I agreed. The miles were flying past, and I wanted to get the story while he was in the humour.

'Exactly! As a matter of fact, she fooled even me for a long time. I learned quickly enough that I'd married the wrong woman, but it took me two or three years to fully realize the pickle I was in. She won other people so easily that I always felt a bit guilty after our first little quarrels. I thought that all I had to deal with was a nagger. A nagger with a heavy leavening of house pride and acquisitiveness. She was forever picking at me over trifles, but all men complain about that when they get together, and I used to console myself by thinking that I wasn't a special case, and that she'd probably grow out of it anyway.

'She didn't grow out of it, she got steadily worse. She used to dwell on me, catch me out in all kinds of little misdemeanours: coming into the house without wiping my shoes clean, not putting things away after me, leaving a tap dripping, letting a hole grow in my socks without telling her, leaving a light on after I'd been into another room. Fair enough, but she used to chip me without making a joke of it, without a smile, and that made all the difference. She used to drive me, too. I had a good job, head storeman with Leckie Electrics. I made good money, but it was never enough. There was never any pleasure in putting my pay packet on to the table. She was always talking about what some other woman had, how much some other woman's husband was earning. She kept a good house, no doubt, but it was never a home. Everything was done with an eye on the woman next door, if you get what I mean. She'd never ask me for something straight out. She'd tell me how some other woman had just got it — and keep on telling me. And as fast as I met one need she'd bring up another. If I kicked back, as I often did, she'd get upset, start dabbing her eyes, and make me feel the offending party. Whereabouts are we?'

'Malvern.'

'But all this wasn't the worst of it. What exasperated me more than anything else was the fact that she made no concessions whatever to me as an individual in my own right. She took not the slightest interest in anything that interested me. She'd smother me with all the fiddling tittle-tattle about other people's affairs, but the minute I mentioned something that concerned me, or ourselves mutually, she'd go as flat as a pancake. All her miseries were at home, all her joys outside. She was a woman for whom adulation was the very spice of life. Adulation, no matter how worthless, as long as she was getting it. Any pool, never mind how small, as long as she was the big fish in it. That was one of the reasons for her systematic housekeeping, she wanted plenty of time for gadding about. She was always up to the ears in some local organization. You know these women's groups and auxiliaries: hospitals, Red Cross, Liberal Party, Labor Party, Animal Welfare, Progress Associations. Don't misunderstand me, I'm not passing judgement on them. They do good work, and there's a lot of fine women in them. But my wife would never stay put. She went through them all, picking them up and dropping them one after another as she got cut down to size. Same thing with the churches. One time or another she tacked herself on to them all: Church of England, Methodist, Presbyterian, there was even a Salvation Army period. Anything at all as long as she could carry a banner, blow a trumpet, or beat a drum. Anything for a bit of limelight. She'd take them all in for a little while, then, as soon as she tired of it, or found her stocks dropping, she'd get out and take up with something else. And while each one lasted I got it morning, noon and night, breakfast, dinner and tea. She used to drive me mad with her piddling boasting and gossip.

'It was the same with individuals, odd connections picked up among the neighbours and around the shops. Her life was a long procession of transient friendships. She had a talent for attracting people, but she won them by deliberately laying herself out to win them. She'd pick up with strangers anywhere, flatter them by getting them to talk about themselves, asking them the kind of questions that people like to be asked. Believe me, in her own shallow way she was clever. She understood some human weaknesses and how to exploit them. She was a fantastic liar, one of those pathological liars who begin by deceiving themselves. She was always repeating to me nice things which she'd heard that people were saying about her. She would invent them, and immediately incorporate them as facts into the image of herself that she was forever building up. Nobody could tell her anything, she was an authority on everything under the sun. She got by through sheer brazen cunning, and the reluctance of people to drive her out into the open.

'When we had visitors she used to put on an act, join in by repeating things she'd heard me say on other occasions, all shrewdly designed to convey an impression of a devoted wife sharing her husband's life. Sometimes in her eagerness she'd draw the long bow, add something quite absurd, turn to me for endorsement, and get annoyed when I denied ever having said such a thing. The onus then was on me to smooth things out, but she would yield in a way that always made it look as if it were she who was giving in for the sake of peace. Oh, she was clever, clever! She had a genius for putting me in a false position, for winning people's sympathy. Can you understand all this? Is she beginning to take shape?'

'Yes, I'm beginning to see her.'

'Good! She'll take on lifesize in a minute.' He gave my arm another appreciative squeeze. Whatever the story was worth, I knew by now that I was going to get it in full. He was a man released, in full tide. I noticed that each time we pulled into a station he stopped for a moment, cocking his head sideways, mentally checking where we were. 'You're sure nobody else can hear me?' he enquired anxiously.

'Quite sure. I'd warn you.'

'Yes, give me a nudge —'

'You were saying she had a genius for winning people's sympathy.'

'It was her whole life. She just couldn't help herself. It was behind everything she did, everything she said. I told you that we lost a child and that she could never have another. She used it directly by fussing over other people's children in a way that almost brought tears to their eyes. And she used it indirectly by pretending I was holding it against her that she couldn't give me a family. It was one of the wicked whispers that kept coming back to me. The truth is that it was one of my great grievances that she would never agree to adopt a child. I wanted to right from the first, but she couldn't be objective even about that. She said she could never bring herself to treat someone else's child as her own, which wouldn't be fair to the child. See how clever she was? That was the story for me. For outsiders the story was that it was me who wouldn't agree. One night I challenged her with all this. I told her that she wanted to keep up the existing situation because it was a perfect cross on which to crucify herself. From that moment she really hated me, because she knew I was seeing into her. No doubt Balzac had something to do with it too. It was about that time that I read *Père Goriot*, and the whole nature of the woman was revealed to me in a flash. What station was that?'

'Ormond.'

'She loved an open quarrel, not because it gave her an opportunity to get things off her chest, but because it made me say things, gave her fresh ammunition. It endorsed the image of herself as a long-suffering wife. Perhaps it was bad for me getting on to that piece of Balzac, because my reaction gave her what she had always wanted. It made me fight back, and she took a great plunge for the worse. Believe me, she wanted a bad husband —'

'She was a neurotic.'

'Yes! Most women like to be envied. She didn't, she wanted

to be pitied. And when I began to fight back in real earnest she was happy, in her own vicious, miserable way. She had something to complain about, true stories to tell her cronies. You must understand that all the time she kept her windows clean — follow what I mean? She knew how to lay money out, and she had good taste. The house was like a new penny, but it was a showpiece, not a refuge. I never went short of a clean shirt, because other people would have noticed that, but I never had a cosy hearth to sit at. One of her most provocative tactics was to be up to the ears in work just as I walked in of an evening. Going for the lick of her life with the vacuum cleaner or at a pile of ironing. And she could glance at the clock, then glare at me, in a way that made my gorge rise. The whole implication being that she'd never stopped for a minute since I went out in the morning, and would have been finished if I'd come in at my usual time.

'There was another one of those tales she put around about me, that I was liable to fly into a rage if I walked in and found that all the work wasn't done and my dinner ready to sit down to. The truth was that she was a very good cook and my dinner was always ready. She had to invent persecutions. When we had visitors she was, of course, a different person. She was quite shameless and uninhibited. She'd call me "dear", fuss over me, fetch and carry for me, take on the role of the meek and mild little wife whose only desire was to please her husband. For my part I never could relax, never pretend. I did the best I could, for the sake of the visitors. But people could hardly fail to get an impression that I was sulking over something. Which was precisely what she wanted. See the impossible situation I was in?'

I could indeed. Actually there was a lot more than I have set down. I can't recall everything. He was talking fast, with only a murmur of assent from me now and then to show I was listening. We reached Mordialloc, and he went on to tell me how things got to such a pass that he began to take to drink.

'My friends were falling away. We rarely got asked out, and people don't like coming around a house where man and wife are obviously not getting along together. I began to do what a lot of men in trouble do, look for comfort in the pub. I'd always been in the habit of having a couple with a mate after work. Just two, never more. But I began to dread going home at night, and the two became four, then six. On odd occasions, even eight. That was always enough to light me up a bit, keep the dinner waiting, lay a charge that never failed to go off. I could hold my drink, you know. I was never helpless, but I found I could always face her better with a few under the belt. It suited her, too. People would see me coming along the street a bit the worse for wear — more strength to her arm! Another stick to flog me with, and the certainty of a ding-dong quarrel if she felt like it. I think the one thing she wanted more than anything else in the world was for me to strike her.'

'Why didn't you leave her?' I asked. It was the question that had been with me for the past few minutes. It was immediately evident that it was also one he had been expecting. I might almost say steeling himself for.

'Leave her? Yes, why didn't I?' He faltered for a moment, and I knew that what he was feeling was shame. Shame of having confessed to putting up with such outrage for so long.

'I suppose it was because I was a certain kind of coward. A man can be a hero in some ways, yet lack the guts to make a big decision the consequences of which he can't clearly fore-see. He keeps deluding himself that something will happen which will solve the problem for him. Micawberism takes many forms. I despise myself for it now. Think of it — of course I thought of it. I was always thinking of it, but when it came to action I always put it off. This week, next week, sometime, never. All I did was provoke her, particularly when I had a few drinks in.

'I used to challenge her to get out if I was such a beast. She loved that. It used to put new life into her. She had different ways of meeting it. Sometimes she'd burst into tears, seize her hat and coat, threaten to go out and throw herself under a train, jump into a river, poison herself. All so real that she would terrify me, and I'd grab her, prevent her by force from rushing out into the street. At other times she'd just stare at me, cold as an icicle, and tell me she'd known for years that that was what I wanted. 'Now we're getting the truth!' she'd say. 'Now it's coming out. You've got another woman, haven't you? You want me out of the way so you can fill the house up with her and your drunken mates.' And as often as not I'd put myself further into the red by going out there and then and getting real plastered. Is this Aspendale?'

'Yes.'

I felt him gather himself together as he took a big leap forward in his story. 'I'll have to skip a lot. I want to tell you how it all ended. You aren't bored with this, are you?'

'Far from it. Please keep going.'

'Well, believe it or not, I kept my nose to it for twenty years before I decided in cold blood to bring it to an end, no matter what happened. I realized later, of course, that I shouldn't have said anything to her. I should have just packed a bag and cleared out one day when she wasn't in the house. But it's easy to be wise after the event. One evening I told her I wanted to leave her. We weren't quarrelling at the time, and I was stone cold sober. She was knitting and I was supposed to be reading the paper. I'd thought out exactly what I was going to say and how I was going to say it. Without any preliminaries I just lowered my paper and asked her, quietly and very seriously, if she thought there was any sense in us carrying on any longer. And — listen, this is interesting — do you know how she took it?'

'Tell me.'

'She took it as calmly as if I'd said I was going out for a packet of cigarettes. She didn't even lift her face and look at me. Her brows came down, and the needles clicked a little faster, that was all. She just sat without saying a word while I pointed out, as gently as I could, that we'd both been wasting our lives, and that the best thing we could do now was call it a day. I didn't reproach her, I didn't drag anything up. I took half the responsibility by saying that the simple fact of the matter was that we'd been totally unsuited to each other from the beginning. I talked to her for quite some minutes, and there was never a word out of her. She just sat listening to me with tight lips and cold eyes, not a muscle flickering in her face. It was too late when I realized how her mind was working. All I felt at the time was elation, relief. I kept thinking: "My God, it's as easy as this after all!"

'I should have known better. When at last I stopped, and waited for her to say something, she looked straight at me for the first time. "I suppose there's another woman in this?" she asked. Believe me, there wasn't a tremor in her voice. And I gave the wrong answer. I said there wasn't. It was true, there wasn't, but I should never have told her. See what she'd been thinking?'

'I'm not sure. Just keep on telling me.'

'Don't you see,' his hand closed on my arm with such strength that he almost made me wince, 'it was what she wanted! Another woman! It was what she'd always wanted, and for a few precious minutes she'd been thinking she was going to get it. Another woman, after all she'd put up with from me. What a story to put around the neighbourhood! What a role to fill! Abandoned, after all the best years of her life. All the time I'd been talking she'd been building up the vision, meeting people down the street, putting a brave face on it as she'd put a brave face on everything else I'd done to her, wallowing in pity. And in one little sentence I'd blown it all to smithereens. I was going to leave her and live on my own. No woman at all rather than her, and everybody would know it. If you could only have seen what that did to her! She scared the daylights out of me. I'll never forget it as long as I live. She gave one heartrending yell and jumped up: "My God, that makes it worse!"

'Tell me, why should it have made it worse, for any woman except her? Even after all those years her mind was still beyond my reach. I thought that would have helped to console her, smooth the way. Instead, it drove her into a fury. Into hysterics. She shouted some terrible things at me. When I tried to calm her she rushed for the sideboard and dragged open the drawer, yelling she'd cut her throat and be finished with me once and for all. And, like the damned fool I'd always been, I seized her, struggled with her, made her drop the knife she never had any intention of using. She really did go over the wall that night, though. I had to put her to bed and send for the doctor. He knew, but doctors never tell. They're always afraid a time will come when you'll quote them to the patient. They just button up, prescribe a sedative, and leave you to it. Where are we now?'

'Almost into Chelsea. Only one more after that, for you. You didn't leave her?'

'No. As I said, I'm still with her. Only a week after that scene Providence took over. I had my accident, and that was the end of it. And this is what I really want to tell you — she came good.'

'She what?'

'I was terrified when it happened, you know, when I knew my sight was gone. I saw myself delivered body and soul into her hands —'

'Well, you were, weren't you?'

'Of course I was. But, don't you see, I'd become God's own gift to such a woman! A stage on which she could strut and perform to her heart's content. Imagine it! Stuck with a blind husband after all she'd been through. She slipped smoothly into the part even while I was lying in hospital. She visited me every day, often twice, and nothing pleased her as much as to find other people with me. I was never to see her face again, but everything came to me through her voice. She used to fuss over me, fiddle about with my pillow, sit combing my hair, stroking my hand. Over and over again she would assure me, usually in a voice just loud enough to carry to the next bed, that everything was going to be all right, I had nothing to worry about as long as she was alive. I'm afraid I wasn't very receptive. The whole performance used to nauseate me. I dreaded her coming in, and was always glad when the bell rang for visitors to go. I lived in mortal fear of the day when I would have to go with her. I thought it would all come to an end then.'

'And it didn't?'

'No!' For the last time I felt his urgent grip on my arm. 'Don't you see, she'd found a part which suited her so perfectly that she didn't have to play it. It fitted her needs like a skin. For the first time in her life she was a bona fide martyr, and let anybody deny it! She no longer had to rely on winning and fooling a fresh set of cronies from month to month. All she had to do was keep close to me, the helpless one, and the light of pity was never off her. All the adulation and sympathy her miserable heart had ever craved for. I wasn't to see the faces of my own close friends again, but from things they said to me I could read a changed attitude even in them — perhaps they'd been wrong about both of us after all. Everything she had ever longed for had fallen right into her lap. That's how I saw it, anyway. And it's how I believe it really was in the first few months.'

He stopped, and I knew he was waiting for me to say something. His face was turned full towards me, the sightless eyes wide open as if they might help him to read me.

'In the first few months?' I repeated in some confusion.

'In the first few months. Even when she continued to smother me with kindness after I went home, I couldn't see it as anything but an act which would come to an end as soon as she got tired of it. It was inconsistent with everything I knew about her. After all those years of stormy torment it was a weird experience, like waking up and finding myself in a glass jar. Exhibit number one. She had me exactly where she wanted me. I'd never been so precious. She loved taking me for walks, particularly on a Saturday morning, shopping, when everybody else was on the streets. Like a mother out with her first baby. Every now and then she'd stop and talk to somebody. One morning when it was a husband and wife I got snatches of what was going on between the two women while I was involved with the man. They were keeping their voices down, but we all have a special ear for a voice we know well. I heard my wife explaining how necessary it was for her to get me out as much as possible. "He mopes a bit if he's left too much by himself. I could get through the shopping quicker on my own, but I give him a little basket to carry, and he thinks he's helping me. It's good for him, gives him a sense of independence." I overheard a lot of things like that. See the skilful building up of herself? That, at least, was characteristic. Can you blame me if I was suspicious? I think she was disappointed when they found a new job for me.'

'But she did keep it up?' Only seconds to go now, and something in his manner told me he hadn't quite reached the end of his story.

'She kept it up. Ten years now, and I've never had it so good. That's what I meant when I said it was the best thing that ever happened to me. And — listen, this is the very essence of it — for her too! For her too. I may be wrong, but it's a long time since I began to give her the benefit of the doubt. Whatever it was in the first place, I don't think it's an act now.'

'You mean —'

'Yes, yes, yes! Remember what I said — the compassion that is in all women. They must have something to look after, something to nurse, something to hold in their arms, whether it's a baby or a man.' He sat forward in his seat as the train ran into Carrum station. 'I believe she's as happy as I am. You'll keep all this to yourself, of course?'

'Of course.' I got up to open the door for him. A Carrum acquaintance stood ready to receive him on the platform. 'Thank you for telling me. You've given me a lot to think about.'

He had indeed. But there and then I was left with two clear reflections: how fascinating it would have been to go home with him and meet his wife, and how little of life some men are driven to settle for.

• Man in the Night •

I'd heard him before this happened, of course. You grow up with a lot of odds and ends of experiences you never really notice until something occurs which focuses your attention on them. The focussing process which is the very essence of childhood, the tremendous adventure of discovering the everyday elementals of life. Sometimes it hurts, sometimes it doesn't. It all depends on what you were expecting; on whether an ideal has been destroyed or transformed into fact. I'm thinking of two of my own early discoveries — that Santa Claus wasn't real, and that the Man in the Night was. One wounded; the other healed the wound and planted a faith which hasn't been destroyed to this day.

I was a toddler at the time, I can't say how old. Just getting over a sickness, and back again in my own little room after a few weeks under the maternal eyes in the double bedroom. I had a window that used to look the full length of the front verandah. A real Australian verandah that creaked like the very devil when you walked over it. Worn sun-baked boards and blistered posts. All kinds of climbing plants rioted over the front of it, but it had an easterly aspect and plenty of heat used to get through early in the day. It was always littered with dead petals — jasmine, bougainvillaea, rose, wisteria — as fast as one finished falling another started. My bed was right alongside the window. I could lie there watching the brown lizards darting about wherever a patch of sunlight fell, and making all sorts of noises to frighten away the mynas eating the ripe figs on a branch that drooped right out over the steps. We had an old Irish setter that kept me company too. He used to come tearing round the minute dad let him off in a morning and poke his big wet nose over the window-sill to make sure I was still there.

He'd lie down then for the rest of the day, bumping the dry weatherboards with his tail every time he heard the slightest movement from my bed.

They were good days, but it was the Man in the Night that really made them live. After so much rest and sleep I was very easily disturbed. But only momentarily, the way a child is disturbed — turn over, muttering, and plunge straight into sleep again. I'd know nothing about it till the morning, then I'd start thinking. After a day or two I noticed that the same thoughts were coming every morning — a sound in the night. I kept going back to it at odd times during the day, then at night when I was being put to bed. I didn't ask about it, because I wasn't frightened — only curious. Possibly I already had the explanation in a hazy kind of way. However, thinking about it going to bed meant that I was subconsciously prepared for the sound when it did come. I was nearly well again, then, and a healthy child is awakened only for a second by a passing sound. But I knew all about it next morning. I knew the instant I looked out of the window and saw the blue enamel billy at the top of the verandah steps. That was when the mystery ceased to be just a sound in the night, and became the Man in the Night. More, it ceased to be a mystery — it became an adventure.

I said nothing about it to anybody. I'd just had one precious illusion smashed. I'd lost faith in the veracity of grown-ups. The Santa Claus myth had just been exploded. It was during the Depression, when Santa Clauses could be hired for sixpence an hour by any tinpot shopkeeper. The time when the very factor which prevented most children from getting any toys at all produced also a super-abundance of the great giver of 'free' toys. Even my young eyes had perceived the anomaly of pinched faces above the woolly beards, and ragged trousers showing below tawdry red robes. I decided to investigate this Man in the Night myself. I'd known long enough, of course, that milk didn't drop out of the sky, that it was connected in some vague way with 'milkman'. But milkman was just a word; I hadn't got to the point of investing it with human form, hadn't even begun to wonder about it. But it takes things to make sounds, and put milk in an empty billy, and I knew very well now what it was that had kept waking me up during the nights of convalescence. I wanted to find out for myself what this thing was like. It didn't take long, but it was good fun while it lasted.

First I tried keeping awake waiting for it, but that didn't work at all. So I tried waking up properly when it did come. That was better. A night came when I sat bolt upright in the darkness the instant the billy was moved. The window was open, but the steps were half the length of the verandah away, about five yards, and I couldn't see a thing. But I could follow every movement 'it' made. It took off the billy lid, set it on the verandah alongside, dipped seven times into the big serving bucket, poured seven times into the billy, put on the lid, hung up the dipper, shut down the bucket lid, and went off. I heard footfalls going swiftly away down the garden path, the bump of the wooden gate, and the coming to life of a horse and cart out on the road.

I was a bit confused that first night, but not for long afterwards. Three nights, and I had the whole routine complete. It wasn't 'it' any longer; it was a man, and there was a horse and cart in the story too. Sometimes he'd speak to the horse. I got to know its name — Baldy. I thought it a good name, funny and friendly, like Dumper, the dog. I used to lie awake for a long time after he'd gone, trying to work out what he looked like, what Baldy was like. I used to enjoy hearing the splash of milk in the billy; used to count the dippers — it wasn't for years afterwards that I solved the mystery of the little seventh one that came at the end. I learned the number of steps he took to get to the gate, and tried to work out what house it was he stopped at next in the street. I found out that he always came round about dawn; very often light was breaking before I fell asleep again. One morning when he came a little later than usual I had the thrill of seeing him — a bit of him, anyway. Unfortunately for me, the billy used to be placed against the verandah post at the top of the steps, so that he didn't have to come right up. He used to stand on the bottom step and reach up. The light was very weak, but I did see his hands as he replaced the billy and put on the lid. I couldn't tell whether they were big hands or little hands, white hands or brown hands — but they *were* hands. They gave indisputable reality to the Man in the Night, and nothing else mattered. I started praying for the day when the dawn would come very late and I'd find out a bit more.

It never entered my head that the Man in the Night came at slightly different times. Everything else about him was so dependable, how was it possible for me to doubt his watch? The noises he made were the same every night, and in exactly the same sequence. Even to that curious little seventh splash of milk in the billy, and the number of steps he took to the gate. Even on the night it was raining.

I was in a fever of anxiety that night, quite ready, though, to make full allowance. All kinds of other things had been different during the day; I understood quite clearly that rain stopped all manner of things. But he did come, and I very nearly shouted out to him in my relief and admiration. From that moment he was infallible. He was a hero. He was the one constant thing in a very uncertain world. Far better than Santa Claus or any of the fairies I was always being told about. He never disappointed. Everything else stopped and started and altered, but the Man in the Night went on forever.

He became the biggest thing in my young life. I used to think about him half the day, and go to sleep dreaming about him. Him and Baldy. I had a very clear picture of a big kind-faced man sitting up on a fine cart painted in bright colours, behind a funny bald-headed horse. I got that way I used to wake up as he put his foot on the bottom step of the verandah, then as he came along the path, then as he opened the gate. Finally, and every night, I used to sit up in a ferment of anticipation the minute Baldy came trotting down the street.

Then came the day I'd been praying for, a day when the whole firmament was out of joint. Something went wrong with the sun, moon, and stars, and the Man in the Night came in broad daylight. I know now he'd been sick, or involved in a collision, or his wife was having a baby — but no such explanation would have done me then. Explanations didn't matter, anyway. Nothing mattered except that he came in broad daylight. I'd been lying awake for years waiting for him, and was almost in tears when the music of Baldy's hooves sent me leaping out of bed. You didn't get a false dawn every morning; and I wasn't taking any chances on this. Out of bed, then! And not for the first time that morning, either. I'd already been up once to make sure the billy was indeed empty, and had been torn by conflicting emotions ever since — fear that he wouldn't come, and excitement over the way I was going to trap him if he did come.

Everything went perfectly. My door opened on a passage leading into the kitchen at the rear. I had to run the full length of the house both ways. Through the passage and kitchen, out by the back verandah steps, then back again by the path running along the side fence. I was in nightshirt and bare feet, but that didn't matter for it was a fine sunny morning and the path was just dry earth. Everything was fine that morning. Dumper very nearly dragged his kennel over as I shot past, but I didn't have a thought for him. I was after Baldy — I'd never seen a bald-headed horse. That was the reason for the flank attack. I could have confronted the Man in the Night at the front verandah, but Baldy would have been hidden by the trees in the garden.

He was quick, that fellow, but not too quick. He'd filled the billy when I got round, but I was at the front gate well in advance of him. And there I met him face to face — my Man in the Night.

No, he didn't disappoint me. He *was* a big man — and young, and hatless, and fair-headed, and active, and smiling. He was everything. I wanted to say something, but the words stuck in my throat. But he spoke! He even touched me. I'd taken up a position on the bit of lawn near the path where I wouldn't be in his way, but he broke his stride for an instant to reach out a long tanned arm and pat me on the head. The first time he'd ever taken more than twelve steps to reach the gate. 'Hello there, Nugget!'

Hello there, Nugget! He had a name for me already, a smile that was like a fire on a cold day, and a hand that ruffled my hair with grand familiarity. Hello there, Nugget!

Everything was just right. Even to the big coloured cart, and the wise grey horse that started to walk without being told to giddup. It wasn't bald, but that was good too, because I hadn't quite liked the idea of a bald-headed horse.

That was the day that I learned for all time that the creatures of fable and fantasy are never half as nice as the creatures of real life.

• Christ, the Devil and the Lunatic •

I was an atheist for several years before I met Hester, and never at any time during my courtship did I make a secret of it. She herself was a devout Anglican, and we married under an agreement that we would pursue separately our spiritual paths, and that our children would be taught to follow her. My paganism wasn't as clearly reasoned then as it is now. I couldn't, therefore, see how cruelly wrong it was to deliberately put into a child's mind beliefs which I myself had long ago rejected. Perhaps it was the influence of Hester herself. She was the serenest creature I have ever known, and I fell into the very forgivable error of ascribing her serenity to Faith. I wanted my children to grow up just like her.

Anyway, our arrangement worked very well, so well, indeed, that only once in all our married life have we had occasion to review it. That was when, in the bad year of 1931, I took a job as personal attendant to an imbecile.

It is of this that I wish to tell, because I believe it embodies an interesting, even if grim, study in the contentious subject of faith.

We were living in Richmond at the time, with two children, and having a desperately thin time of it. I had been a musician in a picture theatre, but the arrival of the 'talkies' had put me out of a job, and for more than twelve months Hester and I had barely scratched an existence. My profession placed me at a tremendous disadvantage in competing for other kinds of work, and all that came my way was an occasional day's gardening and Saturday mornings helping a friend who owned a wood-yard. I had a few pounds saved, but they soon went, and before long we had to move out of our little cottage into a flat. Our clothes wore out; we became shabby. We lived on porridge, bread and jam, mincemeat, and cabbages and potatoes, considering ourselves fortunate indeed when we could afford a little butter or a few chops. Hester and I didn't mind much for ourselves, but it was hard seeing the children go short. They were both boys, six and eight years old, ages when there is no bottom to the appetite.

Through it all Hester was splendid. That congested flat, with the boys sleeping in the living-room, and the constant worry of seeing that they didn't annoy other tenants, must have been heartbreaking for her after the little four-roomed cottage with its garden full of flowers and vegetables. All through two stifling summers she cooked at an open fireplace, for although we had a gas stove we found wood to be cheapest. Of a winter's night we used to go to bed very early, that being the only place where we could keep warm for nothing. Yet never once did I hear a word of complaint or criticism. Hester was the real true-blue Christian, consoling herself in adversity by reminding herself of those still worse off. Some knowledge of the real causes of social suffering made me bitter, but there were times when I envied my wife her faith. 'If ignorance is bliss, 'tis folly to be otherwise.' To me, the monster so euphemistically known as the Depression was something wholly horrible and unjust; to Hester it was but the working of a Divine Scheme. Now and again she would appeal to me to try to cultivate faith, but that's impossible. Reason insisted that I was right and she was wrong. Yet, I repeat, I envied her, because faith gave her peace and courage, however spurious and thereby she suffered less than I the pagan.

All of which is not to suggest that she did not suffer at all. Perhaps deep in her indomitable heart she felt everything, but I was rarely allowed to see it. On returning home after a futile search for work — that was the time. A woman has a way of looking at a man then. Question and answer are so unnecessary. Hester would hear me coming, and always I would find her in some attitude of arrested action, facing the door, her expression a study of mingled hope and fear. One glance at me was always enough. We simply smiled at each other and didn't talk about it. What was the use?

One morning I saw in the paper an advertisement requiring the services of 'a respectable young man as attendant to a mental patient, afternoons only.' The position was, of course, far out of my line, but in the past year or so I had chased stranger jobs. I therefore wrote a letter begging the favour of an interview. That, as is well known, is the correct procedure. One 'begs.' Three hundred years ago, Rousseau lamented that 'Man, who was born free, is everywhere in chains.' He should see us now, begging for the chains.

However, the favour was granted me, and I kept an appointment at an address in Cotham Road, Kew. On enquiring for 'Mr Storey', according to instructions, I was shown by a housemaid into an apartment, half office and half sitting-room, where a little bald-headed man was writing at a desk. He attended to me immediately, laying down his pen and asking me abruptly, though quite civilly, if I had brought the originals of my references. I had. His keen eyes examined me frankly as I held them out. I liked him immediately. Experience had taught me that men who look straight at you and don't fumble for words are to be respected.

After the papers came the usual questions. How old was I? What occupations had I followed besides those mentioned in my testimonials? Was I an Australian? How long had I been out of work? Was I married?

To all except the last I returned a truthful answer, believing that as a single man I would stand a better chance of getting the job. When he asked me what I proposed to do with the rest of my time should he engage me, I knew he had already made up his mind. Here again, however, I deemed it wisest to prevaricate, saying that most of my mornings were already taken up. He gave me a searching look.

'The wage,' he said, 'is only twenty shillings a week.'

I nodded, and he proceeded, without taking his eyes off mine: 'It's necessary that you should not be wholly dependent on this position. There are opportunities for — ah —' He hesitated, then went on with a dry smile, 'It is, in a very modest way, a position of trust, Lewis. No considerable sum is involved, admittedly, but it is essential that I have an honest man. Your charge — his name is Peter Lawson — comes of very wealthy people, and an allowance of ten shillings per day is made solely for his amusement. It will be one of your duties to handle that money.'

Mr Storey paused, as if to allow this to sink in. I remained silent, returning his gaze as frankly as I could.

He resumed, 'That ten shillings I will give to you each day, and you will lay it out as far as possible in accordance with Peter's fancies. Your job, in short, will be to take Peter out every afternoon and help him to spend his pocket money. Spend all of it, and manage it so that it lasts until it is time to come home.'

'What does he usually buy?' I naturally enquired.

Storey smiled and shrugged his shoulders. 'He spends it just as a child would, in Coles's emporium and in sundae shops. The job has its amusing side, I assure you. You'll come back every day full of chocolates and ice-cream and loaded with toys and rubbishy knick-knacks. I'm taking it for granted that you have your own mind made up — you want the job?'

'I certainly do, Mr Storey.'

'Excellent. You'll find Peter erratic, difficult at times, but quite harmless. Take him round the shops with his few shillings and he won't give you much trouble. If he takes a fancy to something which is too dear, just tell him it costs two pounds. He'll believe you.' Here Storey leaned forward, solemnly wagging his forefinger at me for emphasis. 'Now listen carefully, for this is something you must thoroughly understand. Peter has a currency all his own. It has four values, and it would be useless to talk to him of any other. To him everything costs either six and elevenpence or two pounds, every coin is either a "penny" or a "silver penny," and every note is one pound. Anything which he can buy costs six and elevenpence; anything which he can't buy costs two pounds. Therefore — mark this particularly — it is not a ten shilling note which I give you each day, but a pound note. Be careful always to refer to it as a pound, because mention of anything else would only confuse and upset him. Get to know him as quickly as possible; he has many little peculiarities you must find out for yourself. The all-important thing in the treatment of the mentally afflicted is to avoid the unusual, keep to routine, amuse them without exciting them. Peter, like all of them, is inclined to be suspicious, but once you've gained his confidence you'll be able to do as you please with him.'

There was quite a lot more in the same strain. Storey was

a man with his whole heart in his work, and I had to sit listening to him with an appearance of absorbed interest while really I was itching to get away to break the glad news to Hester. For it was glad news. One pound a week was a tragically inadequate income, but at least it would secure rent and insurances. Besides, I still had every morning in which to look for a real job.

That night we had a modest celebration, squandering two precious shillings on pork chops, butter and bananas.

'Perhaps this is the turning of the tide,' suggested Hester.

'Perhaps!' I assented dryly. 'To him that hath shall be given!'

'Cynic! The only time I ever hear you quoting the scriptures is when you wish to be sardonic.'

I was musing on the ten shillings a day squandered by a lunatic.

'Tomorrow,' I said thoughtfully, 'I'll help an idiot to eat ten shillings worth of lollies; afterwards I'll come home and watch my children eat bread and treacle because I can't afford to give them butter.'

I was speaking more to myself than to Hester, but must have sounded particularly bitter, for she came round the table and laid her hands on my shoulders. 'Tom, you don't really look at it that way, do you?'

'It's a grand world! I know a little family — so do you! — not far from here, who have an imbecile child, and they love every hair of his head. They wouldn't part with him, although they've only got to say the word and he'd go into a Home tomorrow. They go short themselves to feed him the best. Peter's people have everything, but they won't suffer the indignity and inconvenience of having him attached to them. And I, because I have nothing, must shoulder their responsibility.'

'Last night,' said Hester quietly, 'we were in the dumps. There was no job at all, and we were talking of selling the bedroom suite and your mother's wedding present. Now we don't have to do that, and — you grumble.'

'But you must admit it's terribly unjust, dear,' I protested.

'To you, yes, because you see no object in it. Tom, we mustn't question. Let us be thankful, or even this little may be taken from us.'

'By Him who ordained in the first place that I receive it!'

Nevertheless, I was in good humour when, punctually at one o'clock the next day, I presented myself at 'The Glen', as Mr Storey's private mental hospital was called. Peter, all wriggles and smiles, was formally introduced to me and we set off immediately, the 'pound' note reposing hypocritically in my trousers pocket.

I'd had some novel jobs since leaving the theatre, but before we'd gone a hundred yards Peter had made it painfully clear that I had yet to learn how some poor devils make a living. Dignity, I decided sadly, must go by the board. Considerably bigger than myself, grotesquely ugly, and without a scrap of physical discipline, Peter Lawson was a living hell-broth of all the monsters I had ever read of. All through the first hour I was constantly expecting him to dilate his horse-like nostrils and wag his piggish ears; both feats would have been horribly becoming. His brutal and disorderly energy frightened me. He was like a villainous marionette out of control. He didn't walk; he lurched and staggered and shambled, rolling his head, swinging his arms, and flapping down his slovenly boots as if there were no feet in them.

Never as long as I live will I forget that first outing with Peter. The whole enterprise was so odd, so fraught with petty anxieties, and so utterly lacking in decorum, that the wonder is I didn't push the crazy fool under a tramcar. He was as stubborn as a cow, as clumsy as a baby, and as helpless as a dead dog. At Victoria Bridge, where we changed from an electric into a cable tram, he immediately made for a front seat so that he could pretend to be driving, with me hanging on to the seat of his trousers. At the Town Hall, where we alighted, I had to wait a full half hour before he got tired of watching the policeman on point duty. From there we turned north, pursuing a devious and troublesome course along the crowded pavements as far as the Royal Mail Hotel. Here, from the familiar display under the green tiled walls, Peter selected his first purchase — *Truth, Smith's Weekly*, and *Sporting Globe*. In a tone of peevish authority that made me sizzle with rage I was instructed to give the news-vendor six and elevenpence — and carry the papers!

A few minutes later at the Bourke Street Post Office he said he was tired, sat down, and began to scan one of the papers upside down. When, thinking to calm myself, I began to roll a cigarette he instantly demanded one.

'Sure. Have this one, Peter,' I said, holding it out.

But he insisted on making one himself, and I had to watch anxiously while he spilled my precious tobacco and mutilated several papers. Then, without the slightest warning, he got up and started off across the road. Faithfully I followed, up Bourke Street to Swanston Street, then southwards as far as the Capitol Theatre, where I was doomed to pass one of the most wretched hours of my life. Peter wanted to go in, and Storey's definite instruction was to keep him out of theatres.

'We'll go in here,' announced Peter with disarming confidence. I had been assured that he understood perfectly well this was forbidden ground, but would probably try to take advantage of a new custodian.

'They won't let us in there, Peter,' I replied. 'It costs two pounds.'

I kept walking, but the bluff didn't work, for when I looked back he was standing stiffly at the booking window glaring at me with an expression of sullen defiance. I returned.

'It's time we had something to eat, Peter,' I suggested hopefully. 'We can come back this way later.'

He indicated the painted beauty in the box, who, with the commissionaire, was watching us delightedly. 'Give her six and eleven. I'm going in.'

Argument, I now knew, was useless, so I settled down to try and wear him out. The commissionaire, who seemed to see nothing but humour in the situation, persuaded the accursed fool to stand away from the booking window, while I took up a position on the opposite wall. And there we remained for a whole agonizing hour. Now and then I took a turn up and down the pavement, or passed a word with the commissionaire, but Peter never once moved. Idiots must have the physical hardihood of religious fanatics, for Peter's posture was one I couldn't have sustained for ten seconds. Every time I caught his eyes he scowled.

'He's harmless, I suppose?' said the commissionaire.

'That depends on what you mean by harmless!' I fumed. 'I'm the dangerous one at the moment. If it doesn't move soon you can take it home and whack it up with the wife and kids!'

Heaven alone knows how long the stalemate would have

lasted had not a group of lascar seamen come along. Their out-landish costumes and excited yabberings and gesticulations completely bewitched Peter, drawing him as the Pied Piper drew the rats. And without as much as a glance at me he fell in behind and tailed them along the street. My luck seemed to have turned, for the seamen actually entered Coles, where Peter soon lost them in the crowd.

Any hopes I had, however, of an easy run home were soon dissipated, for it was in Coles that the real adventures of that day really began. Storey had warned me, but Peter far sur-passed my most gloomy anticipations. He handled everything, wanted to buy everything, barged all over the place like a vul-gar woman, giving voice every now and again to a crazy high-pitched cackle that made everybody stop to stare at us. He bought balloons and wanted them blown up on the spot. He bought a large kewpie, threw away the bag, and gave the damned thing to me to carry. He paid sixpence for a mouth-organ and created a traffic block trying to play it. He bought a box of tacks, went to count them, and spilled the lot. He bought a mousetrap and got his fingers caught trying to set it. Every purchase he immediately and ruthlessly divested of its wrapper. He bought a feather duster and began to sulk when I objected to being tickled with it. In an effort to restore his good humour I bought him a packet of petunia seeds. The pretty little envelope delighted him.

'That's cheap for six and eleven, eh?' he beamed, and promptly ripped off one end, scattering the tiny seeds on the floor.

We must have made a sensational picture when, about five o'clock, we came out onto Swanston Street again. Peter had the handle of the feather duster rammed down the front of his trousers, with the bunch of scarlet feathers ornamenting his chest. In one hand he held aloft a vivid and fully extended toy sunshade, in the other the mouth-organ on which he gave an occasional hideous blast. From one jacket pocket protruded a packet of lunchwraps, from the other a smelly bundle of fire-lighters. My share was the kewpie, a wooden Mickey Mouse on a swing, a bottle of turpentine, and the newspapers. I was utterly exhausted, and trying hard to decide what to say to Mr Storey when I got back.

I had yet to learn that Peter could keep it up until the final gong. While waiting for a tram at the intersection he discovered that something was pricking his leg. I had to run him over to the public lavatory near the Town Hall and take down his trousers. He must have rescued some of the tacks off Coles's floor, for I found several in his underpants. Coming back he insisted on buying a bunch of flowers, which he graciously gave me to carry. In Victoria Street his sunshade was blown away, and he made such a hullabaloo that the gripman stopped the tram while I raced back along the track. Then he took to playing with the Mickey Mouse, finishing up by stamping the thing to smithereens because it wouldn't work to his satisfaction. At Victoria Bridge I had to blow up the balloons and tie them with his bootlace, while all the way up Cotham Road he tickled me with the feather duster. Several people — more lunatics, I assumed — were in the grounds of 'The Glen' when we arrived, and I regarded it as an ominous sign that they took little notice of us. Mr Storey wasn't about, so I handed Peter over to an attendant and fled.

That night I told Hester everything. Dear girl! Her calm voice was celestial music to me after the crazy cackles of Peter.

'Tell me what you bought,' she said.

I named everything from the newspapers to the bunch of flowers. Every now and then she shook her head, murmuring sadly, 'God help him! God help him!'

'God undoubtedly is helping him!' I once replied shortly. In the sane atmosphere of my home I was quickly losing my ill humour, could even see something to chuckle at in Peter's antics. Nonetheless there was a rankling sense of injustice and ignominy that became stronger as I thought of it all. I said: 'A few hours ago, in Bourke Street, an ice-cream nearly choked me; you and the boys haven't tasted ice-cream for months.'

Hester looked at me reproachfully. 'Tom, you're brooding on this.'

'My dear, that only half describes it. I'm rebelling at a — a tyranny that's so terribly subtle one can hardly name it. I suppose a beetle feels like this when it's being poked around a box with a bit of stick. This afternoon Peter and I were Waste and Want parading hand in hand. Imagine it! That Frankenstein with a sunshade! Newspapers he can't read! A mousetrap

he can't set! Fire-lighters, and no fire to light! Dolls, turpentine, flower seeds!'

I really was angry, but thank heaven for the grace of humour.
Even as I spoke I saw again the ludicrous figure of Peter,
trousers down over his boots, with his scarlet feathers and
sunshade, patiently and smilingly waiting while I picked tacks
out of his underpants. I burst out laughing, Hester joined in,
and for the rest of the evening we talked of Peter only with
pity and amusement. Hester appealed to me to be patient with
him.

'It's only for a little while, dear,' she said. 'By and by we'll
get over our troubles, but poor Peter will always be like that.'

I spent the following morning in the usual way, looking for
work, and with the usual result. At one o'clock I returned to
'The Glen', feeling, no doubt, just as Daniel must have felt
entering the lion's den.

That was the day Peter tried to sweetheart me. At the Victoria
Bridge tram terminus we had ice-creams, and for five minutes
my precious lunatic studied me with a brooding and silent
intensity that made me wonder what devil's scheme he was
hatching now. He began the performance by sidling coquet-
tishly along to the far end of the seat.

'I like you!' he announced with a mirthless smile.

'That's nice of you, Peter,' I replied cautiously.

'Do you like me?'

'Sometimes, when you're a good fellow and do as I tell you.'

He frowned. 'I like you all the time.'

'How much, Peter?'

The next instant I could have bitten my tongue off. Laying
his Caliban's head on the back of the seat he half closed his
eyes.

'I love you!' he whispered.

Two tram conductors standing within earshot tittered. I
didn't mind that much, for they probably knew Peter. What did
worry me was the question of where the little comedy was
going to end. Evidently Peter had been overhearing things and
was giving me the benefit of it. I tried to wriggle out of the
trap by winking at him and nodding significantly in the direction of the conductors.

'You shouldn't tell me that now, Peter. Wait till we get on the tram.'

He scowled again. 'I'm not going on the tram.'

I exhibited the 'pound' note. 'What about this? Don't you want to see the shops?'

'I want to stay here with you. I love you.'

I went to get up, but he caught me by the arm, stretching his great bull neck and protruding his thick and slobbering lips. 'Kiss me!' he grunted.

I kissed him.

That same day he stopped outside a big delicatessen in Swanston Street and pointed to some saveloys. 'How much are they?'

'Two pounds each!' I gasped. 'Come on!'

His last tamer, however, must have indulged him, for he began to sulk. 'I want some.'

I defied him for a little while, but had to yield in the end. I bought three, which he promptly dragged out of the bag with a savageness that made me shudder. Fair in the middle of the crowded pavement he giggled and shook them at me, three wretched saveloys.

'How much were they?' he screamed.

'Six and eleven. Put them in your pocket. The dogs will snap at them.'

He cast a wild and predatory look at the shop window. 'I want some more.'

It was frightful. Five times he drove me into the shop, finishing up the proud owner of two dozen saveloys. In the midst of hilarious spectators I baulked at giving him the last lot.

'I'll carry these, Peter,' I said affably. 'The dogs —'

'I want them!' he bawled, snatching, and in an instant saveloys were strewn everywhere.

It takes the responsibilities of married life to develop self-control in a man. Thinking of Hester and the boys I cleared a ring while my poor idiot gathered up his precious bags of mystery. And off we set again, Peter with saveloys sticking out of every pocket and as many as he could clutch in his ape-like paws. Thus laden he made me steer him into Sargent's Cafe, where he dumped all the infernal things on a table and called for crumpets and tea. The wonder is that we were allowed in.

Perhaps they took pity on me, for I must have looked pretty haggard. Staying there, however, was another matter. Peter followed his afternoon tea with a passionfruit ice and one of the seeds got under his top dental plate. I saw immediately what he was going to do, and reached out a restraining hand, but he shook me off.

'Leave me alone!' he screeched. 'I know what I'm doing.'

Everybody had stopped eating. From the far side of the cafe a manageress was watching me resentfully, but I was helpless. There was a barbaric violence about everything the idiot did that frightened me. So I just sat and simmered while he painstakingly cleaned the dental plate with his handkerchief. Then, just as he was about to return the thing to his mouth, he got one of those fantastic ideas which can come only to the utterly demented. His hysterical gaze fixed itself on the nearest saveloy, he gave a shrill crazed laugh, and before I could move a finger to stop him he jammed the teeth fair into it. And as if that weren't enough he had to whip out his lower plate, turn the saveloy over, and complete the bite on the other side, driving the teeth in with a thump of his fist that shook the table.

We were ordered to leave, of course. The manageress wanted to ring for the police, and only after some persuasion accepted my assurance that the situation was not quite out of control. I had to bribe Peter with chocolate éclairs before he consented to follow me out into Swanston Street. That used up the last of his money, yet at Victoria Bridge he refused to board the tram until I had bought him a cauliflower. That came out of my own money, as did the fares. Moreover I had to carry the cauliflower, and between it and the saveloys our homecoming was little less spectacular than that of the previous day. We finished up with a magnificent dog-fight right outside 'The Glen', a pack of mongrels losing all interest in a little bitch to follow the trail of Peter's saveloys. It made my blood boil when Peter began to feed them, for in spite of all ill-treatment they were still good saveloys. I rescued four by pretending to have a couple of poor starving dogs of my own at home.

Storey showed nice understanding when I told him of having spent some of my own money. He advised me to deduct it from the ten shillings next day.

'You find him a bit difficult?' he enquired.

'Mr Storey, the job's worth a pound a minute!' I replied vehemently. 'Couldn't you get his people to raise my pay a little?'

'My boy, I've already tried. Your predecessor asked for an increase, but I had to let him go, although he understood Peter as no one else has ever done.'

'And his people are wealthy!' I exclaimed bitterly. 'It's a hard world, Mr Storey.'

Quite kindly he laid a hand on my shoulder. 'Young man, never generalize about morality. The world's a very beautiful place, only it has some very mean things in it. It's a bad thing to get bitter at your age. Don't wait until too late, as so many of us do, to discover that the ideal philosophy is to make the best of things as you find them. Don't run your head against the inevitable. Understand?'

I understood I was being lectured, but didn't mind that very much, even though I found the argument rubbish. Storey had a way with him. His steady friendly gaze had a soothing effect on me after the crazy antics of Peter.

I nodded resignedly. 'I took the job at a pound a week, and if I'm not satisfied I don't need to stay, eh?'

My tone was still bitter, but he replied patiently, 'It comes to that, although I'd be sorry to lose you. The situation is that Peter's people allow three pounds a week for his pocket and one pound for special attendance, and I've been unable to get them to improve on it. You see I admit the position is worth more.'

'It ought to be one pound for his pocket and three pounds for special attendance,' I said. Storey's candour, however, had got the better of me, and I smiled. 'Thanks for the admission, anyway!'

He gave me a friendly pat. 'Go home and refresh yourself, my boy. Troubles are always a little smaller when you've rested and eaten. Ask for me tomorrow if there's anything you want to tell me.'

Not until I laid the four rescued saveloys on the table at home did I observe that one of them bore the clear imprint of Peter's teeth. Thank heaven again for the gift of humour. My first impulse was to throw out all four, but when I got to telling Hester about the scene in the cafe, I had to laugh, and the three unblemished specimens went into the pan. Hester laughed also, but afterwards I knew by her subdued air and the thoughtful glances she kept giving me exactly how she felt about it all. She gave the boys one each and made to lay the other on my plate.

'No thanks,' I said. 'I've had all sorts this afternoon. You have it.'

She demurred at first, but gave in when I insisted, and began to eat. Watching her covertly I saw a pathetic study in the martyrdom of pride. She really did carry her scruples to ridiculous lengths. Those saveloys had been begged for; I had used cunning and falsehood in order to wheedle them off a helpless idiot. For her, therefore, they held no relish. On the other hand she knew also at what cost to my own dignity they had been acquired, and wanted to eat to please me.

'They're not very tasty without sauce,' I remarked drily.

She smiled weakly. 'It's quite nice. I just don't seem to be very hungry tonight.'

I knew better, though, and without speaking picked the saveloy off her plate and threw it into the bucket under the sink. She uttered no protest, and as I sat down again her hand stole across the table and settled gratefully upon mine.

'I was thinking of you, Tom,' she said quietly.

Nevertheless, I didn't regret bringing the infernal things home, for the boys enjoyed their portions. Later, when we were alone, Hester and I fell into discussing the problem of living. We rarely talked of anything else those days, for nothing else mattered. All the talking in the world won't increase one's income or bring down the cost of commodities, yet in the anxieties of poverty it is impossible to leave the subject alone. One returns to it again and again in the wretched unreasoning hope that, perhaps, on investigation things will prove to be not quite as bad as appeared.

Therein, incidentally, lies the explanation of the comparative lack of fine taste in the working class. For, in the name of creation, how can a man give his mind to exalted things when his boots are worn through and his belly empty? Anxiety is the great sickness of the lowly, for no organic disease causes more universal suffering than the prolonged and dreadful scheming to make ends meet, and the abiding fear of what tomorrow may fail to bring forth.

That night Hester suggested quite seriously that I give up the job. She contended that it was doing us no good, that even in two days I had become horribly cynical and irritable.

'Confess,' she said, 'that it hurts you to help Peter spend that money. You're brooding over it. You think it outrageous that the poor fellow should waste it so when we and so many others are in serious want.'

'Yes, in want!' I echoed emphatically. 'Our boys are at an age when they should be building constitutions to see them right through life. And they aren't doing it. They hardly know the taste of eggs, while that pop-eyed barbarian —'

'At least they're sane, Tom. It's God's will —'

I made an impatient gesture. 'That's all very well, my dear, but I can't see God's purpose. Less than ten shillings a day would raise two useful citizens, yet what have we? Good meat thrown to the dogs! Mousetraps! Sunshades! Flowers! I can't grasp it at all.'

Hester eyed me sadly. 'If only you believed!'

I kept silent, because she'd have been hurt by the only thing I could honestly have said.

'Don't go back, Tom. It isn't worth it,' she said a moment later.

'The rent,' I reminded her.

'We'll manage somehow. We'll sell the suite. Something must come along soon.'

'No.' I was beginning to feel ashamed, and made an effort to throw off the black reflections which oppressed me. 'I'm not grumbling at the job itself, sweetheart, as much as at the — the wicked — oh, ethics of it all. It's so preposterous. But never mind. The point just now is that you're broke?'

She smiled ruefully. 'I have fivepence, and there's hardly anything in the house. I thought Mrs Baker would have paid me today, but she said she didn't have it. Fivepence to get lunch and tea with tomorrow. You'll have to try to bring something in yourself if Peter pays you.'

Mrs Baker was a neighbour for whom she sometimes did a little sewing.

'I'll pay myself,' I said grimly.

It was Wednesday night. Counting what I had loaned Peter, we had exactly thirty pence on which to live until Friday.

On the following morning Mr Storey's greeting was particularly affable. Obviously he was out to placate me, and I wasn't surprised when, in the course of the short conversation, he admitted that the position was one which he had experienced some difficulty in keeping filled. After I'd listened patiently to another of his invigorating 'tonic talks', he cautioned me not to mention my little debt to Peter.

'Just take what is due to you and put it in a separate pocket. He wouldn't understand if you attempted to explain, and it isn't in the least necessary.' He gave me one of those warm frank stares that I found so attractive. 'It should do you no harm to learn that I liked the way you told me about that last night.'

'I had to recover it, Mr Storey. I'm broke.'

'That isn't what I meant. Some fellows wouldn't have mentioned it at all. They'd just have taken it, probably a bit more than their due. And the temptation to repeat the practice would have been irresistible. I know now that I'm dealing with a very straightforward man. That's why I don't want to lose you.'

He wouldn't have said that had he known what was in my mind. I thanked him, passed some inept remark about thieves never prospering, and felt a miserable hypocrite. Between thoughts of Hester and Storey, and the usual antics of Peter, I passed a mentally strenuous day. Paganism doesn't imply immorality. In all my life I'd never been guilty of stealing, and the certain knowledge that two very good people had unbounded faith in my integrity made my first transgression infinitely difficult. The fact is, however, that I did transgress. Perhaps if Peter had been at all merciful that day I would have remained honest, but he made me carry a bowl of goldfish and a bundle of rhubarb all the way from Victoria Market to the Town Hall, and — the Devil won.

That evening Hester and I had our first really serious difference when, on returning home, I laid five packages on the table. Suspecting nothing at first, she gave me the customary kiss, told me to sit down and rest for a few minutes before washing, and turned to inspect my purchases.

'You seem to have got good value,' she remarked smiling.

The boys were climbing all over me, but I hardly noticed them. Hester's smile didn't last long. There was half a pound of butter, a pound of lamb chops, six eggs, two pounds of apples, a pound of tomatoes, and a wholemeal loaf. She looked at them for quite a minute, turning them over again and again, no doubt totalling up their cost, before turning her puzzled face to mine.

'Wherever did you get them, Tom?'

'I earned them.'

'But how?'

'Taking care of a raving maniac for four benighted hours!'

The boys transferred their attentions to the packages. I got up, and with affected unconcern began to take off my collar and tie. But Hester took hold of me by the arms, turning me around so that I was forced to look down into her face.

'Tom, you used Peter's money?'

I understand better now just what it meant to her, but at the time the implied reproach seemed outrageous. I'd anticipated something of the sort, but had hoped that she would, at least, let us all enjoy a good meal and postpone discussion until the boys were in bed.

'Look here, Hester,' I said, 'there's less than four shillings' worth of tucker there, and I've earned it a thousand times over in the last few days. We haven't had a decent meal for weeks. There's one there, and nobody else a hoot the worse off —'

'It's stealing, Tom, no matter how you like to look at it.'

'Hush, the boys are listening!' Annoyance came quickly, for I'd been reasoning the thing out all the afternoon and was thoroughly convinced of the justice of what I had done. I believed that only a coward or a religious fanatic would have acted otherwise. Nevertheless I controlled myself, and fell to appealing. My immediate concern was to get the frying pan onto the fire and see Hester and the boys digging into the chops. Even now Dick and Bob were clamouring for apples. I told them to help themselves, and tilted my wife's chin so that her worried face was raised to mine.

'Couldn't we eat now and talk afterwards? Maybe I'll promise not to do it again.'

'You meant to do this when you went out this morning.'

'I did. Are we going to eat, or shall I throw them out? I can't return them either to the shops or to Peter.'

'Please don't be angry with me, Tom. I can't help it. I never thought — I didn't want to come down to this. We —' She broke off, biting her lip, on the point of tears.

Torn between pity and exasperation I clasped her to me, and for some moments we stood thus in silence. Dick, the eldest boy, asked me with a mouth full of apple what was wrong with Mummy, and I told him to shut up. It's a wicked thing to snub a child, and his timid and curious gaze as he backed away cut me to the heart. My eyes fell on the contentious packages. Beyond them there seemed to hover, ugly and menacing, the distorted image of Peter. I felt his vile presence, I heard his insane laugh. I tasted again his graveyard kiss, and reflected that since then I had kissed Hester. Strange fears gripped me. I sensed contamination and calamity. Peter had followed me home! Something nameless and unclean was in the air, and with a smothered curse I tore loose from my wife's arms.

'Tom, what are you going to do?'

'I'm going to do what you want me to do. Willingly! Hand me that bucket, Dick!'

'No, you mustn't! Please —' Hester, with tears streaming down her face, fastened her arms around me again. 'Tom! Wait ... I'll cook them! Don't throw them out ... please ... this once ... we can talk it over. Dear ... listen to me! ... I was selfish ... I wasn't thinking of the boys ... I know you did it for them ...'

I had one hand free and had already swept some of the things into the bucket before self-control returned. Hester and the boys were clinging to me, coaxing and whimpering. The whole scene was horrible, so foreign to our home. The simple fact is that we had momentarily broken down. Two years of ceaseless anxiety, that was it. People can't live under such conditions without changing. We had, without knowing it, got to that stage where any sudden emotional strain was liable to precipitate collapse. In Hester collapse took the form of fear and despair; in me it awakened a fiend of hate and destruction. I wanted, more than anything else, to get my hands on something I hated ... to rend, to smash, to destroy. If, by any extraordinary trick,

Peter had walked into that room just then I would have killed
him.

But Peter didn't walk in, and firmly disengaging myself from
Hester I sat down. She, poor girl, turned the chops into the
frying pan and the butter into a dish with a haste that shamed
me. I watched her in silence, feeling inexpressibly weary and
nauseated. Everything oppressed me all at once — the cramped
room with the wretched remains of our furniture, Hester's
shabby frock and down-at-heel shoes, the threadbare table-
cloth, the frayed sleeves of Dick's jersey, the patches in Bobby's
pants, and more than anything else, the long vista of
tomorrows ... poverty, anxiety, little hopes, big disappoint-
ments. We seemed to have travelled so far from the little cottage in Powlett Street.

Meanwhile Hester was busy. The table was laid, bread was
cut, the chops sizzled. I caught her anxious sidelong look, and
not knowing what to say I got up, rolled up my sleeves and
went out to wash.

Neither of us referred to the matter as we sat down and
began to eat. We talked, of course, but it was the boys who got
things going and brought us back to normal. Children are great
peacemakers, and in the irresponsible chatter of Dick and Bob,
Hester and I found ourselves again. At the same time the meal
was hardly a success. It was the case of the saveloys all over
again. Hester smiled whenever I looked at her, but I knew her
too well to be deceived. I still believed that I had done right,
but her scrupulous loyalty to her faith compelled respect. This,
I knew, was an issue on which she would never yield.

Later, when the boys were asleep, there came the reckoning.
For half an hour I read a newspaper and my wife knitted without either of us saying a word. Each of us was waiting for the
other to begin, and I was relieved when she asked quietly, without looking up, 'Were you very angry with me tonight, Tom?'

'I wasn't angry with you at all,' I replied. 'I was simply exasperated at the predicament we found ourselves in.'

She knitted for a minute or two. Then, in the same quiet
tone, 'What are you going to do about it?'

Welcoming this straightforward approach, I laid aside my
paper. 'If you mean am I going to rob Peter again, the answer

is no. Not without your full approval, anyway. I don't want any more scenes like that one. They're right out of our line.'

Hester gave me a caressing glance. 'It was horrible, Tom.' She came and sat beside me, laying her hand on mine. 'You must give in to me in this, dear. You must promise not to do it again.'

'Of course I promise, but under protest!'

'But this is so unlike you. You used to be so ... so fussy. It's stealing, no matter how you try to justify it. You'd keep on doing it, and there'd be so little difference between stealing from somebody else. You'd take away the only precious things we have left, our pride and honesty. Don't you value them?'

'Hester,' I replied confidently, 'I haven't stopped thinking of this for twenty-four mortal hours. And for the life of me I can't see how I'm offending God or hurting anyone on earth. Peter went home today as happy as a schoolboy. Mind you, I am giving in; I won't touch his money again. But I still maintain that all this fuss is uncalled for. Our first duty is to those two children.'

'That's just what I'm concerned about, only we see it in different ways. I wish you'd never taken this job.'

'So did I a couple of hours ago. I had an uneasy feeling that Peter had somehow got between you and me. But I've been turning it all over again. We're still soft, kid, that's what's wrong with us. We're too sensitive, too conscientious. We'll have to toughen up or we'll go under. Christianity wasn't made for this social order. The great captains of industry they talk about ... professors of exploitation I call them ... are they Christians?'

'Christianity was made for all time,' murmured Hester sadly. The simple sentence was spoken with a depth of sincerity and conviction that almost awed me.

'If Christ came back to earth tomorrow,' I exclaimed bitterly, 'there'd be a bigger clean up than ever there was in the temple.'

'Christ is always with us.'

'I can't believe it, my dear. If He sees all this, and is indeed omnipotent, then what is His object? All this inequity, and useless suffering. Why, why, why?'

Hester's hand came up reprovingly. 'Tom, you promised ...'

'I promised never to attack religion. True, but ...'

'Wait! We can leave religion out of it. There's something else. Do you want me to think of you as a thief?'

'A man isn't a thief when, in order to feed his family, he takes what no one else needs.'

'His family doesn't want it. Yes, I'm speaking for the boys too.' Hester spoke confidently and quickly, as if afraid of losing the thread of her argument. 'I want them to grow up respecting you. They needn't know the truth, I admit, but I couldn't bear hiding something from them that I was ashamed for them to know. And if I'm to teach them, then I must respect you myself. I want to keep on admiring you, as I've always done. I don't mind going hungry, you must know that by now. And it hurts me as much as it does you to see the boys going short. But, Tom, it can't last forever. Work must come sooner or later, and then we must have nothing to regret. We've lost so much; let us, at least, keep our self-respect. There's Mr Storey too. Don't you value his confidence? He also trusts you. You told me Storey gives an impression of honesty. Those were your very words. That doesn't spring from nothing, you know. Storey *is* honest. Don't you want to impress people in the same way? Storey trusts you. How could you look him in the face if you were secretly betraying that trust? If the temptation is too much for you then give up the job.'

'Not on your life!'

'You intend to go on with it?'

'I do.'

'And you'll play fair?'

'I'll play fair . . . according to the lights of society!'

Hester smiled ruefully. 'I know you're not a bit impressed by what I've said. Still, you've made a promise, even if it was . . .'

'Extorted!' I smiled. I was weary of the whole business, and wanted to put Peter right out of mind until tomorrow.

'Some day you'll be glad I . . . kept you in order. We've had some bad luck, and God will reward us.'

I laughed. 'They say the Devil also looks after his own!' And before she could reply I had caught her in my arms and closed her lips with a kiss.

'You're a frightful heathen, Tom,' she gasped a moment later.

'And you're a darling to bear with me!'

Hester's relief at what she regarded as a victory over sin must have infected me, for there was a happier atmosphere in the home than there had been for many a long day. Later in the evening she asked me for some music, and I wiped the dust from my long-neglected violin and played to her. Afterwards we fell to talking over old times, of the cottage in Powlett Street, of the flowers we used to pick from the tiny garden, of Sunday mornings when we used to loaf in our pyjamas on the sunlit back verandah, of Saturday nights, when Hester always used to come to the theatre and walk home with me. Great days. Talking of them didn't make us at all sad, and we went to bed with the firm, though quite unreasonable, conviction that better times really must come soon.

Better times did come, but not until three months later. In those three months three forces combined to torment me: Christ, the Devil, and the Lunatic. Christ in the faith of Hester, the Devil in the temptation provided daily by Peter's money, and Peter himself. I knew no peace, but that one pound a week was indispensable, and I carried on. Never again did I appropriate a penny of Peter's money. Every weekday for three months I took him out and deliberately squandered ten beautiful shillings. It was grotesquely infamous. Often I came home sick from eating ice-creams and chocolates to sit down with Hester and the boys to a meal of tea and bread and jam. For I reasoned that the more Peter and I ate the less conspicuous would we be. Better a shilling's worth of candy in my stomach than a balloon or a bundle of rhubarb in my hands. Each day I could have taken two shillings out of Peter's allowance without him being a whit less content, for I acquired quite an art of interesting him in cheap trifles.

'Spend it all every day,' Storey had said, and faithfully I did spend it all. It was criminal. I got to a stage when meals at home were an ordeal, when I would sit gloomily reflecting: we could be eating meat and vegetables, perhaps even a pudding. And eggs for breakfast!

There was the indignity of the job, too. Most nights I came home looking like an idiot myself — grimy, perspiring, and dishevelled. No wonder Hester told me I was losing pride in myself. She said I was getting vulgar and careless. A score of times she begged me to give up, but there was nothing else and I would tell her gruffly to let the matter rest. We talked little of an evening. As often as not I fell asleep on the sofa. We took each day as it came, a makeshift hand-to-mouth existence. Storey's one pound a week paid rent, firewood, and insurance. For the rest we depended on what Hester could pick up with her needle and I at odd jobs.

The end came with a completeness that sent us both almost hysterical with joy. A friend got me a position in a warehouse in Flinders Lane at four pounds a week. Constant work at four pounds a week! Hester handed me a letter with the glorious news when I came in one day, and we did a jig round the table with the boys watching us in bewilderment. Four pounds a week! It was explained, moreover, that I was to begin as soon as possible. It was then Tuesday night and, quite naturally, I decided to drop Mr Storey and Peter there and then, and begin the new job next morning. By so doing I would collect two pounds on Friday night instead of Storey's one. When Hester began preaching to me about fair play in regard to Mr Storey I exploded, 'Hang Mr Storey! Would he consider himself obliged to give me warning if he had no further use for me?'

'You needn't take your morals from other people, Tom,' she replied quietly. 'In your own heart you know what's right, and you must do it.'

'My first duty is to provide for this home. Mr Storey comes second.'

'Your duty is to do as your conscience tells you. Mr Storey has treated you fairly. He trusts you. Tomorrow he will be waiting for you . . .'

'He'll just have a job to fill. That'll be easy, with a thousand other unfortunates choosing between looking after Peter, or starving.'

'It isn't worth it, dear. Give him notice tomorrow and finish on Friday night. God has sent you work; let us be grateful. We've come through without being unkind to anyone. Don't betray a trust for a paltry twenty shillings.'

'A paltry twenty shillings!' I ejaculated.

Still, she prevailed, as she always had. My ultimate capitulation was, I suppose, only a just reward for her fortitude. Her example throughout had been so consistently brave that it would have been unkind to ignore this final appeal.

At nine-thirty on Wednesday morning, therefore, I presented myself at Mr Storey's establishment. The throwing up of a thoroughly detested job is, I declare, one of the few pleasures of life exclusive to the working man, and that summer morning I gave myself over to it with epicurean enthusiasm. This was my moment, and I lived it. I had a job, a real job, dignified and remunerative, and I approached 'The Glen' warm with the wine of independence.

A housemaid, immaculate in black and white even at that hour, answered my ring and I asked if I might see Mr Storey. She thought Mr Storey was busy just then with one of the patients, but if I would step inside for a moment she would take him a message. She knew me, of course, but I didn't tell her my business.

'Just ask if I could have a few words with him, please,' I said. 'It's important, but I won't keep him long.'

She departed, returning in less than a minute to say that Mr Storey could not come immediately but if I would wait in his office he would be glad to see me as soon as he was at liberty.

Grandly assuring her that time was of no value to me that morning, I allowed myself to be shown into the same cosy little room where, twelve weeks ago, I had had that momentous initial interview. Here, after seeing me settled in an easy chair, and indicating with a friendly smile the morning paper lying on the desk, the housemaid left me.

I didn't touch the paper. In a mood of luxurious indolence, I just lay backwards, heaved a sigh of contentment, and fell to musing on Mr Storey's charming office. It was comfortable, simple, and above all orderly, like the man himself. Nothing ornate, nothing superfluous, nothing out of harmony with the whole. A settee in the window recess, three easy chairs and a plain chair, a plain green carpet, a big cedar bookcase. On the mantelpiece two white plaster casts of classical figures, a pair of Chinese vases, and a marble clock. Lastly the desk, with its daily calendar, its stationery rack, inkstand and blotter, and morning's mail ... the latter opened and sorted into two or three neat piles ready to begin work on.

I felt a pang of envy. Everything breathed rest and security, the work-room of a man at peace with himself and all the world. Outside birds were singing in the garden, and faintly

I could hear the clatter of dishes in the dining-room. It was odd to reflect that this was a mental hospital. By turning sideways I could read the titles of some of Storey's books: Lord Avebury's *Pleasures of Life*, *The Meditations of Marcus Aurelius*, Wordsworth's *Poems*, and an apparently complete set of the works of Henri Fabre the great French naturalist. Here again was something characteristic of the man — simple philosophy, simple poetry, simple science, elementary text-books on exalted subjects. It was easy to picture Storey taking down the *Meditations* and conning it, leisurely and reverently, by the fire-side of a winter's night. What a contrast to the life I had been living during the past three months! It came to me suddenly with terrific force that this room had been just like this all the time. That afternoon, for instance, at the very moment when Peter had sunk his mouthless teeth into the saveloy, this room had been just like this. A little pool of peace and knowledge, with the muffled songs of birds, and the sunlight, filtering through the trees in the garden, making a pattern on the half-drawn curtains. Just like this.

I think it was at this stage in my reflections that my eyes fell on the name 'Peter' occurring on the top sheet of one of the little piles of correspondence. Had it been any other name I probably wouldn't even have noticed it. As it was, though still quite idly, I read the few words immediately following. They interested me. I looked at the address at the top. Then at the signature at the end. Finally, with a peculiar tingling sensation at the roots of my hair, I slowly read the letter right through. It was as follows:

Dear Mr Storey,

I thank you for your letter dated January 14th. It came as a surprise to me to learn that it has been necessary to engage a new attendant. Peter is, I well know, a big handful, but in these hard times I would have thought the remuneration sufficient to retain the services of any man seriously mindful of his welfare. It is unfortunate you did not inform me immediately of Arthur's impending depar-ture, as I have lately been involved in some financial loss and find it necessary to curtail Peter's expenditure. As you are aware I have always allowed more than I was legally obliged to, but circumstances now compel me to come down to the exact terms of Father's will.

It would have been convenient if the new attendant had been engaged on those terms; nevertheless an adjustment must be made. Will you, therefore, inform him that his wage is forthwith reduced from forty to thirty shillings per week? Peter, on his part, must content himself with ten shillings per day instead of the fifteen he has been accustomed to. This latter is, of course, a matter for yourself alone.

I am sorry to have to impose on you what will doubtless be an unpleasant duty, but I have no alternative. Will you please inform me of the working of the new arrangement as early as possible? I will be in Melbourne on business some time in April and will make a point of seeing you.

Yours faithfully,
Herbert Lawson.

Comment on the letter is unnecessary. Before leaving that room I compelled Storey, under threat of exposure, to hand over to me a cheque for all the money he had wrongly appropriated while I was in the job, a total of thirty pounds. Hester still thinks I won it on a racehorse, for I never had the heart to tell her the truth. I've never been a racing man, and she hasn't even yet got over her amazement at the one little flutter I was unable to resist.

• The Ticket •

It was 1924. I didn't know much at the time. I'd been out from England only six months, all of which had been spent on a struggling dairy farm near Sale. But I was young, anxious to test myself and see the country. So I came in to Melbourne, hung about the registry offices for a few days, received a lesson in card-sharping at the quite reasonable cost of £15, and took a job as groom — milk, kill, and generally useful — on a sheep station out from Beeac in the Western District.

I'd been in hopes of something better, but funds were almost exhausted, time otherwise was on my side, and it was five shillings a week better than I'd been getting. There was a bit of magic, too, in the word 'station'. I felt I was getting nearer to the Australia I was after, the Australia of sheep and cattle and horses and boundary riders. And big cheques. I was sick of doing a man's work for a boy's wage.

It was late winter. I left Melbourne in the early morning under grey skies, and at about three o'clock in the afternoon the train pulled up specially to set me down at one of those lonely little bush railway stations where intending passengers wave a flag in the daytime or a hurricane lamp at night.

It was a cheerless beginning. The rain still held off, but a cold wind blew along the platform. The country didn't seem very different from that around Sale. About half a mile away a house and outbuildings huddled against a group of pines. Everywhere else was grey-green plain, with here and there a dead gum tree and patches of those tough dark grasses that grow in swampy places.

I was met by an old man with a horse and jinker. An old man wearing a chaff-bag cape and a hat dented into a peak to shed the rain, who talked almost incessantly over the eight miles'

90

drive out to the property, first along an unmade road with pot-holes full of water, then through paddocks where the track wound between outcrops of stone and where heavily-woolled sheep lifted their heads to stare at us as we went by.

He said his name was Joe and that he was 'cutting a few thistles' on Meelah, as the place was called.

'I don't do much now. I've only myself to keep and I've got me own little joint in Beeac. I wouldn't be working now if it wasn't for Mr Bailey. He was stuck for a man to get the thistles down, and I like to help him out when I can. I'm finishing up tonight.'

'What's he like to work for?' I asked.

He gave the horse a flick with the bit of twig he was carrying. 'Git up there, Rose! What's he like to work for? He's a gentle-man. I've worked for Mr Bailey off and on for twenty years, and if anybody can show me a whiter man anywhere I'll be glad to meet him.' Joe turned to give me a prolonged stare.

'You ought to know,' I said agreeably.

'I know all right. And I'm warning you now you'll meet blokes in these parts'll tell you he's a bastard. All right, that's what they think. But I know what their form is — no-hopers! There's some blokes you could give the whole world to, and they'd still moan. Gimme, gimme, gimme — they never stop. All they can think of is squeezing as much money out of a man as they can get away with. Spare me days, you got to work in this world if you want to get on. And you got to have bosses. If there wasn't any bosses there wouldn't be any work. Anyhow, Bailey's only a battler himself. They think because he lives in a decent house and drives a car and has a few sheep . . .'

'How many?' I asked in an effort to give the conversation a more constructive turn.

'He'll be shearing about ten thousand this year. Git up there, Rose! But you ought to see the way he works himself! Most times he's only got three hands on the whole joint. You'll be one of the shearing crowd, I suppose?'

'Shearing crowd? I was engaged as groom.'

'Groom?' The old man gave me a surprised look. 'We got a groom.'

'What!'

'We got a groom. Sure that's what you came for?'

'Well, I'd know, wouldn't I?'

'Where'd you get the job?'

'Excell's.'

'That's where he generally gets his men. When was this?'

'Yesterday.'

Joe's eyes went back to the big swaying rump of the horse, and for a few seconds I watched him in an uneasy silence. He wasn't difficult to read. He was wondering how much further he should discuss the matter with me before I'd seen Bailey.

'Has the other bloke said anything about leaving?' I asked.

'Leaving — he only started the day before yesterday. Come in off the road and asked for a job. The boss told him he'd give him a try-out. An Irish chap. Bit queer, but a good toiler.'

'Didn't you have a groom?'

'Yes, up to about a week ago. But he had a row with Mr Bailey about his wages and cleared out at a minute's notice. I was doing the milking till he got somebody. I never see Mr Bailey stuck.'

I gave a shiver, and huddled my head deeper into the collar of my overcoat. The cold, which I'd hardly felt coming up from Melbourne, suddenly began to get into me. There was a pattern slowly taking shape, and it was a pattern I didn't like.

'Bailey should've wired Excell's,' I said. 'It looks as if I'll be on the way back tomorrow.'

'Not if I know Mr Bailey you won't. He don't do things like that. He ain't the kind to bring a bloke all the way from Melbourne and then turn round and tell him he ain't got a job.'

'He'd have to give me a week's pay and fares, of course.'

'And Mr Bailey don't waste money like that, neither. You'll get more than a week's pay off him, don't you worry. You just do your own work and don't take no notice of anybody else and you'll get on with Mr Bailey. I bet he's got something in mind for you already. They're starting shearing tomorrow. I thought that's what you was at first, one of the shed hands.'

'I can't shear.'

'The shearers is here, four of 'em. Come out this morning, had a look round, fixed up their gear, and shot straight in to Cressy in an old car they had. I bet they're full as boots by now. You're just a new chum, ain't you? You wouldn't even have seen a shearing shed yet.'

'No.'

'There's other jobs besides shearing, you know. For instance, there's the press. Mr Bailey might have that in mind for you; a big bloke like you would go all right on the press. And this is a long shed here, we shear for a couple of other properties, too. Git up there, Rose! Does some funny things, Mr Bailey. I remember one shearing . . .'

Reminiscence upon reminiscence, while the dreary landscape flowed past and great dollops of mud flew from the thumping hooves of Rose. Now and then I got down to open a gate, fumbling with chilled fingers at an endless variety of chains and wires.

At a distance the collection of buildings comprising the homestead looked inviting and picturesque. A few huts and sheds, with a yard in which several cows stood waiting. A big woolshed with a roof that had gleamed on the horizon long before we could see anything else. A red-tiled house showing above a cypress hedge, and standing in a position calculated to be just out of earshot of the working quarters.

I liked it less as we got nearer. Only the woolshed and house seemed sound. All the huts and sheds were drab and tumbledown, with an aspect of struggle and poverty that I hadn't associated with sheep stations. Three lean odds and ends of dogs rushed to meet us as we drove up, but no men were in sight.

Joe skirted the cow yard and pulled up before an open-fronted barn containing a stack of bags, a lot of gear and rubbish, and a buggy thick with dust and chaff and the droppings of fowls.

'We'll go up and bite Rene for a cuppa,' said Joe. 'Leave your bag there and I'll show you where you doss when you come back.'

I waited while he took out the horse and pushed the jinker into the barn, then followed him along a well-worn track to the cypress hedge, in by a wooden gate, and through a higgledy-piggledy vegetable garden to a kitchen opening off a spacious back verandah. Something else I didn't like. I'd been expecting to meet a male cook, smoking and blaspheming in a kitchen exclusive to men. Here was not only a woman, but painted furniture, china cups instead of pannikins, and a linoleum you could slide on. And a cautious, whispering, don't-disturb-the-mistress atmosphere I'd been in hopes I would never encounter again.

Rene herself was a tidy, solidly-built woman past middle age, and although she received the introduction to me with a friendly smile, told us to sit down, and immediately began putting out cups and saucers, I had an impression from the beginning that she was preoccupied with a grievance. There was a sulk behind her smile, and a lack of real interest in the more or less routine questions she put to me — how long had I been out? — how did I like Australia? — and so on. It was really Joe who kept conversation going. Several times after she sat down with us I caught her with her head cocked sideways as if she were listening for something in the interior of the house.

'Did you ask her yet?' enquired Joe in a moment when all three of us seemed stuck for something to say.

She gave her head an angry toss and picked up her cup of tea. 'Course I asked her.'

'What did she say?'

'Same as she said last year, and the year before, and the year before that. She'll have a talk with Mr Bailey.'

'That means you won't get it. I wouldn't have asked her.'

'Don't you think I'm entitled to it?'

Joe shuffled uneasily. 'I'm not saying you ain't entitled to it. It's just a question of whether they can afford it.'

'They can afford it all right. They'll afford a trip to Sydney or the islands when shearing's over, like they always do. Another pound a week for six weeks wouldn't hurt them.'

Joe, obviously unimpressed, muttered pacifically, 'They might get a better price for wool this year.'

Rene sniffed. 'She told me they didn't expect to get as good a price. And I said wasn't they taking the odds, getting a new Buick when the wool was still on the sheep's backs. She didn't like that. We had a bit of a go-in, I'm telling you. She hasn't spoken to me since. She's in her room now, sulking.'

'She'll get over it,' said Joe, and rose from the table, manifestly anxious not to carry his disagreement any further.

I also was glad to get outside again.

'She's hostile about the money she's getting,' he said as we went down the path. 'It's on every year at shearing time. She says she was engaged to cook for the family and regular hands, and ought to get something extra when there's up to six shearers and rouseabouts to feed as well.'

'It sounds reasonable enough to me,' I said candidly.

'Spare me days, boy, the woman's got sweet Fanny Adams to do for forty-six weeks in the year! And because there's a bit extra the other six she wants more dough. She's worse than the bloody shearers. Anyhow, Mr Bailey just laughs at her, he knows she can't do nothing about it.'

We had reached the group of huts at the back of the barn. Joe stopped and tapped me on the chest. 'Don't you go letting her turn you against Mrs Bailey. Mrs Bailey's all right. Do you know that that woman Rene has hardly bought a stitch of clothes since she come here? That's fair dinkum. Mrs Bailey's about the same size; you just ought to see the things she gives away. Shoes, frocks, jumpers — some of 'em hardly worn at all. The kind of stuff my missus could never afford when she was alive. Ain't that money? I got no time for this "gimme" business.' He stepped forward and opened the door of one of the smaller huts. 'This is where you doss. You're in with Mick. The shearers is in that big one, there's a fireplace in it. Anyhow, you can get your gear fixed up and just hang around for Mr Bailey. He's out mustering with Alec — that's the regular hand. Be careful what you say to Alec, he ain't to be trusted. He's been here thirty years — bit of a boss's man . . .'

'I won't unpack till I've seen Mr Bailey.'

'That's up to you, son. But you'll get a job all right. I'm going over to give Mick a hand with the milking. Too late to start cutting thistles now.'

He left me, and for the next few minutes I diverted myself unpacking a few essentials and taking stock of the hut in which I was to sleep.

It was pretty bare, but more comfortable than I'd expected. Clean and weatherproof, and with a smell of men that went some way towards dispelling the atmosphere of furtive intrigue I'd brought away from Rene's kitchen. Lined ceiling and walls, the latter decorated with a few dusty photographs of film stars of a past generation. Two bag stretchers with a hurricane lamp standing on a box between them. A shelf with shaving gear, an empty wine bottle, and some magazines. A ragged overcoat thrown down as a mat. That was all.

Some blankets and one of those bushman's quilts known as a wagga were on one of the bunks. I took the other, fixed it up in readiness for the night, smoked a cigarette, and wandered out just as Bailey and 'the regular hand' came in.

Dogs were barking over at the yards, and the two men were slowly walking their horses in behind a mob of bleating sheep. I started towards them, and when I was halfway one of the men saw me, shouted something to his companion, threw the reins of his horse over a fence post, ducked between the wires, and came to meet me.

Walking over from the yards he seemed all right. He was a small man, but sturdily built, and wore his oilskin coat, puttee leggings and shapeless hat as if he were never out of them. I felt, though — no doubt rather absurdly — that he was hurrying too much, and when he got close enough to begin speaking everything was wrong.

He had shrewd, restless little eyes set in a round rosy face without any character at all. He talked too much, in the manner of a young salesman sure neither of himself nor of the goods he is trying to put across. I'd applied for quite a few jobs, for all my few working years, and Bailey was a new experience to me in the way of employers. Try as I would I couldn't pin him down to a frank eye-to-eye stare. Between all his fidgetings and chatter and stolen glances I knew from the start that he had taken to me, that I was something he wanted.

'Good afternoon,' he began affably. 'You'll be Johnstone?'

'Yes. Good afternoon, Mr Bailey.'

He was breathing heavily. 'Busy time here — getting them in for tomorrow — start shearing. I suppose you know there's been a bit of a mess-up. Did Joe tell you?'

'He told me you've got a groom.'

'I wired Excell's two days ago. Next thing I hear is there's a man on the way up. Too late to stop you. Mind you, I'm not obliged to keep this other fellow on.'

'I'd as soon you did, Mr Bailey.' I'd already made up my mind there was going to be no struggle for the job.

'Hold on ...' he held up his hand and beamed at me in a

wait-till-you-see-what-daddy's-got-for-you kind of way. 'I'm a man who likes to do the right thing. You came here as groom; all right, the job's yours if you want it. But I'd like to do something for both of you if I can. Did Joe tell you the other fellow came in off the road?'

'Yes.'

'Nice fellow, too,' he glanced vaguely across at the huts and gave me a conspiratorial wink, 'but a bit queer. To tell the truth, I was sorry for him. Bad time of year for a man to be out on the road. Didn't even have a decent swag. I wanted to give him a go. He's turning out all right, too. Good worker. Now what I'm getting at is this: is there something we can fit you into, and make everybody happy?'

The cool assumption that my happiness lay so completely in his hands almost made me smile, but I kept a straight face and waited for the rest.

'You're English, aren't you?'

'Yes, Mr Bailey.'

'Ever worked in a shearing shed?'

'No.'

'Where have you worked?'

'On a farm.'

'Would you like to have a go in the shed? We're starting tomorrow.'

'I'd like to try it.'

His eyes dropped to my feet and swept upwards to somewhere near my chin. 'A strong young fellow like you wouldn't have much trouble with a wool press. Give it a go?'

'Yes, I'll give it a go.' I still hadn't warmed to him, but I liked the way things were shaping.

'I had a feeling you'd say that. It's what appeals to me about you young fellows from the old country — you're keen. Even this man who got your job. He's Irish. Work — that's all he asked for. And, mind you, he can work. That's why I wouldn't like to put him off. We can't afford to have good men tramping the roads here. We need all the good workers we can get . . .'

There was a bit more in this strain. I kept silent, waiting for him to get back to essentials.

He had a look to see what was going on at the yards. 'Anyway, we'll see how it turns out. You came at a good time. Always something to do at shearing-time. There may be a bit for you afterwards, too. I'll show you the press in the morning; you'll be handling it like a veteran by lunch-time. Between you and me I had this in mind for you yesterday and was hoping they'd send me the right type of man. It isn't light work, you know.'

'I'm not worried about that, Mr Bailey,' I assured him. I had something else in mind, but before I could say it he reached it himself.

'Good. Now one other thing,' his smile was almost affectionate, 'there'll be something better than thirty shillings a week in it for you if you do a good job. I'm not in a position to pay what they call the award; this is only a small shed. But I'll tell you what,' he tapped me impressively on the chest, 'you do the right thing by me and I'll make it fifty shillings. And keep, of course. How will that do you?'

'It sounds all right to me, Mr Bailey,' I replied. It did, too.

'Right. Straight question, straight answer. That's how I like to do business. A golden opportunity here for a young fellow. There's good money in pressing once you pick it up and get into the big sheds.'

I nodded my satisfaction and prepared to go, but there was still something else. His keen little eyes really held mine for the first time.

'Now just a word of warning, young man. Keep your own counsel and don't listen to mischief-makers. We get some bad men in the shearing sheds. You might know the type, you get them in England, too. The kind of men who're always grumbling about their jobs and running the boss down. They'll never get you anywhere. Follow me?'

'I think so, Mr Bailey.'

'I try to be a fair employer. If a man does the right thing by me he's got nothing to be afraid of. Don't you worry, I'd never try to put anything over you. You'll find worse places than Meelah to work on as you go around the country. Most of the year we're just a nice happy little family here. But at shearing-time we get strangers in, and there always seems to be trouble. I want to dodge it this year if I can. Enough said?'

I smiled. 'Enough said.'

A nice happy little family. I'd heard that one before, of

course, and thought of Rene and Joe and Alec. And wondered. All in all, however, things were turning out better than I'd expected, and I went back to the huts feeling a good deal more content than I had ten minutes ago.

I found Mick, the other 'groom', in the hut when I arrived, but he was no company. He was Irish all right, with a brogue that was sheer music but hard to follow. He was quite young, say in the middle twenties, with a face the shape of an inverted pear, a pink complexion, and a small mouth set in that vacuous gape that usually indicates a nasal disorder. He also had the most ecstatic smile and the most innocent blue eyes I'd ever seen in my life.

He showed little inclination to talk, but was a good listener, ejaculating 'Mother of God' in a tone of rapt astonishment and on a softly falling inflexion every time I told him anything about myself.

We sat for a long time waiting for the call to tea, but all I got out of him was the startling bit of information that he didn't know what wage Bailey was paying him. He told me without a flicker of the lovely smile that he wouldn't know 'fernent Friday'.

'You won't know before Friday?' I interpreted with a poker face.

'Niver a word did he say about wages.'

'And didn't you?'

'It was his place for to tell me that,' he said in the tone of a man pointing out the obvious.

I let it go. In all lines of reasoning there must be a starting-point, and I could see no starting-point here.

He certainly wasn't prejudiced against me, and that was the main thing. I hadn't been looking forward to meeting him. I'd told myself that the other fellow would naturally assume that my arrival involved his immediate departure, and would have read something like a notice to quit in my suitcase thrust possessively under the empty bunk.

On the contrary, his warm wondering stare was embarrassing, made me feel like a god. His vivid blue eyes shone like lamps. He watched every movement of my fingers as I rolled a cigarette, followed the first puff all the way to the darkening ceiling, then waited with childlike eagerness to see what I'd do next. The idea came to me that he was a half-wit, but I rejected it immediately.

I couldn't place him. I made what conversation I could, but there were long silences while the daylight left us and I grappled with another darkness that seemed to be closing in on me with the falling night. He had the eyes of a child but he frightened me. When someone rang a cowbell up at the house I felt as if I'd been rescued.

It was a good meal we sat down to — roast mutton followed by jam roly-poly — the kind of meal men like, but much of the pleasure of eating it was lost through the atmosphere of secret antagonisms and dissatisfaction that hung over the table. There were five of us: Joe, Mick, Rene, myself, and Alec the regular hand. Only Mick seemed to be happy. He ate heartily, and with a certain grace and fastidiousness that surprised me and that went well with his serene smile. He took no part whatever in what passed for conversation, but I noticed that his placid eyes were always resting on whoever happened to be speaking.

Joe talked more than anybody else, too much indeed, and too irrelevantly, the way a vindictive woman talks in the presence of two other women who she knows don't like each other. It became evident within a few minutes that he was performing largely for the benefit of Alec and that he had Rene with him.

Alec, a lean little man with grey hair and a sneezy worried face, seemed to have reached a stage where he didn't care whether anybody liked him or not. He was seated opposite me, bolt upright and tight-lipped. Several times I caught him watching me with a thoughtful frown, as if trying to work out if I'd been got at already and lined up one way or another in the happy little family of Meelah. He didn't speak to me once after the first curt 'How are yer?' when we were introduced. There was a barely detectable but significant difference between the way Rene placed his food before him and the way she placed it before the rest of us. He was well aware of it, too. 'You don't have to slam it down at a man!' he seemed to say, but each time Rene managed to get her back turned before his protesting face came up.

He was wearing his going-out clothes, bushman fashion —

blue serge suit and white open-necked shirt. I gathered that he was getting a lift in to Beeac with Joe, and that he was returning first thing in the morning with a young relation who was to be rouseabout in the shed. The very idea of those two men sitting side by side in the jinker over the eight miles' drive in to the township struck me as altogether incredible.

'And how will you come out here in the morning?' I asked, remembering that Joe was not returning.

'Young Jimmy's got a turnout of his own,' said Joe, before Alec could answer.

'Ain't I got a tongue?' demanded Alec.

'You ain't using it too much,' retorted Joe, but he said it in a low voice, and a remark from Rene covered it up.

'I don't know why Mr Bailey couldn't run in and get Jimmy himself. It wouldn't take more than a couple of hours in the car.'

'Don't you reckon Mr Bailey's got enough to do?' asked Joe.

Rene pouted and didn't answer, and after a short silence, in which I believe all three of them were trying to think of something to say, Alec pushed back an empty cup and said in a tone of finality: 'That ain't the point. Jimmy's got to have his turnout here; he'll want to go home at weekends.'

'And I do all the weekends in the kitchen on me own!' snapped Rene. 'Eight men, and them inside. Last year, when young Dick was here ...'

'You won't see much of the shearers after lunch Saturdays,' Joe assured her. 'You know their form, and this crowd's got a car.'

'What's all this got to do with Jimmy?' asked Alec. 'Jimmy's coming out to work in the shed.' He was looking at Joe, but he was speaking to Rene, and she knew it.

She was gathering up the empty plates, and stopped to fix a belligerent stare on the regular hand across the table. 'And what was I supposed to do when I come here — cook for a whole damned shearing shed?'

Joe held up a warning hand. 'Break it down, Rene — they'll hear you inside ...'

'What do I care.'

'You can take it.' It was the end of the meal. Joe got up,

looked deliberately at the table in front of Alec, and demanded abruptly: 'How about it — you ready?'

'I been waiting for yer for the last five minutes,' snarled Alec.

It was my first meal on the place, and I felt I couldn't walk out without saying something. Of them all, Rene had my sympathy, and I remember well the expression of startled gratification on her face when I thanked her for a good feed.

It was a relief to get back to the hut and the saintly smile of Mick. It had got very cold, and we turned in immediately. I had a good book, and was pleased when Mick anticipated me by saying: 'Pull the light over towards ye. I just go to slape.'

All the same, I wanted him to talk for a little while, not only because I was curious about him, but because I was fascinated by the sound of his voice. I began by asking him how long he had been in Australia.

'Eighteen monts,' he said. He was lying flat on his back, but turned his head to beam across at me.

'Do you like it out here?'

'Oh, yes, I loike it all right. It's a great counthry.'

I waited, but he just kept on looking at me, all ready for the next question.

'This is a funny place, Mick, isn't it? They all seem to hate each other.'

'Who?' His eyebrows went up a little in surprise.

'Why. Joe — Alec — Rene —'

'They don't mane one half of it.' He said it quite patiently, but the wide staring eyes suddenly made me feel I'd said something mean and foolish.

'Perhaps you're right, too,' I agreed, and lifted my book. I wanted to think him over.

It was very quiet lying there, just the two of us in the little hut, with the lamp burning steadily between us. The wind had fallen, and between those little puffs that always find something to move in old buildings there was absolute silence. Some minutes passed, and I was trying to imagine what it would be like tomorrow night, with the shearers and Alec and young Jimmy, when I heard Mick say something.

'What was that, Mick?' I asked, looking across at him.

'I saw a rabbit's funeral.'

He was lying quite still with his eyes fixed on the ceiling, and the smile of a man looking at a vision of paradise.

'Eh?' I exclaimed.

'I saw a rabbit's funeral.'

Something like a chill flowed over me, and I laid down my book. I'd heard him correctly — he'd seen a rabbit's funeral.

'You see some funny things in the bush, Mick,' I observed hurriedly.

I thought of the empty wine bottle on the shelf, but as he rolled his head over to face me I knew that whatever intoxication it was that had gripped him it wasn't the intoxication of alcohol.

'It's true!' he whispered. 'A rabbit's funeral! A dead rabbit was being buried, and there I stand while they all march past me, just as if it was a rale man that was going to his last grave.'

'Where was this, Mick?'

'Out on the plain there beyont the dam. There was I, walking out for to bring in the cows, and niver a sowl in soight or a thought in me hade, and — Mother of God, it starts! Such a wailing and squealing as niver you heard in all your born days. And over the grane grass they come, tousands and tousands of rabbits, all in the long, long lines. B' the Holy, it must have been the King Rabbit of thim all!'

Here was the vision he had been staring at all the afternoon. No wonder the petty bickerings of the dinner-table had passed over his head.

'How close did they come to you?' I asked breathlessly.

He'd turned in in his singlet. Out from under the blankets came an arm round and slender as the arm of a woman.

'I could've touched thim — loike that!'

'You kept still?'

'Niver a breath did I draw. They're loike the wee people, they niver see ye if ye stay fast. And call on the Holy Trinity. Ye're safe if ye spake the Holy Trinity.'

'And they were weeping and wailing?'

'Wailing? . . . the loike of it was niver heerd on earth. There he came on the grane branches, high up on the showlders of four rabbits big as hares, and walking on their hindmost legs loike lions. I can see him as he passes, roight at these fate of moine, lying with his wee paws folded on his chist, and the long ears of him all limp at his hade. And after him the Quane Rabbit, sobbing loike a lost sowl, and held up by her two ladies at aitch soide. And behoind thim all the rabbits of the reaim, squealing and stumbling among the stones away back as far as mortal oiye could say. It was a strange, strange soight.'

'Where did they go, Mick? Did you follow them?'

'Mother of God — no! They're all roight if ye jist watch, but niver a move must ye make.'

'And they went out of sight?'

The long arm waved once and was withdrawn under the blanket. 'Out and out across the plain till ye couldn't see thim any more.'

He fell silent, totally absorbed again in his procession of squealing rabbits passing across the ceiling. I could have listened to more, but was at a loss for the next question. Without the actual burial the picture was complete. I, too, lay still, my book turned down on my chest, marvelling how any man could so vividly people the clear Australian bush with the fantasies of the bogs of Ireland. But that other darkness had deepened. I felt lonely and depressed. The only sound, the persistent piping of one frog somewhere close by, irritated me, and I began to long for that hum of a car which would indicate the return of the shearers.

Truth to tell I never heard it. I fell asleep, and woke up with some kind of a clatter ringing in my ears. There were voices and a shuffle of footsteps. The lamp was still burning. Mick lay just as I'd seen him last time I'd glanced across.

It is the only time I can recall not being annoyed over being jolted out of a sound sleep. I'd been dreaming, dreams that vanished without a trace the moment I opened my eyes. But I do know that they were uneasy dreams, and that in the immeasurable fraction of time between waking and realizing that the shearers had arrived I thought not only of Mick but of the entire company of Meelah.

I sat up so suddenly that the book slid off my chest and bumped to the floor. A second or two of utter silence, then the whole brooding atmosphere began to dissolve.

Out of the night, only a few yards away, there came, of all things, the sudden blast of a mouth-organ, followed instantly by a gruff and urgent, 'Break it down, Alf, for crissake! There's blokes sleeping here.'

Then another voice, saying something I couldn't distinguish, and a confusion of approaching footsteps. They stopped at a point which I guessed to be just outside the big hut, and the same two voices came quite clearly:

'Hold on, Frank. He wants . . .'

'Spare me days, not here! Not right outside the bloody huts!'

Footsteps again, shuffling away, and more talk, at a distance. Then they came back, and after a bit of fumbling and whispering the other door scraped open and they went in. Last thing I heard before the door closed again was a third voice, 'They ain't all in bed. There's a light in that one over there.'

I lay still, interested in the peace that seemed to have crept in and laid down at my side. It was a long time since I'd got off the train and climbed into the jinker beside Joe, since I'd heard people saying things that weren't in one way or another disturbing. At the blast of the mouth-organ Mick's face had twitched as if he were going to wake, but all he'd done was roll over away from the light and give a long contented sigh.

I began to dally with the idea of getting up and going in to make the acquaintance of the men, but thought better of it, and after a few minutes I blew out the lamp and fell into a deep and dreamless sleep.

It interested me, and disappointed me, next morning to see how the shearers kept to themselves. I was in a hurry to talk to them, to get to know them, and fondly believed that the simple fact that I was on the press would establish an immediate basis of friendship.

It wasn't like that at all. When I came out at seven o'clock to wash in the tin basin standing on a case near the door, the door of the big hut also was open, and two of the newcomers stood at the foot of the steps, smoking, looking towards the woolshed, and talking in low voices.

I was all ready to walk over and engage them in conversation, but something in the way they responded to my 'Good morning', and in the non-committal way they looked at me, stopped me in time. I had a wash with a feeling that they never took their eyes off me.

All four of them were just in front of me as I walked up to

the house when the bell rang for breakfast, but although one of them glanced back at the sound of my footsteps they didn't wait for me to catch up, and we entered the kitchen still complete strangers.

I was expecting casual introductions. None came. They were a community in themselves right from the beginning. They didn't talk even to each other, and replied to the occasional remarks that were addressed to them with the rather excessive politeness of men moving in an environment they don't trust. They sat in a row opposite me, and although they ate heartily I could see that they were like me yesterday, impatient to be finished and get outside again. They were much the same age, somewhere between thirty and forty, and there was an expression of calm and guarded self-sufficiency common to all their faces. They were even dressed alike: 'twist' trousers whitened by repeated washings, and frayed jackets over heavy flannel singlets. I learned later that they were mates of long standing and had followed the sheds all the way down through Queensland and central New South Wales.

Jimmy turned out to be a youngster just left state school, with a shock of red curly hair and a cheeky face. He was the only one at the table who tried to make talk, but nobody encouraged him. I was sitting too far away from him, and after several vain efforts to get Rene and Alec to notice him he turned to the shearer just around the corner and announced brightly, 'I'm the picker-up.'

'You'll be all right, son,' replied the man in a slow deep voice. He smiled, but the smile vanished as he turned his attention from the boy and swiftly scanned the rest of us, as if enquiring if anybody else would like to say something.

It was little enough to go on, but I think the others felt as I did, that some kind of a warning had been issued to the whole company of Meelah. Alec, I believe, would have liked to come in. I saw his sour eyes move vindictively from one to another of the quartet of shearers and knew precisely what he was experiencing. Rene must have comprehended too, because when, a moment later, she gave Alec his second cup of tea, she placed it before him with unaccustomed gentleness.

'Thanks, Rene,' he said.

I could have fallen out of my chair with astonishment. It was the most pathetic closing of ranks in the face of a common enemy I'd ever seen. Only Mick seemed unconscious of what was in the air. Rather amusingly, he was also the only one who managed to unsettle the newcomers. Several times I saw one or other of them shuffle uneasily under the Irishman's persistent stare. He kept looking at them as if they were men from Mars.

It all made me wonder where I was going to stand. I knew which side I wanted to be on, but with Rene already, and rather ostentatiously, beginning to call me by my first name I knew I was moving off under a handicap.

From the kitchen we went straight to the woolshed. Alec had left the table a few minutes before the rest of us, and as we crossed over from the huts I could see him and Bailey herding sheep in the yards at the back. I'd made up my mind, though, to take my cues as far as possible from the shearers and was close behind them as they went up a ramp at the side of the big shed.

They still took no notice of me. Young Jimmy, running late, went straight through to the other side and began helping in the yards, and for a few minutes I was left entirely to my own devices.

Everything interested me, and in spite of my isolation there came over me a pleasant sense of being on the threshold of worthwhile experience, of having got into a man's world.

A young man in a white dust-coat, who proved to be the classer, stood with his back to me, looking into the nearest pens. There was a breath-catching smell of ammonia, a bedlam of bleating and barking and shouting from outside, an endless wooden tapping of the feet of sheep already penned. Near me was what I guessed to be the press, a heavily-constructed wooden box about head height, fitted with gadgets that as yet meant nothing to me. There was a big table, a series of cubicles against one wall, a stack of new packs, and a few finished bales of wool in one corner. Tufts of wool were caught everywhere, and all the woodwork had a greasy polished appearance.

One long side of the shed was the actual shearing board, with the driving-rod just overhead and the four arms still hooked back against the wall. Two of the shearers were occupied with combs and cutters, one sat on the floor pulling a pair of rough moccasins of hessian on to his feet, and the other could be seen working over an engine in a doorless compartment at the far end.

It had got to twenty-five past seven. Bailey and young Jimmy were now inside, urging sheep to the outermost pens, and I was just beginning to wonder what I should do when work actually commenced when one of the shearers walked over to me. I'd seen this particular man taking an occasional curious glance at me, and knew beforehand that he was going to speak to me.

He began by asking me, quite pleasantly, if I was on the press. I said I was.

'You've got a ticket, I suppose?' he went on, as if it were just routine.

'Ticket', I repeated, 'what kind of ticket?'

I can still smile when I remember the expression of blank astonishment that came over his face.

'What kind of ticket — why, a union ticket.'

'I've got no union ticket,' I replied innocently. 'What union?'

'A.W.U., of course.' His expression hardened. 'You're not a member?'

'I'm not a member of any union.'

'Spare me days, mate,' he scratched his head and waved his hand at the press, 'you can't work that without a ticket.'

The assumption that I knew I was doing something wrong irritated me. The other two shearers on the board were now both looking towards us, and in a distant pen Bailey suddenly straightened up.

'Then what about telling me something?' I said. 'I've never been in a shearing shed before. What am I supposed to do?'

'You're supposed to be in the union.' His voice was much less aggressive, though. I even thought I detected the beginning of a smile on his tough face. 'You're a new chum, aren't you?'

'Yes.'

'Been out long?'

'Six months.'

'Jeeze, you're new all right! Where'd you come from? I mean, how did Bailey get you?'

'Excell's Agency in town. But I came up as a groom. When I got here . . .'

'I might have guessed it!' The smile broke out, a smile full of irony. 'I was warned about this joint. There's trouble here every year. The greatest nest of crawlers this side of the black stump. You prepared to take a ticket now? Cost you twenty-five bob.'

'Sure, I'll take a ticket.'

We went for our pockets together. At the same moment a whistle blew and I looked over to see Bailey's hand just leaving his mouth. He was facing us, and I knew he'd been watching us all the time.

My companion, who had brought out a little book and a stub of pencil, turned swiftly to his mates on the board. 'Hold your horses a minute, boys! What's your name, mate?'

I liked the 'mate'. 'Tom Johnstone.'

He began to write, while out of the corners of my eyes I observed Bailey pushing towards us through the pens.

'Got a permanent address anywhere?'

'No.'

'I'll put Meelah Station, that'll do for now. I'll tell you all about it later. I'm the rep here. I've got to see that everything's in order. What's Bailey paying you?'

'Fifty shillings and keep.'

'Fifty bob and keep!' He kept his attention on his writing, but I saw the corners of his lips drop grimly. 'The rate on the press is four pounds nineteen and eightpence — and keep. He's got to pay you that or we don't start.'

Four pounds nineteen and eight — or *we* don't start. It was beginning to make sense.

By this time Bailey had reached us. He arrived blowing hard from the exertions of fighting his way through three pens of frightened sheep.

'What's the hold-up?' he demanded. 'I blew the whistle.'

The shearer leisurely tore off the ticket and gave it to me before he answered. 'Just joining him up, Mr Bailey,' he said civilly. 'We're right now. Everything's in order.'

Bailey was glaring at me as if he'd like to cut my throat, but I met him with a confidence that in the last few minutes had been flowing into me like wine.

'This man isn't experienced, you know,' he said to the shearer. 'He's got everything to learn.'

'Well, I didn't engage him. I'm only joining him up to the union. He's the presser, isn't he?'

'I'm going to teach him . . .'

'You've still got to pay him the award. Why didn't you get an experienced man? There's sheds cutting out everywhere.'

Bailey's eyes were darting from one to the other of us. I felt a bit mean standing silent while the dispute went on over my head, but could think of nothing to say which wouldn't have sounded childishly insolent.

'Anyway,' said the shearer in a tone of finality, 'you know as well as I do what the position is. We don't start with a presser who isn't working under the award, and that's all there is to it. What're you worrying about? You've got a man.' He gave me a sly wink. 'All you want on the press is a strong arm and a weak head. If he doesn't suit you can sack him.'

Next moment it was all over. Bailey gave an exasperated snort, glanced angrily at the idle board, and passed the back of his hand over his upper lip as if his nose were dripping.

'All right, damn you!' he burst out. 'Let's get on with it. I'll sack him if he's no good, you needn't worry about that.' And after relieving his feelings by giving a second and prolonged blast on the whistle he headed for the press, muttering, 'You won't get me paying good money . . .'

'Into it, mate!' The shearer gave me a hearty dig in the side. 'You're on full money — it's up to you now. Give him a go.'

It was an hour or two before I got a civil word out of Bailey, but he did get over it. And I can savour yet the warm feeling of comradeship that was on me when, at twelve o'clock, I walked up to the house with the shearers for lunch.

The big moment for a youth is not, as we are so often told, when he first does a man's work. It is when he first receives a man's wages and finds other men standing beside him as equals.

· This Freedom ·

Jim and I had been talking about Abbs only an hour or two before the fire started. Jim and his wife Olive are old friends of mine, with a pleasant little place between Sassafras and Olinda in the Dandenong Ranges. I've known them for many years, and am always welcome to spend a day or two with them when opportunity offers.

On this particular occasion I'd had the usual cup of tea in the kitchen on arrival, and on getting up from the table had strolled over to the window to look again at a prospect that never failed to refresh me after the dusty road — the little Dutch home of the Abbs.

It lay on the opposite side to us of a long-burned-out fern gully, and so close that Abbs, standing in his garden and cupping his hands, could call a message to us across the litter of blackberry, dogwood, and fallen trees that had replaced the once-lush tree ferns.

Only Mrs Abbs was Dutch. Joe was as Australian as they come, but it was the woman who had imposed her nationality on the home. People referred to it as 'the Dutchies' place'. Behind it a great waste of bracken, wattle, and dead gums swept up to Mernda Road along the top of Hacket's Hill, and on that casual Australian landscape of grey, dusty green and russet red the Abbs' house and garden stood out like a coloured picture postcard. By all the laws of good taste it should have been offensive to the eye, but it wasn't. You can get away with these things sometimes, and I wasn't the only one who found it pleasant to look at. People in cars often stopped on the road just above Jim's place, from where there was an unobstructed view, so that they could enjoy the novel miniature of blue-painted roof, yellow weatherboard walls draped with climbing roses, casement windows, water tanks wire-netted and heavy with passion vines, brick paths, and surrounding garden laid out with Chinese economy and full of vegetables, fruit trees, and all the old-fashioned flowers out of the book. Pink hollyhocks stood against a woodshed sheeted with bark, and on a moist evening in early summer the scent of the lilacs drifted as far as Jim's kitchen. Both the Abbs were keen gardeners and tireless workers, and in that sheltered spot were never without colour even in the depths of a Dandenongs winter. They had some fine camellias, and weeks before the first cootamundras lit up the cold hills their back fence glowed with the yellows of cassia and othonna.

Most neighbours, like Jim and Olive, had at some time or other been inside the house, and all agreed that it was impossible afterwards to think of the place as anything but a little bit of Holland. I'd been there once, and, in spite of the Abbs' very real hospitality, came away interested rather than warmed. It was a home you just couldn't relax in; it was too clean, too tidy, too obviously a show place. You felt you had to be too careful with your cigarette ash, your feet on the polished floor, your fingers when you lifted anything that could possibly spill. I was only in one room, the kitchen living-room, and came away with a memory, more vivid than anything else, of a fireplace that could have been a set-piece in a museum of antiques: andirons, a great steel fender, copper kettle and preserving pans, coal scuttle and shovel, pokers and tongs, bellows, a mantelpiece loaded with vases and pewter jugs and, hanging at one side, an ancient long-handled bed-warmer. I had to ask Jim afterwards what the latter piece was. He told me that Mrs Abbs had a lot of stuff sent out to her from Holland when she was married, and that it was Joe's job every Saturday morning to 'do' the fireplace with blacklead, red ochre, emery paper and Brasso.

I could believe it. Joe was a big, slow-moving, good-natured bushman, working locally for the Forests Commission, and appeared, like his wife, to have no interests in life outside job, home and garden. Mrs Abbs, plump, cheerful and always as speckless as her gleaming floors, ruled the roost, but it seemed to be a benevolent rule. From all I'd gathered from Jim and his wife the couple lived in a kind of mutual domestic slavery, always making something, mending something, cleaning something up, but with it all quite happy and well respected in the neighbourhood.

It came therefore as rather a shock when I heard Jim say just at my shoulder, 'There's only Joe there now, you know.'

I looked at him in enquiry. I'd been watching Joe's head bobbing up and down in the garden, and imagining Mrs Abbs vigorously polishing something in her museum of a kitchen.

'Only Joe?'

'He lost the old girl a couple of months ago.'

'Dead?'

'A stroke of some kind. Went out like a light, coming down from the township. They found her on the track. She was dead by the time they got a doctor.'

The news depressed me. She was a nice woman, her home a not unimportant part of the background of my visits here. I looked now with quickened interest at the quilt-like little garden on the brown hillside. Nothing seemed changed.

'How's Joe?'

'He took it badly, but he's beginning to steady up again. You'll have to say something if you meet him, but don't get talking about it. He's still liable to break down.'

'How's he living . . . looking after himself?'

'Well, he's pretty domesticated, as you know. Cooks a hot dinner for himself every night when he comes in. Keeps the place like a new pin. You'd hardly know she wasn't there.'

'He'd be pretty busy.'

Jim shrugged.

'He's used to that. Anyway, he's talking of leaving the Commission next year. He'll be sixty-five and due for the pension.'

It occurred to me that a man of Joe's habits and industry might not be altogether dependent on the old-age pension, but I let the thought pass without comment.

'He'll never retire,' said Jim positively, 'not as long as he can stand up. Joe wouldn't know how to relax.'

'Does he still do the fireplace on Saturday mornings?'

Jim returned my smile.

'Perhaps not every Saturday. But I do know he keeps it

shining. I've got a notion he feels she's watching him. We'll go down and have a yarn with him in the morning. He likes to see you.'

But we never had that yarn, because only a couple of hours afterwards the fire broke out.

Had it happened a little earlier we would almost certainly have been aware of it before it got properly going, for the sink and draining-board in Jim's kitchen were at the window which overlooked the gully, and Olive had been there preparing a salad. It started while we were eating, and Abbs himself, after the evening meal, had gone out again to work in the garden.

It was Olive who, first up from the table, brought us rushing to the window.

'Jim . . . quick! Where's this smoke coming from?'

We were at her side in an instant. At first I couldn't see that there was anything to get excited over. A bit of smoke was certainly going up from Abbs's, but all of it was in the vicinity of the little chimney set in the corner of the roof nearest to us. I knew there was a wood-fire stove under there, and as the chimney itself was smoking I thought it was just a bit of wind driving down onto the roof.

But country people are far more fire-conscious than city dwellers, and Jim sized up the situation at a glance.

'It's coming from under the eaves . . . come on, Bob!'

An exciting hour followed, my first experience of a burning house, and I hope the last.

It was a steep pitch down one side of the gully and up the other, even though there was a bit of a track through the blackberry and fallen trees. Jim is younger than me, too, and set a smart pace, so that by the time I reached Abbs's he had already roused Joe out of the garden, been inside, got an idea of what had happened, and was charging out of the wash-house holding an axe. Joe himself was in the kitchen; I could hear great blows as if he were smashing a wall down. The place was wide open, with the fly-wire door unhooked and swinging clear. Only a bit of smoke drifted out, but overhead it was now pouring from the eaves with a force that showed the fire was already making its own draught.

Among the many things I learned that day was that you never

know any man until you see him in a crisis. Easy-going Jim was transformed. His eyes were red and streaming, his fresh shirt soiled with soot. He seized me by the arm and shouted at me as if I'd done something to annoy him.

'Stand out in the open and give Olive a yell — she'll ring the brigade.' I pulled away, but he hung onto me.

'Wait — there's some boards lying behind the wash-house — grab one and pass it up to me — quick!'

He pushed me off, and as I raced along the side of the house I heard him give the alarm, three long piercing coo-ees that set up echoes all among the surrounding hills.

Olive hardly needed telling. She was expecting the call and had taken up a position out on the lawn where she would be seen at a glance. She threw up one hand in understanding and was running inside even as I began shouting.

When I got back to the kitchen all that corner of the house was hazy with smoke. A thousand-gallon water tank stood there on a stand breast high, and by this means, Jim had managed to reach the roof. I could hear him up there as I rushed past and seized one of the several hardwood boards lying behind the wash-house only a few yards away.

'Give me one end!' yelled Jim, and when I reared it up pulled it off me with such force that he drove splinters into my fingers. He looked fantastically big standing there on the edge of the roof with smoke swirling all round him.

'Get a bucket — two if you can — anything to bale with — and hop up here.'

I got a bucket and a cut-down kerosene tin from the wash-house, hoisted myself onto the tank stand, and found that Jim had laid the board across the top of the tank, and with one foot on it and one on the roof was flailing away at the sheet iron around the chimney. He knew how to use an axe, and the heavy blade was going through the roof like a can opener.

'Up here with you — stand by to bale —'

In the township a bell began to toll. Here and there, on the track leading down from the road and across the paddocks, people were running towards us, some thoughtfully carrying buckets.

Abbs was still inside, making a great racket. He must have

got to something, because there was a sound of splashing water
and hissing, and a smell of steam began to mingle with the
smell of smoke.

Jim had cut away a piece about three feet square and hooked
it up with his axe. Heavier smoke billowed upwards and for
the first time I felt the heat.

'Water, Bob!'

Helped by the passion vine and wire netting I was already
on top, and as the tank was nearly full it was an easy matter
to kneel down and bale from the board. Jim sent several buck-
etfuls swishing into the hole from all angles, then took a look
around to size up the situation. Smoke was streaming out now
all around the eaves. He gave me a desperate glance.

'I think he's going to lose it, mate. He's got a lot of three-ply
in those inside walls.'

The first of the helpers, a big man in flannel singlet and over-
alls, showed up below.

'What's the score, Jim?'

'Hop inside and see how Joe's going. Better tell the rest of
them to start getting his stuff out.'

We got a ladder and cut in again above the seat of the
trouble, but had to give up and retreat when the iron got too
hot to stand on. Flames were coming now from the hole at the
chimney, and when we reached the ground we found that Abbs
and the other man had been driven out of the kitchen. A frightful crackle came from inside. On the other side of the house
a bucket-passing line had been organized between the bathroom tank and the casement window of the next room. Several
people were around Abbs, trying to comfort him and urging
him to leave further efforts to the younger men. The old fellow
was half-dazed, wet and blackened and scorched from head to
foot. He kept trying to fling off the restraining hands, but not
attempting to return into the house.

'It's no good, no good — got right up through the roof —
inside the wall —'

Some of them managed at last to drag him away to the side
of the garden. Others turned on the taps of the wash-house
troughs and began carrying out buckets of water and flinging
them onto that little outbuilding.

In the front portion of the house there was a great thumping of moving furniture and calling out of voices. Men dragged the stuff out while women hauled it away to a safe distance. All the beautiful little garden was trampled underfoot and crushed under a jumble of tables and chairs and chests and beds and all kinds of outlandish knick-knacks.

It was an old house, dry and combustible as matches, and minutes before the arrival of the little volunteer fire brigade we were all standing back from the heat, watching great flames leaping up from the weatherboard walls, and waiting for the roof to collapse. Even the wash-house caught, and when it was all over there remained only ruins, the chimney stack, and, at the end of the short path, the little privy under a bower of singed roses. I found it a deeply moving experience, that swift destruction of a man's home.

There were plenty to offer Joe immediate shelter, and long before evening of the next day all his saved possessions were safely distributed and under temporary cover. I gathered, moving among the local people, that there was a community sense of loss, for, in a way understandable in a tourist resort, 'the Dutchies' place' had belonged to all of them. Jim told me before I left that there was already talk of a working bee to put up another home for the old man, but that he doubted if anything would come of it.

'I don't suppose he's got anything to worry about as far as getting another roof over his head is concerned. And he's an independent old coot.'

'He might not need another roof,' I commented, recollecting Abbs as I had last seen him, babbling and wild-eyed, being helped into a car at the foot of the track.

Jim agreed.

'Between this and the loss of his wife he could very easily pop off in the next week or two.'

But Abbs didn't 'pop off.' On the contrary.

About four months passed before I was in Victoria again. Heading for Jim's, and taking the lower road from Ferntree Gully because it involved going up the lovely Clematis Avenue turn-off at Kallista, I saw a familiar figure trudging along near the Red Mill just beyond Belgrave. Glad of a chance to render Joe a service, and full of curiosity as to how he was weathering his misfortunes, I pulled up.

I knew the minute his face beamed in at the opened door that he was very much on deck. He seemed younger, sprightlier, and there was an unaccustomed heartiness in the way he greeted me.

'Well, if it isn't Jim Jennings' mate! Very nice of you to stop — I always was lucky.'

Before climbing in he laid a fairly heavy kitbag on the floor, a typically-weighted Australian kitbag that I identified instantly, and with a mild shock, with his breezy manner. He was tidily dressed in black hat, open-necked shirt, and blue suit, and seated himself beside me with the air of a man on whom all the world is smiling.

'There ain't a bus for half an hour. I knew somebody would pick me up.'

'And how are you, Joe?'

'Never better. I been down to the Gully. Sam Wills give me a lift up here. You wouldn't know Sam ... nice bloke. He wanted to run me right home, but I don't like putting people out. Everybody's busy on a Saturday.'

I remarked that he was looking very well.

'And so I should be! I give up the Forestry, you know.'

That much I'd had in a letter from Jim, but little more. I had a feeling that there was something interesting here that Jim either hadn't observed or just hadn't told me.

'You were due for it,' I said. 'Still living on the old block?'

'Yes, I'll be there till I turn me toes up. I just got a little place now, though, just big enough for me and me cat.' He looked at me with twinkling eyes as he said this, as if there were some special significance in it not yet clear to me.

'Well, that's all you need, Joe.'

'They wanted to put up another house for me after the fire, but I wouldn't let them. Very nice of them, mind you, but what would I want with a whole house now?'

'And how d'you put in all your spare time now?'

'Spare time ... I got no spare time! Fair dinkum, I can fill every minute. Only difference is I got nothing to worry about. I got the garden and the wireless and the papers. But I don't hang about much. I get around. You know how it is ... a bit of a yarn here and a bit of a yarn there. Time never drags if you got somebody to talk to. And you can always do somebody else a turn if you haven't got too many things of your own to think of.'

'You wouldn't have much housekeeping now, anyway.' It was, of course, deliberate probing on my part, and a sudden quickening of enthusiasm showed that I was getting near the bone.

'Housekeeping ... I got no housekeeping now. By cripes, it makes a lot of difference when you don't have a lot of things to look after.' He placed an odd emphasis on 'things', just as a woman might have said 'children'.

'Things?' I repeated.

'Yes — Things.' My eyes were fixed on the road, but I knew he was watching me.

'That's what puts people into the grave ... Things. They get themselves that cluttered up with Things they got no time to live. Always wanting Things, and every time they get another Thing they got another worry. Something they got to sort of take care of. You see what I mean, don't you?'

Yes, I saw what he meant.

'Fair dinkum, the stuff people get around them! You don't seem to realize it till you wake up one morning and see you've got nothing to worry about any more, because ... well, because you got nothing!' In a growing excitement Joe pulled himself together and let loose a great exclamation.

'Spare me days, I'll never forget it! I'm sitting on Ted Craven's back verandah one morning — Ted took me in, you know — and I'm looking down on the old block and very nearly crying. That's all I did for days, just sit there and stare at the ashes, thinking of all the little rooms, and the things that was in them, and the missus, and the times we had. And it come on me all of a sudden: we was always working! We put in all our lives just looking after a lot of Things! And when we wasn't working on them we was talking about them.'

I took my eyes off the road just long enough to look into Joe's, and found them bright with laughter.

'I'm fair dinkum,' he assured me.

'I know you are. Go on.'

'Well, that's all. Things. You must have seen that old-time bed-warmer that hung alongside the fireplace?'

'Yes, I remember it.'

'Believe it or not, I polished it every Saturday morning for nearly thirty years. I was still polishing it after the wife died. And what did the bloody thing ever do for me?'

This made me laugh outright, but Joe knew why, and he chuckled with me.

'Marvellous how a couple of pots makes a man talk,' he said with a quaint air of contrition. 'I know what I'm saying, though. And don't you worry, I'm not taking to the booze. I got more sense than that. I go down to the Gully every Saturday morning now, but it ain't the beer. It's the company. I get up to the bar there and I got mates all round me. They're better than Things. Old blokes like meself I hadn't seen in years. The minute I walk in it's "How are yer, Joe!" and "Have one with me, Joe!" all round the joint. It'll do me. Joe nudged the kitbag at his feet. 'I'm going down to see Andy Carruthers at Monbulk in the morning. He's got a birthday. We used to cut wood together before I got married. Nobody's taken any notice of Andy for years. We're going off on a week's fishing trip soon, just the two of us.'

'You've got the game by the throat, Joe,' I said warmly.

'You reckon?' he replied with great satisfaction.

I realized, of course, that much of it was sheer rationalizing. But I knew also that deep within it was a core of wisdom that went back beyond Aesop.

Joe Abbs was a happy man, if ever I'd seen one.

· The Man on the 'Bidgee ·

We'd come up from Melbourne through Bendigo, Wedder-burn and Ouyen, crossed the border at Robinvale, cut north to a place called Lette, and followed what is known as the Prungle Mail Route, through Bramah and Bruno Stations, back to the Murray River Highway a few miles out of Balranald.

Most of it was new country, at least to me, but Balranald had little of interest for either of us, so we went straight through to make camp on the Murrumbidgee just outside the township.

We had a trailer caravan, and as we came around in a wide circle to bring the door facing the river I noticed the tall, dark figure of a man watching us from beside a drover's wagon at the foot of one of the big red gums with which the area was covered.

'We've got company,' I said to my friend Gordon.

He nodded indifferently.

We lost sight of the man as we made the turn, but when we finally straightened up on a piece of level ground we were again facing him. He was a good hundred yards away, but it was possible to see that he was engaged in wiping out a frying pan with a sheet of newspaper. Actually all his attention was on us. Alongside him a small fire sent up a thin column of blue smoke, and with the wagon and the red gum as a background I thought he made a wholesome and arresting picture. I said so to Gordon.

'He'd look better still if there was a hobbled horse in sight, and a couple of dogs,' he replied testily. 'Can't you see that wagon's a derelict?'

'Drovers don't travel in wagons these days,' I reminded him. 'They go in utility trucks.'

I was tempted to add that he was letting his nostalgia for old

121

times spoil his enjoyment of the holiday, but let it pass. Years ago, before a few successful novels had given him an independence, he had worked in the pastoral industry, and was finding nothing quite the same in this revisiting of old scenes.

As we got out I waved a greeting to the still watching stranger. He waved back, then turned away rather hurriedly, as if suddenly realizing that he had been staring too much.

It had been a long hot drive, and after uncoupling and jacking up the caravan we opened a bottle of beer to sharpen our appetites for the evening meal. Gordon sat at the little let-down table. He had turned the car away, as he always did where possible so that he could see out of the front window, and I observed that the glances he directed now and then towards the derelict wagon were full of curiosity.

'Ask him over for a drink,' I suggested.

All the reply I got was a shrug of the shoulders, so I didn't press the matter. We'd been around a lot together, and had made a success of it simply by being sensitive to each other's whims.

I'd seated myself on the bunk alongside the open doorway. There wasn't even a whisper of a breeze, and no sound except an occasional chatter of parrots somewhere over towards the road. The summer had been a long one, and in those parts they were still waiting for the autumn rains. Far down between the banks of crusted mud the shrunken river lay dark and still, and edged with scum and debris like a lake. Yet there were flood-marks on the trunks of trees showing that not so long ago water had covered even where we stood. I noticed that there were no young trees coming up — only scattered veterans with great smooth buttresses and knotted limbs, many of them with long-healed scars where, before the coming of white men, Aborigines had cut out their bark canoes and coolamons. This must have been a favourite camping place with natives from time immemorial, and more recently with white men. All was silent and deserted now, but the bare brown earth held something of the odour and aspect of a place used and worn and loved, like an old house.

I had just fallen to musing on how much ash from camp-fires was mingled with the warm dust when Gordon said suddenly, 'Better get that other bottle out. He's coming over.'

I just had time to reach under the bunk and set the bottle on the table before the man stood in the doorway.

He was older than he had seemed, seen from a distance, probably closing seventy, but tall and straight and spare, and dressed in patched old clothes that placed him instantly in the ghostly company of bushmen I had just been evoking. I liked his diffident approach, his lean, gentle face, and the big brown hand he rested on the jamb of the door. I noticed that with a natural courtesy he kept his head well back so that he would not be looking right into the caravan. He asked me if we had an old newspaper to spare.

'I thought you might have one you was finished with. I ain't seen one for days, and a man likes to know what's going on in the world now and then.'

'Tell him to come in and have a drink,' said Gordon.

He couldn't see Gordon, but the bottle and glasses were well in his line of vision and he was trying hard to pretend he hadn't noticed them.

'No, no, mister, I wasn't looking for a drink. I just wanted a newspaper . . .'

'We've plenty of papers,' I said. 'Come on in. There's only the two of us.'

He came in then, ducking his head to clear the top of the doorway, and seated himself carefully on the edge of the bunk.

'This is very nice of you, I'm sure. I wouldn't like to run you short, though.' He gave Gordon a shy nod, then looked around him with frank interest. 'My word, you are comfortable, aren't you!'

Gordon smiled his appreciation. I knew that, like me, he had instantly taken to the visitor. 'You're having a dry season up here?'

'The driest we've had since forty-two.'

There was a pleasant twinkle in the old man's eyes as he watched me pour the third drink. He held up the glass.

'Here's to your very good health. Very nice of you to put me in. How far have you come, if I might ask?'

'Melbourne,' I told him. 'We've been up as far as Lette. Do you know Lette?'

'Yes, I know Lette. You got off the beaten track a bit, didn't you?'

'Well, we're on holiday, and that's how we like it. I'm interested in birds. I wanted some photographs of emus.'

'Emus — did you get 'em? You'd have done better if you'd gone out towards Homebush. The dry season's bringing 'em right in.'

'We found plenty on Bramah,' said Gordon. 'Are you travelling alone?'

The old man gave us an amused little smile.

'A man ain't got much choice about that these days. Blokes don't take to the roads the way they used to; everybody seems to have got cars now. Years ago I've seen this place lousy with men, all with the swag up, waiting for the sheds to start. So close together you couldn't make camp without hearing what they was saying round the next fire. Now? Well, spare me days, I've been here nearly a week and never spoke to a soul till you fellows came along. There's a few cars pulled in off the road now and then for a bit of lunch, that's all. Everybody's in a hurry these days.'

'You came down by Homebush, did you?'

'No, I was just going by what they tell me. I've come from Deniliquin.'

'Deniliquin?' Gordon smiled with quickened interest. 'I classed around there many years ago — Wanganella, Murgha, Baratta . . .'

'Wool-classer — was you now? Well, just fancy that! And how far back might that have been, if I might ask?'

'Early thirties.'

'That's a long time ago, mister. You'd find a lot of changes around there now. Some of them big holdings have been cut up.'

'So I've heard. Different crowds everywhere, too. All the old-timers will be dead. Sam Tyers of Murgha . . .'

'I was never on Murgha . . .'

'Caroonboon? Colin Bryant — ever meet Colin?'

'Colin Bryant! You knew Colin, did you? Well now, there was a hard case for you, eh? Yes, he's dead now. I knew Colin when his first wife was alive. I don't think they got on too well. They had a bit of a place at Moulamein. I stopped with them once or twice when I was travelling through. Ever hear the story of when he put the rooster down the chimney? By God, that was a funny turn! He goes to light the open fire one night, and the chimney smoked that much he had to put it out. "Leave it till the morning," he says, "I'll fix it." And first thing in the morning up he gets, grabs a big black rooster, climbs on the roof with it, and rams it feet first down the chimney. Well, was it on! His missus was still in bed. She come flying out in her nightdress. You just should have heard the racket! Soot! . . . that rooster brought everything with it except the bloody bricks. And Colin's missus very nearly tearing her hair out. She threatened to report Colin to the Society for the Prevention of Cruelty to Animals. That only made him mad. "Cruelty to animals!" he yells, "what's cruel about that? It won't do it no harm, it'll forget all about it in five minutes. You don't know what cruelty is. That rooster don't have to live with one silly hen for twenty years!" '

The old man took a drink of his beer and wiped his mouth with the tips of his fingers.

'I started to laugh then, and that was the finish of me. I got chased out, and I was never game to go near the place again. Last time I saw Colin he had a stand next to me on Quiremong.'

'He was a good shearer,' said Gordon. 'The year I was on Wanganella . . .'

I sat in contented silence while reminiscence flowed easily between the two of them. Each of them had been around a lot, and they made good talk. Gordon and I are both romantics, and the old man was giving us something we had been wanting ever since leaving Melbourne. A whiff of the fast-vanishing Australia of Lawson and Furphy, the Australia of wagons and bullocks and horsemen, of blade shears and billy and broad axe. He knew it all, and spoke with a sad contempt of boundary riders who went out on motor cycles, of machine-cut sleepers, of axemen who went into the bush with thermos flasks, of drovers who followed their mobs in trucks carrying mattresses and kerosene stoves. Nonsense, if you like, but as easy to listen to as an old sailor lamenting the passing of windjammers. His simple phrases and colourful idiom intensified the mood that had been on me just before he arrived. Every time my eyes came back to the interior of the caravan after looking out at the darkening river I felt something of the guilt of an intruder. We were the hosts, but it was the old man, not us, who belonged here.

In an effort to get him to talk more specifically about himself I asked him how work was in those parts.

'No good,' he said promptly. 'Things is crook.'

We both looked at him incredulously.

'What, no work?'

'Nothing. I came all the way from Deniliquin.'

'You should have made south. They're screaming for labour…'

'I know, down Melbourne way. But that's no good to me. I never could stand Victoria. I've only been south of Echuca twice in my life.'

'And things are really as quiet as that up here?'

He scratched his head in some confusion.

'Well, maybe I'm wrong when I say there's nothing doing, but I'm danged if I can get on to it. There's a new bridge starting here next week. I heard about it in Denny and come all the way over. I know the game backwards, I've worked on timber construction all over New South Wales. But d'you think I had a hope? Locals only, that's how it is here. If you don't live around Balranald you ain't in the hunt. Now that don't sound too much like prosperity, does it?'

'But what about the station properties? Wool's booming …'

'I know, money ain't scarce there. I think it's the times that's changed. A man never was no good battling on his own, and you can't pick up a mate on the road like you used to. I never called myself a contractor, either, like they all do now, and I've put up miles of fencing all over the Riverina. In the old days two of us would just roll up to a station and give a price for a job, and all we had in the world was on our backs and in our swags. All we give was a price for labour. They'd take us out and supply us with everything. Shovels and bars and posts and wire. Tucker you, too. If you was far out from the homestead they'd send out once or twice a week, flour and meat and sugar and tea, and take it off your cheque when you cut out. But that's all done away with now. They tell you what they want, and you give your price, and they don't want to have nothing more to do with you till the job's done. You find all your own gear and wire, cut all your own posts and run 'em out, or sublet for somebody else to do it. And tucker yourself. The squatters find it works out cheaper in the long run. All right, it means you've got to have a truck to begin with. Now where would an old bloke like me get a truck from?'

'But the contractor would need labour, wouldn't he?' I said, filling his glass.

'Thanks, mister. Your very good health again. Very nice of you, I'm sure. No, these contractors is mostly two or three young blokes working in together. They ain't mates, like we used to be in the old days. They're sort of business partners, if you see what I mean. They've all got the idea into their heads that they're all going to be real rich some day. They put in together for the deposit on a truck, and it's head down and bum up to get it paid off. Rip, tear and bust, from dawn till dark. They wouldn't want the likes of me. I'll put up a fence with any man, but I've got me own price and me own pace, and I don't like being pushed by nobody. The bosses ain't changed a bit, they're still looking for the cheapest job — and getting it.'

Without any warning the old man placed his empty glass on the table and stood up. 'But this ain't fair. You ask me in to have a little drink with you, and I finish up taking all your good time.'

Both of us protested that we were enjoying his company.

'And how do you go now?' I asked him. 'No work in Balranald . . .'

'Oh, I'll be all right.' Out of a mesh of fine wrinkles his grey eyes smiled at us with complete serenity. 'I got put on to a bloke this afternoon that wants his garden cleaned up a bit. I'm starting in the morning. There might be two days in it. Then I'll make over to Robinvale. I heard there's a road job on.'

'There is. We just came through there. Gardening would be a bit out of your line, wouldn't it?'

'Fair dinkum, mister, I don't know the first thing about it. But this bloke says that all he wants is a good tidy-up. And I've got to get myself a pair of new boots somehow.'

We followed his gaze downwards to the worn old bluchers. For the first time a note of bitterness crept into his voice.

'The thing that's sticking in my crop is the pay. Thirty bob a day! He says it's all he can afford. You ought to see the joint he's living in! And the basic wage about twelve quid a week.' I'd given him a rolled-up bundle of newspapers, and for emphasis he pointed it first at Gordon, then at me. 'See what I mean when I say they still want labour as cheap as they can get it? Thirty bob a day. And what can I do about it? I got to have them boots. But, by cripes! I've seen the day I'd go barefoot and hungry before I'd take it.'

He went out and stood on the ground before saying goodbye.

'Well, thanks again, gentlemen. That drink really did do me good. There ain't many want to be bothered with an old-timer now. Everybody's far too busy making money. Good luck to you both, and I hope you get all the photos you want.'

'There goes a real Australian,' said Gordon, as, through the window, we watched him stride away through the gathering night.

Afterwards, when I went outside to throw away some scraps, my glance went immediately to where the wagon stood in the darkness. A few coals glowed there, and just as I looked a little flame flickered up and I got a momentary glimpse of the old man crouching forward on what appeared to be a kerosene tin, drawing on a cigarette, and staring straight before him into his lonely fire. It came to me that he had been sitting like that ever since he left us. What was he thinking about? The past? Or tomorrow, and the contemptible thirty shillings he was going to get for his bit of gardening?

Hours later I turned out the lamp, wondering if he was sleeping on the ground or if he had spread his blankets on the floor of the wagon ...

In the early morning, at daylight but before sunrise, there drifted in to me a rich odour of burning leaves and bark. Throwing open the fly-wire door, I lay on for nearly an hour, picturing the old man boiling his blackened billy and eating whatever modest breakfast the brave new world had provided for him.

Everything promised another hot day. Some magpies were singing in the distance, but in the immediate vicinity of the caravan there was absolute silence. High over the misted river, on an out-thrust branch of a red gum, a cormorant sat preening itself, craning its long neck, quite indifferent to the occasional splash of a fish in the river below. Every now and then a single black duck flew round the bend and headed swiftly downstream as if it were the last duck on earth and afraid of being left out of something good.

Suddenly there was a shuffle of footsteps, a discreet little tap on the wall, and the old man stood before me. All dressed for the road. A professional-looking swag hung from one shoulder, and he carried his billy as you rarely see a billy carried these days. Was it the daylight that made him look younger, or was it something else?

'Good morning!' I exclaimed. 'You're moving early, aren't you?'

'Good morning to you.' He peeped in until he could see the motionless bundle of my companion at the far end of the caravan, and held up his hand to stop me from speaking too loudly. 'I wasn't sure if you'd be up yet. Don't wake your mate. I just didn't like to go past . . .'

'He'd like to say goodbye too . . .'

'Fair dinkum, I'd rather you didn't, mister. I ain't stopping a minute. I want to get a good leg in before noon.'

'Before noon?'

'I'm going straight out to Robinvale.'

As he said this his face lit up with such a spontaneous don't-give-a-damn smile that I knew instantly what it was that made him look different. He was excited, under restraint. He was hard put not to yell at me. This was why he had called. This was what he wanted to tell us. He had felt a need to vindicate himself.

Putting one foot on the step he leaned in and reached me easily with his long arm. And as I grasped the strong hard hand I felt something of a lost and almost-forgotten youthful exhilaration flow into me.

'He can keep his gardening. Thirty bob a day's no good to me.'

'All the best, old chap,' I said jealously.

'My regards to your mate . . .'

A moment later he was gone, and I was left again with the cormorant, the gleam of the risen sun on the river, and the faint smell of a dying camp-fire.

· Black Night in Collingwood ·

Mrs Brady turned from the stove and hurriedly placed a roasting-dish on the table. 'Phew, that's hot!'

A rich odour of roast lamb filled the little kitchen. Mrs Woods, in on a neighbourly visit from next door, sniffed appreciatively. 'It smells good.'

'It ought to. I paid plenty for it. Fifteen and six. You could buy a whole sheep for that once, wool and all.'

Mrs Woods, with an expression of disapproval, watched Mrs Brady baste the sizzling joint. 'I don't know how you can be bothered to cook a hot dinner Saturday night.'

'You'd be bothered all right if you was in this house. You wouldn't get them two blokes of mine to sit down to this at twelve o'clock Saturday. Not young Jimmy, anyhow — not in the football season.'

'I heard he was playing for Mordialloc again this year. I thought he was going to turn it up.'

'That'll be the day! He'll turn it up when he gets his damn neck broke, not before.'

'I suppose Pop's following Collingwood — they're playing Footscray, aren't they?'

'Fair dinkum, I wouldn't know if they was playing Dudley Flats. I've had football. I'm always glad when it's over. I get a bit of peace then.'

Mrs Brady returned the joint to the oven, glanced at the clock, and began moving the pots around on the stove.

Mrs Woods, for the third time in half an hour, got up to go. 'My God, just look at the time! That lot of mine'll be in any minute.'

Mrs Brady, just as reluctant to end the session as was her

130

friend, promptly came back to the table and enquired, more affably, 'Going out?'

'I wish I was. We've got Harry's folks coming. His old man's all right, but you know how I get on with his old woman. What're you doing?'

'Depends on Collingwood. Joe's been talking all the week of going to the flicks, but it'll be another story if that damn football team loses. He gets a bit full when they win . . .'

'They were leading thirty-two points to eleven at half-time.'

'Thank God for that!' Mrs Brady, after another glance at the clock, sat down. Mrs Woods also sat down, but on the extreme edge of the chair, as if ready for instant departure.

'That Marlon Brando's on. I've never seen him yet . . .'

They got talking of pictures. It was very peaceful. Through the quiet give and take of the two gossips the clock ticked steadily on, the pots bubbled and hissed on the stove, and a muffled voice rose and fell on a radio in another room.

An inner door opened and a young girl came in. She was wearing a highly-coloured floral dressing-gown and pink mules, and had her hair set in butterfly-pins.

'Hello, Mrs Woods.'

'Hello, Dulcie. I was wondering who was in there.'

Mrs Brady was observing her daughter critically. 'How're you feeling now?'

'All right. I told you I was all right. Done my frock?'

'I said I'd do it as soon as I got the table cleared, if you'll stop worrying. He isn't coming till after seven, is he?'

'Keep your wool on. I only asked.' Dulcie rubbed her mother's cheek with the back of her hand and seated herself on the edge of the table.

Mrs Woods was smiling at her in the interested, slightly-envious way of a matron watching a girl prinking herself up for an outing. 'Still going with Bill, love?'

Dulcie smiled back, and winked. 'He'll do me!'

'Good on you! What's up with the football this afternoon?'

'Oh, Mum says . . .'

'She come in with a sore head and a bit of a sniff last night,' put in Mrs Brady. 'I told her if she wanted to go out tonight she could just content herself in the house for the rest of the day. It's no day to be standing looking at a football match.'

Dulcie looked round at the yellow evening sunlight streaming in at the window, and winked again at Mrs Woods. 'They're
winning, anyway. They had a nine points lead at three-quarter
time. Bobby Rose got a beaut goal in the second quarter.'

'It'll be about over now.' Mrs Woods's eyes sought the clock
again, and she fairly jumped off her chair. 'Jeeze. I'll get turfed
out! Have a good time, Dulce. See you tomorrow, Ruth. You
can tell me about Marlon Brando . . .'

'If Collingwood wins! Ta-ta, Peg.'

Dulcie, after a bit of chatter with her mother about what she
was going to wear, went back to her room — and radio. Mrs
Brady began to clear a litter of dishes and cooking utensils
from the table.

Five minutes passed. Then the radio suddenly stopped and
the door was flung open. Dulcie didn't come in. She just stood
there, looking in at her mother with an expression of horrified
astonishment, wide-eyed and open-mouthed.

'Mum!'

Mrs Brady faced her in guarded silence from the other side
of the table. She knew.

'They got beat?'

With a grim face, she picked up the electric iron and tested
it for heat by shooting a bit of spittle at it.

'That Trusler got a goal — oh Mum, Dad'll have a fit!'

He came in at a quarter-past six. He was a big, slow-moving
man, and entered with the weary 'Thank God I'm home!' air
of a workman at the end of a particularly exhausting day.

Mrs Brady, seasoned veteran of a football home, brewed a
pot of tea as soon as she heard him coming along the side of
the house, and managed to be at the stove with her back to
the door as it opened. By the time she turned round it was
understood that he had already looked towards her, and both
were saved the initial embarrassment of meeting each other's
eyes. For the next few minutes she could study him to her
heart's content; he wouldn't look at her.

'By jeeze, it's cold outside!' he said as he pulled off his overcoat and hung it behind the door.

Her lips tightened as she noted that his voice was deliberately lowered to hide the rasp in it.

'Get a cup of tea into you then. I've just made it fresh. And your slippers are there on the side.'

'That'll do me, mate. Me feet's like blocks of ice.'

He had his head down now, and she watched him closely as he settled into an armchair near the stove and began unlacing his boots. She had changed into her going-out frock, not to save time later, but just to remind him.

'So we lost,' she said sympathetically as she poured a cup of tea and placed it at the end of the table where he could reach it.

'Lost?' Struggling with his laces, he repeated the word thoughtfully, as if it were the clue to a problem. 'Yes, we lost. We lost all right. Three-quarter time we had it in the bag, and we finished up losing. I'm satisfied now we got the stiffest side in the League.'

'Dulcie says Bill Twomey got hurt.'

'Two goals in two kicks, in about five minutes. Then goes off hurt. Wouldn't it! And they don't need to talk to me no more about Jack Collins. Seven behinds and one goal — God spare me days . . .' in his excitement he raised his voice and it immediately cracked. He coughed in an effort to cover up, and picked up his cup of tea. 'Anyhow, what's the use of worrying you about it — you wouldn't understand. We lost, and that's all there is to it. Jim in yet?'

'Not yet. What d'you want to do — wait for him?'

'We might as well, there's no hurry. I'm not particularly hungry, anyway.'

'There's a good hot dinner. You haven't been going and getting yourself upset again, have you?'

His head came up suddenly, and for the first time they looked straight at each other. 'Now what d'you suppose I'd be getting myself upset over?'

'You sound like you've been bawling your head off. You can hardly speak.'

'Well, that's all right, ain't it? I've been to a football match. What d'you want me to do — stand like a stunned duck all the afternoon?'

'All right,' she said pacifically, 'there's no need to get shirty about it. What about a gargle with an aspirin? I'll mix you some.'

'Look, Mum, me throat's all right. I had a bit of a tickle in it this morning when I got up. I might have a cold coming on.'

'If you thought you had a cold coming on you shouldn't have been to a football match,' she said incautiously, and turned quickly to the cupboard so that she wouldn't meet the exasperated stare the retort was sure to provoke.

A minute or two passed while he rolled a cigarette with great concentration.

Then, in an effort to dispel an atmosphere which had already become difficult, she said, 'Peg has just gone out. She was here all the afternoon.'

'Did she say anything about Geelong?'

'All she said was that Harry's still working on the truck. He thinks he might have it on the road next weekend.'

He nodded, and silence fell again.

He was sitting crouched forward with his eyes fixed gloomily on the base of the stove. She could tell by the speed with which he was burning up his cigarette that he was thinking furiously, living over again the last fateful moves of the game, yearning backwards to that blessed moment around three-quarter time when it had been in the bag. Observing him at leisure from the far side of the table where she stood whipping an egg, she saw him involuntarily move his head forward, brows knitted, eyes fairly popping as if he were following a snake vanishing into the ash-pan. Then, as if the snake had suddenly turned and lunged at him, he drew back, with eyes tightly shut and face twisted with horror — Trusler's goal.

Absurd though it all was, she couldn't but feel sorry for him. 'I wish you'd let me mix you some aspirin, Joe. It would help to steady your nerves, even if you haven't got a cold.'

'Look, Ruth,' he exclaimed irritably, 'I wish you'd leave a bloke alone. I'm not worrying nobody, am I?'

'You're worrying *me*. You shouldn't be getting yourself stewed up like that at your age.'

'Who's getting stewed up? Stone the crows, I'm just sitting here having a nice quiet smoke. I've told you before I don't like taking them aspirins unless I've got to. They play my guts up.'

'They never did you any harm that I know of,' she said stubbornly. 'You're in no fit state to be going out like that, anyhow.'

She was going to say something more, but pulled herself up as she realized she had already conceded precious ground. And the fact that he let the remark pass in silence showed that he was wide awake to it.

She took Dulcie's frock through to the girl's room, and came back and began laying the table for the evening meal.

Ten minutes later the son came in. They could hear him whistling all the way up the side of the house from the front gate.

'Sounds like Mordialloc won, anyway,' she remarked cheerfully, glad of a chance to break the long silence.

He just grunted, but raised his head with a glimmer of interest as the door opened.

Jim came in with the headlong exuberance of youth, heeling the door behind him and flinging his leather bag into a corner so that both bumps sounded as one.

'Hi there! Why don't you come and barrack for a winning side, Dad!'

His father gave him a sad smile. His mother, standing where only Jim could see her, was making signs to him to be careful what he said.

He was smartly dressed, more as if he were on the point of going out than just coming in, and after taking off his hat and raincoat strode across the room and stood looking down at the pans on the stove.

'How's dinner, Mum? I've got to be out again in half an hour. Ted's picking me up in the city.'

'Aren't you having a shower?'

'I had all that at the ground. Dulcie in?'

'She's in her room. Give her a call and I'll dish up right away. It's all ready.'

Mrs Brady brought out the plates from the oven, and after going to the passage door and yelling, 'Come on, Dulce, it's on the table!' Jim returned to the side of his father's chair.

'The old Magpies had a bad day, Dad.'

Joe nodded wearily. 'We should've won. Seen the scores?'

'Yes. Led every quarter up to the last, eh. What happened to Bill Twomey?'

'Pulled a muscle in his leg. He got two goals almost before the whistle stopped blowing.'

'What sort of a day did Jack Collins have?'

Joe pulled himself together. 'One goal and seven behinds! Work that out for a so-called star forward! Footscray would have been better off . . .'

'He's still a star forward. You've got to give it in that the best of them have their off-days.'

'They all have their off-days when they're up against Jack Hamilton!'

'I wouldn't say that.' Jim flinched as his mother gave him a warning dig in the back, but finished what he had to say, 'Collins didn't do too bad against Hamilton last time they met. He got eight.'

Joe picked up his tobacco with the air of a man settling down to a formidable but not unwelcome argument. 'How many times have you seen Collins play, mister?'

'I haven't seen a game this season, you know that . . .'

'All right — I have. Now then . . .'

'Collins gets the goals!'

'Pigs!'

'Joe!' Mrs Brady, waiting for the last few seconds for an opportunity to break it up, seized on this just as Dulcie came into the room. 'Can't you two talk football without doing your blocks?'

Jim gave her a hurt stare, caught the appealing wink, and shrugged his shoulders.

'Anyway, come and get your dinners. I want to get washed up.' She shot a sharp glance at Joe. 'We're all going out tonight.'

'How did you go, Jim?' asked Dulcie as they pulled their chairs up to the table.

'We stoushed 'em, kid, we stoushed 'em. Mick Ryan was asking after you.'

Dulcie wrinkled her nose to indicate how much Mick Ryan meant to her, and shifted her attention to her father. She liked the way he was looking at her frock.

'All right?' she asked, spreading the skirt and standing where he could see it.

'You're not bad for a wharfie's daughter, mate,' he grunted.

She sat down. 'Cheer up, we're still in the four.'

'What's special about that for Collingwood?'

'We've got an easy programme left, you know,' put in Jim.

'We should be lying right up with Melbourne. A team that gets beat by the class of football that was played this afternoon . . .'

'Suppose you talk about something else till dinner's over?' suggested Mrs Brady.

Joe was watching her carve the joint. 'Not too much for me, Mum.'

She stopped. 'What d'you call too much? There's only one slice there. I've given you the outside cut. You like it crisp, don't you?'

'Yes. Yes, I like it crisp. But I told you I'm not hungry. And only one spud.'

'You was hungry enough last Saturday when you beat Melbourne.' Then, before he could reply, 'What about peas?'

'I don't think I'll have any at all. Just a bit of meat and a spud.'

'That damn football'll be the death of you yet,' she said as she took the plate to the stove.

Behind her back there was a swift exchange of glances. Jim gave his father a conspiratorial wink and made signs to Dulcie to keep talking. Dulcie showed the tip of her tongue to her father.

'Never mind him, Mum!' she called out. 'He'll be all right once he gets out', and followed up by pulling a face at him that said quite plainly: 'There, that'll cook your goose!'

'I'm not out yet!' he muttered defiantly.

They began to eat, but it was a far from happy meal. Jim and Dulcie ate heartily but hurriedly, with eyes every now and then seeking the clock. Joe 'picked', head moodily bowed over his plate, selecting every portion with meticulous care, and looking at it for a moment before carrying it to his mouth, as if all the time he wanted to stop but didn't dare to.

Mrs Brady sat bolt upright, watching his every movement out of the corners of her eyes, and disposing of her own food with a noisy and ostentatious relish. She'd given up hope, but if there were to be no pictures she would, at least, let him see how she felt about it. Football wasn't going to put her off *her* food.

Jim and Dulcie carried on what little conversation there was, but nothing flowed easily. It was the talk of people playing for time, the forced inconsequential talk of neutrals in the presence of an imminent quarrel. They tried in vain to make it four-cornered, but only Mrs Brady came in. This made matters worse, because she did so with an exaggerated enthusiasm that obviously had no other purpose than to expose the silence of Joe.

When meat was finished, and two bowls, one of stewed fruit and one of custard, were placed on the table, everybody was conscious that another stage had been reached in a situation that was rapidly approaching flash-point. Three pairs of eyes were on Joe as Mrs Brady picked up the serving spoon.

'What about some apricots?'

'No thanks, I'm set. A cup of tea's all I want now.'

'Spare me days, Dad,' exclaimed Jim, 'how would you be if you was barracking for St Kilda! You'd be down to fly weight!'

Joe glared, but before he could say anything, Mrs Brady rallied.

'That's enough from you, Jim. You get on with your own tucker. And for Pete's sake stop staring at the clock, Dulcie! He can come in and wait for you, can't he, if you're not ready?'

'I was just looking,' said Dulcie meekly.

'And see you keep inside, wherever you're going. Don't go running in and out of the night air.'

'I'll be all right, Mum.'

'You wouldn't be wearing that frock if I'd had my way. You'd have had something warmer on of a night like this.'

'I reckon there's a storm blowing up,' said Jim to his sister.

Mrs Brady intercepted the half-concealed smiles, and frowned. 'You was talking of being in a hurry when you come in.'

She brewed a pot of tea and sat down.

'Excuse me,' Joe murmured, 'me feet's freezing.' He retreated from the table to his seat at the stove, and the meal creaked along to a finish.

Everybody gave some indication of relief when a car tooted out on the street.

'There's Bill!' Dulcie got up, cup in hand, and stood hastily sipping the last of her tea.

'Ask him if he's going towards the city,' said Jim.

A little later, after a whirl of last minute titivating-up, and a few perfunctory kisses and not so perfunctory admonitions, the youngsters were gone and Mr and Mrs Brady were alone with their sorrows.

Mrs Brady, with set lips, began to clear the table. She worked quickly, and with a certain intent deliberation as if all this were just a boring prelude to something much more important to be done next. Every now and then she looked at Joe, sitting with elbows on knees and face hidden in his hands.

With the departure of the children there was nothing now for either of them to shelter behind, and their quarrel, though not yet spoken, was right out in the open. Every touch of dish and pan sounded unnecessarily loud. Perhaps it was.

At the end of a difficult five minutes Joe raised his head and gave his wife a long offended stare. She was standing at the sink, in profile to him, and pretended not to be aware of it. But when he relaxed into his former position she seemed to think that an opportunity had been missed.

'You don't have to go out, you know, if you don't want to.'

He ignored the remark, and after a little thoughtful contemplation of his bowed shoulders her expression slowly changed. She dried her hands and took down a small bottle from the mantelpiece. Dropping three tablets into a tumbler she watched them dissolve in a little water, filled up the glass with milk, stirred the mixture, and took it to him.

'Here,' she said firmly, 'get that into you.'

He looked up at the glass suspiciously. The pressure of his hands had driven the blood from his face, making him pale and haggard.

'Go on,' she said, 'drink it up. Why didn't you say you had a headache when you come in, and be done with it.'

Still looking only at the glass, he took it from her and swallowed the medicine. 'Thanks.'

'And if you take my advice you'll get yourself straight into bed.'

He didn't answer that, and nothing more passed between them while she finished washing up and put everything away.

He heard her go into the bathroom, and followed the trickle of water, the dropping of the soap into the rack, and the familiar rattle of the roller as she hung up the towel. Then her footsteps going up the passage to the bedroom, the moving about of things on the dressing-table, and the opening and closing of the wardrobe door.

When, all ready to go out, she returned to the kitchen, he hadn't moved.

'What's it like now? Has it eased off at all?'

'I'll be all right, Mum. You go out and enjoy yourself.'

'I might as well. There's no sense in two of us sitting here moping.'

'Yes, go on. I'll hit the cot.'

'But I'm telling you this, mister' — he kept very still as her finger prodded the nearest shoulder — 'I'm not cooking no more hot dinners of a Saturday night. I've had it. Every damn Saturday night's the same now. You either come in full of beer and wind if they win, or full of pains and aches if they lose. If they lose next week you can just bring yourself in a packet of fish and chips, because ...'

'Did you say you was going to the flicks?' he demanded sharply.

It was what she wanted. 'Too right I am!'

'Then for God's sake, woman, go! Stop talking about it.'

'I'm going all right ...'

He could hear her muttering all the way down the passage, and gathered himself for the bang of the front door.

It shook the house.

She would have been gratified, though, if she had seen the despairing look he cast around the deserted kitchen before going back to his moody contemplation of the floor.

· The Fugitive ·

For several successive days early in the week it was an item of news, but Pop knew nothing about it. He never saw a news-paper, except as wrapping for some of the odds and ends he bought on his Saturday morning shopping trips into Frankston. He had a scratchy old wireless set, worked off batteries, but it was rarely turned on, and never at all for news sessions. So that when Friday evening came he was as well informed about the much-publicized military exercise then taking place on the Peninsula as he was about most other exercises of what he had long ago decided was an utterly crazy society.

At four o'clock he stitched the last bag, poked the big needle through the lining of his ragged waistcoat, threw the few remaining potatoes into the butt of another bag, filled and lit his pipe, cast a long satisfied look over the results of his day's work and, with fork on shoulder and dog slinking at heel, set off up the hill towards his hut.

It was a fine, calm evening in early summer. A few miles away beyond the pine plantation a train whistled as it pulled out of Seaford station; from the Bullarto Road there came the drone of a truck. But Pop heard neither. Any more than he heard the chattering of blue jays and wattle birds over his head as he passed through the first group of manna gums at the foot of the track. Or the thump of a fleeing wallaby. Or the audible fluttering of thousands of Bogong moths feeding on the white ti-tree blossom that clothed the heathlands. Everything was just as it had been on thousands of other such evenings, and all his thoughts as he toiled upwards between the converging walls of scrub were the comfortable, practical thoughts of a simple old man living alone in the bush. Anticipation of the evening meal, estimates of the size of the potato crop he was going to get from the clearing on the edge of the swamp, of the time it would take him to dig it, of the price it would fetch in Victoria Market. A checking up on the things to be done in the next hour or two; feed the fowls, water the vegetable plot, nail a board over the hole in the floor where a possum got in last night, parboil a bit of mutton flap for Jinny the bitch.

Jinny was older than him, as dogs go, and it was his custom to pause now and then in the long climb from the bottom of the hill so as to give her a rest.

And it was in one of these pauses on the Friday night that he first came up against Operation Euphorbia. He had stopped about sixty yards down from where the track ended near the fowl pen. Jinny had immediately stretched out, as was her habit, head resting on extended forepaws, the bloodshot whites of her eyes showing as she stared fixedly up at her master, eyes full of gratitude and unfathomable devotion. Pop contemplated her without thinking of her — looking at a dog, but seeing only chickens, marauding possums, fat bags of potatoes.

Suddenly, with a 'whoof!' that made the old man's pipe jump between his teeth, Jinny's head came up, mongrel spaniel's ears half-cocked, nose pointing straight to where the hut lay still hidden by the six feet high wall of ti-trees.

'What's up, Jinny?'

Pop, not really interested, began to walk again. It had happened before. No visitors ever came here, and the old bitch was even more jealous of their bit of territory than was her master. Another dog, a rare wandering cat, a wallaby poking around the garden fence, were enough at any time to send her tearing off like a mad thing.

She did it tonight, passing him in a flurry of black fur before he had gone ten paces, and taking the turn in the track in a four-footed sidelong skid that threw out a little cloud of fine white dust.

'Come behind, you silly bitch!' yelled Pop.

But in the next instant, and for the first time in years, he himself was running.

Someone was — had been — in the hut. It sounded as if a big heavily-booted man had started suddenly from the middle of the floor, reached the open doorway in two swift strides, and gone out in a great leap that carried him clear of the rickety verandah and fair on to a sheet of old iron that had been thrown down over a muddy spot during the winter.

The crash of the fugitive's landing set up a little echo in Myrtle Valley, a quarter of a mile away, and amid a snapping of dry twigs under running feet, and the furious barking of Jinny, a flock of magpies flapped noisily upwards out of the peppermints over the wood-shed.

So much noise hadn't been heard on Yunki in all the years Pop had lived there. He knew very well that there was nothing to tempt a thief, but indignation and excitement gripped him, and he was shouting with all the strength of his cracked lungs as he reached the top of the track and came within sight of the house.

'Git 'old of 'im, Jinny! Git 'old of 'im! — git 'old of 'im!'

It was no wallaby this time, though, nor any raiding cat or possum. And when, just where the scrub began again about a hundred yards down the other side of the hill, the man turned and made a grasping motion at the ground, Jinny instantly retreated, yapping and dancing at what she judged a safe distance.

A moment later the intruder was gone, and only the receding crackle of ground litter and the swaying tops of bushes marked his passage down to Myrtle Valley.

Jinny remained, barking ceaselessly, every now and then making a brave little rush at the broken scrub where the man had gone in, then stopping to look back to see if Pop were coming.

But Pop hadn't moved. Even when the dog calmed down and came back and stood with hanging tongue at his feet he kept still, breathing heavily, sucking thoughtfully at his dead pipe, and staring angrily out over the now silent bush that stretched away to the yellow cliffs of the sand-pits four miles distant.

'What the hell . . .' he kept asking himself. 'What the hell . . .'

Nothing in the whole extraordinary adventure puzzled him as much as the man's costume. He had seen him clearly just before the scrub swallowed him up; khaki blouse or shirt, khaki trousers pushed into heavy calf-high boots, slouch hat, some

kind of weapons or paraphernalia swinging from the broad
leather belt. Details were hazy, but of the general picture Pop
had no doubt whatever.

Now what, with the war over nearly eight years, was a soldier
doing running about the bush like an escaped convict?

'Jinny, me girl,' he said aloud, 'there's something funny goin'
on out there.'

Shaking his head as at something utterly beyond his comprehension, he turned to the hut, climbing the steps with a vague
fear that another man might still be lurking inside. Perhaps he
heard the sound of the approaching car even as he crossed the
narrow verandah, but if he did the sight of his disordered table
made him forget it before he realized that it was on his own
track and headed straight up the hill.

'The dirty bastard!' he ejaculated. 'The dirty —'

He was still standing on the threshold staring at the litter
of scraps and wrappings when the car pulled up in the only
place where there was room to turn and three men got out.
A fourth, a soldier, remained at the wheel.

'Good-day there!'

All were big men, two in civilian clothes, the third a military
officer.

Pop faced them, scowling, from the elevation of the verandah. It wasn't hard to guess what the 'civilians' were.

The policemen stayed near the car, looking all around them
and taking everything in in the deceptively casual way of
policemen the world over. The officer, the one who had called
out, came to the foot of the steps.

'Which way did he go?'

'Which way did who go?'

The reply came quite spontaneously. Most men when they
tell a lie have some reason, however good or bad. Pop had no
reason at all. He didn't think about it. He just opened his
mouth, and the words came out, as if they'd been waiting there
— for generations. The way, a few minutes ago, Jinny had
reacted to the man grasping at the ground.

Calm, but very alert, the two policemen walked away in different directions towards the scrub, their eyes probing alter-
nately the dry bare earth and the long vistas of silent heathland.

The officer gave an exasperated curse.

'Good damn you — another one! You're all the blasted same out here. You know very well what I'm talking about. Morton!'

The soldier flung open the car door and jumped out.

'Quick — into it!'

The soldier followed the policemen down to the scrub.

Pop, a little anxious now, and wondering what on earth he had got himself involved in, stood to one side as the officer hurried up the steps and into the hut. There was only one room, a room in which everything could be seen from the doorway. The officer faced Pop angrily.

'We're looking for a soldier,' he said authoritatively and with a clipped accent. 'Where is he?'

'How would I know? There ain't no soldier here.'

'There was a minute ago. Which way did he go?'

'I tell you I ain't seen no soldier.'

'What were you shouting at?'

'At the dog.'

'Why? What was he chasing?'

'A rabbit.'

'I've been informed there aren't any rabbits around here.'

'That's all bull. You must have been talking to old —'

'Never mind who I was talking to.'

All the time the officer was staring hard at Pop. Under great restraint, he was manifestly uncertain how to handle this stubborn old man. He took a pace or two across the floor, examining carefully the crude but tidy interior — the single bed with the blankets thrown back just as Pop had left it that morning, the ash-dusted stove with kettle and frying pan standing at one side, the home-built skeleton wardrobe full of clothes, the Coolgardie with its moist drapings.

'Look here, old chap . . .' Suddenly changing his manner, he turned to Pop, extending his hands in an appealing gesture. 'This fellow we're after — he isn't in trouble. He isn't a deserter, or a criminal, or anything like that. This is a military exercise. Do you read the newspapers?'

'I never see 'em.'

'That's a pity. You'd have known all about it. A most important military exercise. And we've asked the public — that includes you! — to help us. You know what a commando is, don't you?'

Pop nodded.

'Well, then, this is one of the ways we train them. We dropped five men out in the bush last night and gave them a start until this morning. They're supposed to be in enemy country — no maps, no food, no friends — they've got to get through to Frankston by midnight tonight. Through our lines. We're all out looking for them — soldiers, police, and public — if they'll play!'

The officer, observing the gradual relaxing of Pop's features, went on eagerly.

'Now you understand, don't you? You aren't putting anybody away. Nobody gets hurt. It's your duty to help us. It's a game, but a damned important one for all of us if war comes —'

Another second, and he would have got what he wanted. But at the very moment when Pop's eyes brightened with full understanding the two policemen came in.

Pop had actually lifted his head to speak as the heavy footfalls sounded on the verandah and the big body of the leading man filled the doorway.

'You feel differently about it now, don't you?' prompted the officer. 'He *was* here, wasn't he?'

But Pop's mouth had snapped shut again, and the dogged expression settled once more on his grizzled face. No doubt it was all right, but every instinct in him cried out against taking part in a game where you helped the coppers to catch somebody. One moment he saw the logic and the innocence of it. The next he saw nothing but two husky poker-faced men striding into his hut — and a fugitive pushing his hungry way through the lonely bush. It was as simple as that.

'I tell you I never saw him.'

'God bless my soul! What are you lying for? We aren't going to hurt him. When we catch him we'll all have a good laugh together, shake hands on it. That's a good soldier we're after. He's doing a job, he was picked for it because he's a good soldier. It's a game . . .'

'I know. I heard you.'

'Then what are you stalling for? We're in a hurry.'

Pop wasn't even looking at the officer now. He was watching the first policeman, who had walked over to the table and now stood looking down on it with great interest. The other policeman remained in the doorway, hands in pockets, watching Pop. The old man felt the eyes on him, as he was intended to, and became even more nervous — also as he was intended to.

'God spare me days! What's up with you all? I ain't seen nobody. I been digging spuds all the afternoon. I just come up from the paddick . . .'

'And found a soldier in here!'

The policeman turned from the table, made a sign to the officer, and approached the old man.

'What did you have for lunch, Dad?'

'For lunch?' Pop, still conscious of those other eyes boring into him from the side, tried to look at the table, but the broad chest of policeman number one was in the way. 'I had — what's that got to do with it?'

'Just an idle question. What did you have?'

'Cold meat, bread —'

'Leave any meat?'

'A bit.'

'Where did you put it?'

'I left it on the table.'

'So that it would get good and blown, eh? You put it back in the safe, didn't you?'

'I tell you —'

'What do you usually drink — tea or coffee?'

'Tea.'

'But not for lunch, eh? What else did you have?'

'A bit of cheese.'

'And bananas, and tomatoes. You do yourself all right, don't you? Don't you ever use a fork or put anything on a plate?'

Pop, who had been trying to stare the policeman out, suddenly flinched. This was different from brazening it out with the officer.

'Had tea yet?'

'No, I just —'

'Yes, you just come up from the paddick, didn't you?'

The policeman, without moving his feet, turned sideways from the hips so that Pop could see the table.

'You wouldn't want much, anyway, after a lunch like that. Would you?'

Tomato cores, banana skins, cheese rind, a bit of string and fat on the plate that had held the corned beef. Pop could have sworn —

'Come on, old chap, we want to get away. Which way did he go?'

Which way did he go? The old, familiar, ominous sentence, falling on the ears of the humble, generation by generation, all the way down through the ages. Slave — peasant — worker — which way did he go?

'Which way did he go!' Pop's lips twisted in scorn. 'What in hell d'you take me for? I never shelfed a man in me bloody life. And, by cripes, I ain't goin'ter start now.'

The policemen exchanged amused smiles, but the officer gave an angry exclamation. 'I knew it! How the hell are we going to defend this country —'

Pop exploded. 'Don't talk to me about defending the bloody country. I fought in two wars and what the hell did I get out of them? Yes, Soldier Settler, fifteen of the best years of my life sunk in the Mallee dust. And have a look at this lot' — Pop spread out his arms to indicate the surroundings. 'Yes, have a look at it all this time round. I'm on me own here. I grow spuds. I mind me own business. I don't know nothin'. I seen nobody. Go and ketch 'im. Y'ain't gittin' nothin' outa me.'

And indeed they did get out, one of of the policemen good-naturedly hushing down the exasperated old man, the other bustling the still protesting officer.

A minute later Pop stood on the verandah watching the car depart. The officer, seated in front with the soldier driver, was speaking heatedly into the mouthpiece of a radio transmitter. In the back seat were the two policemen. As the car completed the circular turn and straightened up to run down the track, one of them turned and looked through the rear window. Pop felt sure he was smiling.

'Which way did he go?' he repeated contemptuously, and went in to see if there was anything left to eat.

Colin Ogilvie and Ron Black were going on a fishing trip.

Assistants in the men's department of a Melbourne store, and old friends, they had arranged for their annual leave to be taken together. Both were married, and they had spent the first week with their respective families on the understanding that for the second week their wives would allow them to go off and enjoy themselves in the nostalgic make-believe way that middle-aged men so often yearn after and so rarely achieve.

Over the years they had often been away for a weekend, and each occasion had been a great success. Ogilvie tall and lean and composed, Black short and fleshy and fussy, they looked an odd pair, but had many simple tastes in common: domestic life, the bush, gardening, watching cricket. Except for two recent little skirmishes, one when Black bought a car and the other when he was promoted to take charge of his floor, they had always got on well together.

Planning for the big adventure had been going on for nearly a year. They proposed to travel, in Black's car and caravan, first to Echuca, and then follow the Murray by easy stages as far as Mildura, perhaps Wentworth. They were to leave on a Friday morning and return on the following Friday for a homely weekend before resuming work on the Monday morning.

The long-awaited day had come at last, and well before the time set for departure Colin Ogilvie sat at a corner of the kitchen table of his Hawthorn home watching his wife put up a lunch to be eaten at some place on the road where they would boil the billy. He had been up since break of day, and preparations were completed down to the last detail. Except for coat and hat he was ready to walk out — second-best slacks, white sports shirt, heavy-duty shoes. He was trying to preserve an air of calm, but his wife did not miss the speed with which he was burning up his cigarette and the restless glances he kept throwing at a pile of gear just outside the doorway: shot-gun and fishing rods, worn suitcase, old army ammunition box, bulging haversack, and neatly rolled swag of blankets.

It was a perfect morning to start such a holiday, still and warm. Through the fly-wire of the open doorway came a twitter of birds and a smell of stocks freshly watered. Colin was a good husband, and preoccupation with his own intimate affairs had not prevented him from giving the garden a good hosing and laying in a supply of kindling wood against the coming week.

Mrs Ogilvie, a capable and substantial woman still in slippers and dressing-gown, worked diligently at a table littered with bread, scones, roast lamb, pickles and sauces, and the remains of the breakfast of two teenage children gone to work.

Colin talked, innocuous little odds and ends of remarks about the trip, every one of which had been made a dozen times in the past week. Mrs Ogilvie hardly pretended to be listening. In her down-to-earth woman's way she was checking up all the time, and every now and then would pull him up with a point-blank question: how many handkerchiefs was he taking? . . . socks? . . . singlets? Did he remember the antacid powder? What about the hot-water bottle? . . . it might be cold at nights. Was he taking his heavy cardigan?

Only when she happened to ask where they intended to stop for lunch did they get on to anything like conversation.

Colin replied that they hadn't definitely decided. 'Not this side of Bendigo, anyway. That'll leave us an easy afternoon's run to Echuca. We want to camp on the river tonight.'

Mrs Ogilvie worked on for a minute or so in silence. Then, 'Do you do any of the driving?'

'No. It's a bit different with a caravan attached, even if you know the car. And Ron's like any other bloke, he likes to drive his own car when he's in it.'

'He isn't having any trouble with it, is he?'

'He hasn't mentioned anything.'

'Is he still nursing it?'

'What, the grievance?' Colin gave his wife a sharp glance. 'I don't think so. He was just a bit sore when he found out it had been in an accident, that's all. He's probably never given it another thought since he found it was performing all right.'

'He still had no right to go for you the way he did. *You* didn't sell him the car.'

'No, I just introduced him to the man who did . . .'

'He should have known you wouldn't put anything over him.'

Colin stirred irritably. 'Ron's all right. Any bloke would have been upset. Six hundred's a lot to pay for a used car and then find it's been rolled. I don't think he suspected I got anything out of it.'

Mrs Ogilvie didn't answer that, which was significant enough for him to give her another disapproving look. She must have been aware of it, for she abruptly dropped the subject.

'D'you want mustard on these sandwiches?' She was carving the leg of lamb.

'Some of them. Make it fifty-fifty. I'm not sure Ron likes mustard.' He was watching her with a dry smile. 'You're still a bit crook on Ron getting charge of the floor, aren't you, Doris?'

'I'm nothing of the kind. It was you . . .'

'Well, perhaps I was — at the time. It was like the car, it didn't look too good at first. But I've admitted since he was in front of me for promotion.'

'You also told me he'd changed a bit since he got it.'

'I didn't say that at all. I said Franks, the manager, had changed.'

'And you seemed to think it was because Ron was putting the dirt in.'

'That was months ago.' Colin, who had been showing signs of increasing annoyance all through this exchange, firmly stubbed his cigarette butt in the ash-tray. 'We're not going to start pulling Ron to pieces this morning, are we? He's the best mate I ever had.'

'I know that, Colin. I'm not saying anything against him. I'm only reminding you of what you said about him yourself.'

'But why remind me? All good mates get sore on each other now and then. They forget it. There's times when Ron must have been crook on me . . .'

'Like over the car!'

But the laugh with which she said this, and the playful

wagging of the carving knife, broke the tension, and when Colin spoke again all the bite had gone out of his voice.

'Yes, like the car, damn it! We'll get over it. And don't forget that's only a lunch you're cutting. We'll be buying fresh meat on the road for tonight.' He stood up, rubbing his hands. 'You beaut — chops grilled over black ashes!'

'That's all right — you'll be glad to get back to a proper meal.'

He went outside, and for the next few minutes she could hear him wandering restlessly about the neat garden paths. Then, evidently unable to think of anything that had been left undone, he came in again and resumed his seat. The cat jumped on to his knees, and he sat stroking it while he and his wife got talking about something the children had been up to.

There was no further mention of Ron until a sound from the street brought both their heads up.

'That sounded like a car door,' said Mrs Ogilvie.

Colin glanced at the clock. 'It wouldn't be Ron yet. It's only a quarter to ten.'

But even as he spoke there came the clash of the garden gate, hurried footfalls along the side of the house, and he was already on his feet as someone thumped onto the verandah and a familiar figure appeared in the doorway.

'Hi there! ... anybody home?'

'Ron! You're early, aren't you?'

'Plenty of time ... don't panic.'

This could have been amusing, because it was immediately evident that he was excited himself. His plump face, below a shining bald head, was moist and flushed, and he didn't smile as his eyes leapt from Colin to Mrs Ogilvie then back to Colin again. He had walked straight in with the ease of a close friend.

'You don't know?' he demanded breathlessly.

'Don't know what?' Colin's welcoming smile began to fade.

'You weren't listening?' Ron glanced at the radio in the corner, as if the silence wasn't enough. 'You haven't heard?'

'Haven't heard what? What's the matter?' Mrs Ogilvie's hands had stopped moving. She was staring at Ron with an expression that was gradually becoming frightened.

Ron pulled himself together. 'Where's that Tatts ticket I gave you last week?' he said to Colin in a strained voice.

'Why?'

'Spare me days . . . you ask me why! Get it, quick!'

Colin and his wife opened their mouths in a simultaneous gasp.

'Ron!'

'Where's the ticket? I want to make sure.'

Colin was staring incredulously at a bit of white paper Ron was fiddling with. 'Jeeze, where did I put it . . .'

'Find it, for God's sake! We're in the dough . . .'

Colin dashed from the room, and Mrs Ogilvie dropped the knife and sank into the nearest chair. 'Oh Ron, it won?'

'My oath it won. I've got the number here. I took it down before I gave Colin the ticket. I thought: you never know.'

Mrs Ogilvie, quite overcome, covered her face with her hands, and for a few seconds all that could be heard was the frantic rummaging of Colin in the bedroom.

It didn't take him long. Ron met him half-way across the floor, seized from him the little coloured slip, held it alongside the white one, and read out the figures in a voice that rose gradually to a triumphant shout. 'Two . . . six . . . one . . . one . . . nine!' He passed the ticket reverently across his lips and handed it back to Colin. 'Ten thousand quid — we pulled it off!'

For the next few minutes the room was in an uproar. Both men kissed Mrs Ogilvie, pumped each other's hands, clapped each other on the back, crashed over a chair doing a jig. All three of them were taken with uncontrollable titters. Ideas for spending the money, some sound and long-considered, others spontaneous and utterly absurd, tumbled from their lips. In self-congratulatory glee they went over every detail of how the ticket had come to be bought and, like so many Tatts tickets, temporarily forgotten.

'I never gave it another thought,' said Colin. 'Just tucked it into my breast-pocket, and that was it. I've had so many . . .'

'It was the wife got on to it,' said Ron. 'She always listens in to the draw, even if we haven't got a ticket running. Tunes in every Friday morning at half-past nine. She said to me, "Didn't you keep the number of that ticket you gave Colin?" It was her made me get it.'

'I bet she was excited,' laughed Mrs Ogilvie.

'Excited — she nearly had a fit. So did I. I almost put the car up a tree getting round here. You know how it is — you just can't believe it till you see that ticket. Anyway, the telegraph boy will be here in a minute.'

That made Mrs Ogilvie jump. 'Gosh, I suppose there'll be a reporter too! And I'm not dressed yet. Colin, tidy up a bit ...', and she rushed out, leaving Colin carrying the dirty dishes and cutlery over to the sink, and Ron dropping with a gasp of exhaustion into a chair at the table.

She was gone about fifteen minutes, and when she came back, neatly groomed and wearing a bright frock, she found the two men talking of putting off their departure until Monday morning. Ron was still excited, but Colin had calmed down considerably. She also had got herself under control, and for some seconds stood at the end of the table, primping the hair over her ears, and looking first at one man then at the other, giving herself time to pick up the conversation before coming into it.

Colin had piled together the packages of lunch, cleared the table, and was sitting opposite Ron rolling a cigarette.

Ron was saying, 'We could put it for an extra week now, without pay, and make a fortnight of it.' He winked, and gave Mrs Ogilvie a sly grin. 'If it was okay with the women!'

She said nothing to that, but remained there, looking down at his upturned face with a smile more thoughtful than warm, as if turning over in her mind something about him that she hadn't noticed before.

Colin chuckled. 'You might have something there, too, mate. How about it, Doris?'

'It would be all right by me.'

'You don't sound very enthusiastic.'

'Well, we don't have to go into it now, do we?'

'Why not? We aren't talking of what we'd do *if* we won Tatts — we've won it!'

'No hurry, Colin,' put in Ron. 'I'd have to see Anne about it, anyway.'

This drew Colin's attention back to Ron, and for the first time he became aware that something new had crept into the atmosphere. He caught his friend watching his wife with an intensity that startled him, and when his glance travelled to her he saw that she had been trying to convey some kind of warning to him.

There followed a moment of caught-in-the-act embarrassment for all three of them. Mrs Ogilvie turned from the table to the sink. Both men started to say something, but stopped as she said casually over her shoulder, 'You're both in it, then, are you? Fifty-fifty?'

It was perfectly timed, when she was directly behind Ron and could look past him straight into the face of Colin at the far side of the table. She grimaced fiercely, but it was gone by the time Ron swung his chair sideways so that he could see them both. She was at the sink then, sorting out the dirty dishes.

Ron gave a nervous little laugh. 'I'll say! You didn't think it was a one-man show, did you, Doris?'

Colin was still looking puzzled, but Mrs Ogilvie, support or no support, wasn't going to be put off. She faced them again.

'I thought you gave the ticket to Colin, Ron,' she said pleasantly.

'So I did ...'

'Well, that isn't fifty-fifty, is it?'

'Oh, break it down, Doris! You aren't fair dinkum, are you?'

'Of course I am.' She was staring frankly at Colin, begging him to come in. He was sitting bolt upright now, with the startled frown of a man who has suddenly realized that something questionable is going on. 'It was a bet. You had an argument about Hoad ...'

'That's right. Colin reckoned Hoad would lose his first professional match. We had a little bet and I lost. And Colin wouldn't take the five bob. So I said we'd have a ticket in Tatts on it. Correct, Colin?' The flush had deepened again in Ron's face. His voice trembled. The speed with which he was reacting to the changed situation showed that it was one he had been anticipating.

'I don't know about the *we* Ron,' said Colin heavily. 'What you said was: "I'll get you a ticket in Tatts".'

Mrs Ogilvie relaxed. 'Yes, I knew that was what you told me,' she said cheerfully, as if the matter were now finally disposed of.

Ron struggled to smile. 'Stone the crows, you're not going to do this on me, are you?'

'Do what?' demanded Colin with growing confidence. 'You're rushing me. Couldn't you have trusted me to cut you in? You'll get something out of it. But not half — not five thousand quid!'

'Something — what d'you call something?'

Restraint was vanishing fast now. Colin pushed the ash-tray away from him. 'See what I mean? I'm not obliged to tie myself down . . .'

'Colin . . .' Ron leaned towards his friend, his face full of anxiety. 'We're not going to fall out over this, are we?'

'Who's talking about falling out? It's you that's getting all stewed up . . .'

'Colin! Ron!' With all the cards now on the table, Mrs Ogilvie felt it safe to jump into the role of peacemaker. 'Now for goodness' sake don't start quarrelling over it.'

'Quarrelling!' exclaimed Ron. 'It was you . . .'

'I only brought it out. I could see from the way you were talking . . .'

'So could I,' said Colin. 'You've been saying *we* from the minute you walked in.'

'What else would you expect me to say? I never thought anything else from the minute it came over the air. I said to Anne...'

'Well, you'll just have to go back and tell Anne you were wrong.'

Pale and tense, Colin was on his feet, shakily rolling a cigarette, and looking everywhere but into Ron's face. Mrs Ogilvie had taken up a frightened attitude, but a light of triumph was in her eyes.

'And if I don't keep a civil tongue in my head I get nothing, eh?' said Ron in a low voice.

'It's you that's saying all these things, Ron. All I'm doing is pointing out that you gave me the ticket. Now that it's won you want half of it.'

'It's made out to Colin, Ron, you can't deny that,' put in Mrs

Ogilvie. 'You should have called it the Hoad Syndicate, or something like that.'

'You don't worry about details like that among mates ...'

'You're worrying plenty about it now!'

'Wouldn't you? I offered you the five bob. You wouldn't take it. But, by cripes, you'll grab ten thousand quid!'

Both men were standing now, with their voices steadily rising and all hope of compromise gone. Mrs Ogilvie tried to hush them down.

'Don't shout, for goodness' sake. All the street ...'

'Don't you worry — there's more than the street going to hear about this!'

Ron made for the door, and in his passage around the table and across the short length of floor all the little poisoned thoughts that had been lurking between the two men came out in a savage exchange that must have been heard further than the adjoining houses.

'There's one thing I found out about money this morning, Colin ... it opens your eyes! I know the form now all right. I know now who it was put that car over me ...'

'Think I wasn't a wake-up you were nursing that? Even when you came rushing round here to tell me about my good luck. Or to get in for your chop — that was it, wasn't it?'

'You can talk — you've got the game by the throat now. You won't have to look for any more suckers to sell bodgie cars to...'

'I never sold any kind of a car in my life, and you know it. What I won't have to do is put up with any more of the muck you've been giving Franks to sling at me. Yes, you can look at me! I was on to it ...'

'By God, it's coming out now, isn't it! And you were going on a fishing trip with me — with all that sticking in your throat! Franks —'

'You know what you can tell Franks when you get back, don't you?'

'Yes, and I know what I can tell everybody else. And, by jeeze, will I tell 'em!'

He was gone, and in the clean sunshine of the quiet kitchen Colin Ogilvie stood looking miserably at his wife, at the little coloured paper lying on the table, and at the pile of fishing gear near the door.

· Bushfire ·

It was one of the most unreal moments I've ever experienced. No doubt excessive weariness had much to do with it. That, and the inevitable relaxation that comes with the smell of victory. But more than anything else I think it was the sudden comparative quietness and isolation. There'd been so much noise, so much violence, so many people. So much blinding light, now the darkness was coming back again.

Now and then, further along the slope, the vague figure of a man with a knapsack pump showed up as he patrolled the edge of destruction. In the other direction a few people moved around the surviving home of the Gregs. At my side was the inert form of Jim, collapsed, already fast asleep.

Footfalls rustle in the dry ferns behind me, and out of the shadows comes a little girl carrying a basket and a billy. Do we want anything? She's like everybody else we've seen in three days, soiled with sweat and ashes.

Eat — no! We've been eating too often. There's always plenty of food around — the women see to that — but only time to gobble a few mouthfuls. We'd give anything to get really empty and hungry, to have a wash, and sit down to a proper meal. Drink? Incredibly, I don't want that either, but the little girl looks so disappointed that I take a cupful of the strong black tea she's carrying. She goes off down the line stumbling in the brittle ground-litter and full of importance. One of the Greg children. We saved their house, anyway.

It comes over me now, the most extraordinary sensation of loneliness I've ever known. It calls to mind something I once read. An English literary periodical asked its readers to say what they considered to be the most awful predicament a man could possibly find himself in. One of the answers stuck with me throughout the years: 'To be utterly alone in infinite space.'

It's something like that. A sense of terrifying emptiness, and a desolation that takes away even the comfort of my own body. I'm aware of the broken end of a fern stalk sticking into my hip, and of something crawling along my neck. But neither one nor the other seems to concern me. Far up on the main road behind me the roar of vehicles goes on unceasingly: rural fire brigades, water tankers, police, trucks crowded with men, pouring up to the raging southern front of the fire. But for me it's over, if only for a few minutes. I'm absorbed by the scene before me, and I sit like a man trying to fix forever the details of a fascinating dream.

Perhaps the northerly is falling at last. More likely it's still blowing; we wouldn't know down here deep on a southern slope. All I do know is that it has become very quiet, and after the sustained violence of three days it's a quietness that intimidates. Only a few yards beyond my extended feet the tangle of parched ferns and wire grass stops as abruptly as along a road, and there is nothing. Little is left on the living trees, but here and there flames still sputter and glow in the high forks and along dead limbs. A stone's throw away the great hollow shell of a long-dead veteran roars like a furnace. It's a good shell, straight and sound as a gun barrel, with a hole near the ground big enough for a man to crawl into. Every now and then the coals on the white-hot inner walls collapse and a blast of flames and sparks belches from the top. I know that the valley is full of such fireworks, but it's full of smoke too, and all that reaches me for a few minutes is an occasional thump as another tree comes down.

Then, high in the darkness of the opposing ridge, a man suddenly calls out, and there's a clanging crash like an empty water tank falling. I didn't think there was anything left to burn up there, but they must still be fighting. The two sounds bring home to me as nothing else does just what it is that has happened. I've been down here so often before, and this is the first time I've heard sounds from that ridge. Every noise carries now because there is nothing left to absorb it. The entire valley has been cleaned out. Not a leaf or a stick or a blade of grass left.

It's just a huge ditch full of ashes, smouldering logs, naked spars, smoke, and the sad wreckage of homes.

And out of it there comes that extraordinary rustling. I'm aware of it quite suddenly, and find it rather soothing after the long crackle of flames and the clash and fury of struggling men. I'm not sure what to make of it, uncertain whether it's the snapping of millions of sparks or the settling down of all these acres of cooling ash. Either way it fits in perfectly with scene and mood. An endless, whispering, papery sigh. A sigh of exhaustion. The dying down of a burned and blighted earth.

Tuesday night. It seems so long since noon on Sunday, when it came over the air that a bushfire was burning at Chum Creek, near Healesville, twenty miles away. Since we heard that a second fire had broken out at The Basin, only nine miles from us on the other side of the Dandenongs. So long since Sunday afternoon when the first smoke haze drifted over, and my wife came in from the garden and showed me the fine ash which had settled on her dress. Yarra Glen and Montrose on Monday, Warrandyte and Dogwood today. We're in an arc of fire extending nearly a hundred miles from Warrandyte and Hurstbridge in the west, through St Andrew's, Kinglake, and Healesville to Launching Place in the east, and Ferntree Gully in the south. And many points within the arc. Only heavy rain can save what's left. And all that we're promised is a possible — just a possible — thunderstorm.

Two men come past, trudging heavily along the dampened edge of ashes. Both are carrying knapsack pumps, obviously empty. One of them looks as if, like my mate Jim, he's been in it from the start. He doesn't walk. He goes in a succession of staggers, leaning forward and catching his weight step by step. His shirt and trousers are ragged and black. One forearm is swathed in dirty bandages. Even so, he notices Jim, and stops to ask in a slurred voice, 'How is he — all right?'

'Yes, he's all right,' I assure him. 'He's just had it.'

'Ain't we all.'

They pass on, but the spell is broken, and I shake Jim into life. 'We'd better get up top, Jim. See what's doing.'

He sits up, passes both hands across his face, and spits. 'Jeeze, me eyes is crook. What time is it?'

'Getting on for ten. It's safe down here now. There's a few standing by.'

As we get to our feet and start off I observe the beater he's carrying. A folded potato bag nailed to the end of a three-feet length of two by one hardwood. Half the bag charred away. It makes mine look like the tool of a novice.

Just before reaching the track that leads up to the road we get close to the Gregs' house. They're a tough crowd, source of endless gossip and speculation in the township. One man, two women, and eleven children, living in a higgledy-piggledy cluster of splintered weatherboards and rusted roofing-iron on an unfenced block. For years all the rubbish of a turbulent don't-give-a-damn household has gone into the surrounding bush, and the fire, which licked the very walls, has laid it all bare. A little way down the hillside a piped fallen tree burns safely but fiercely, lighting up the blackened litter of jam tins, shattered bottles, drums, iron bedstead and metal remains of a derelict car.

A dismal sight, but it's impossible to think harshly of the Gregs — tonight anyway. They fought like tigers.

The younger children had been taken out, and in the final critical moments an attempt was made to get the women to go. I don't know where Joe Greg was just then, or Mavis, but I did see the struggle with Nell. A group of us were battling to save the detached wash-house and privy, with the bush already catching on the far side of the dwelling. No flames at first, just a blast of hot air whistling up at an acute angle through the tall trees. I saw them flinch, stand still again, and a shower of light debris come floating down, as if they'd merely shaken themselves. A few plumes of smoke curled up from the crisp undergrowth. Below us the entire valley was alight, full of flames and smoke and exploding trees. The din was terrific. Some rural brigade had got down to us, and as they ran a line out their urgent shouts were added to our own pantings and blasphemies. But through it all I heard the raging scream of Nell, 'Take your hands off me, you bastards!'

I got a glimpse of her through the swirling smoke, a solid big-boned woman shaking a beater at the sprawling figure of Sam Emerson.

'Where the hell are we to go with eleven kids! This is my

home — it's all I've got in the world — by Christ I'll save it . . .'

And in a frenzy she threw herself again into the line of men flailing away at the creeping flames below the back verandah.

There, now, is the house, still standing. But amid the black nakedness of earth and human debris it looks wretched in the eerie glow of the burning tree. It lacks the warmth even of lighted windows. Power lines are down everywhere, and the Gregs, like so many others, are back to candle and hurricane lamp. Nobody is in sight as we turn and head up towards the road, but there's a sound of children quarrelling, and the voice of Mavis comes to us clearly in the empty stricken forest, 'What's up with you? Everybody else has washed in that dish. You know as well as I do the bloody tanks is empty.'

Jim turns his head to give me a tired smile. 'They've got a house to sleep in, anyway.'

The traffic on the road isn't the unbroken roar that it was some minutes ago, but a lot of vehicles are still going through. No doubt some of the other roads are blocked by fallen trees.

We're beginning to feel the wind again, but that also seems to have weakened. And the air is comparatively clear. There's only a haze, lying among the quiet trees like a morning fog. A newly-arrived volunteer to whom I was talking late in the afternoon told me that there are places in the hills where visibility is better than in Melbourne. He also told me that shipping has been slowed down in the bay since Sunday night, that Moorabbin Airport is closed, and that a leg of the Warrandyte fire got right across to the Maroondah Highway before it was stopped.

For me, anyway, the illusory sense of victory is instantly dispelled as we come onto the road. A police car cruises past with blaring amplifier: 'Attention please! Police here — a wide load is following. Drivers please pull in or exercise great care. Attention please . . .'

'The bulldozer,' mutters Jim. We know one has been asked for.

On the far side of the road stands a shire council tanker from which men are filling knapsack pumps. A little way behind it is a truck with only the driver in the cabin, sleeping over the wheel. The big white letters on the side of it puzzle me:

P.M.C.C. I ask Jim, and he solves it for me — Port Melbourne City Council. I like the idea of the men of Port Melbourne coming up to help us fight fires in the Dandenongs.

Northwards, a few hundred yards away, there is the township itself, the township which has twice been reported as 'evacuated'. A lot of cars and trucks are about, and there is much coming and going around Blacket's Post Office Store on one side of the road and the Mechanics' Hall on the other. The public telephone box has been closed for two days, during which time Ernie Blacket has never left his post. Only emergency and official calls are being accepted.

'Where d'you reckon, Jim?' I ask, because we've come up without any clear idea of where we're going.

He screws up his face. 'I've had it, Bob. I've got to get something for me eyes. I can hardly see.'

'Home?' Jim lodges with me, and my place is out along Sanders Road.

'How about the hall? They've got everything there. I'm euchred.'

We cross the road in the wake of a big ready-mix concrete transport out of which water is slopping. Before we reach the hall the bulldozer also goes past. A monstrous piece of equipment mounted on a low-loader, both marked R.A.A.F. It's ironic that when, in a crisis of peace, men call out for the best weapons, they receive the weapons of war. The Country Fire Authority should have things like these. As it is, the rural brigades have only bows and arrows. One of them, marked with the name of some obscure township I've never heard of, comes along in the middle of my reflections. A modest little red truck bravely panting up into yet another battle. A three hundred gallon water tank, a length of hose, some knapsack pumps, and five or six men clinging to the platform at each side. A pitifully inadequate unit to throw into such a holocaust, but they're trained, organized, fearless, and at home in the bush. Time and again in the last few days we've seen the blessed winking red light picking its way in where no vehicle ever went before.

Outside the cottage of the Nevinsons their ancient Buick still stands, loaded for instant flight, as it has since Sunday. A mattress and blankets roped to its spacious roof, its interior crammed, except for the driving seat, with boxes and suitcases.

These two old people are settling in for another uneasy night. In the weak glow of a kerosene lamp set on a table we get a glimpse of them moving about in the front room. Small shop-keepers from Prahran, they arrived here only last winter to spend their declining years in the peaceful hills.

It's hot. Oppressively hot. When I look up at the sky I'm sur-prised to find that all the stars are gone. They were there, how-ever dim, only two hours ago when we raced up York Road from smouldering Montrose. Taken with the high humidity and the falling wind, the discovery excites me. There's that tan-talizing forecast of a possible thunderstorm. I remark to Jim that it's clouding over, but he doesn't even bother to lift his head.

'Might get another dry one,' he grunts sceptically. We've had several of them lately, all the fireworks and no rain.

From the higher ground up the road, and looking across the Recreation Reserve, we come in sight of the great glare of the fire over Silvan. A lot of pines have been planted around the dam, and they burn as fiercely as the eucalypts. Lit by the surg-ing flames in colours of grey and yellow and russet-red, clouds of smoke roll majestically up into the black sky. At this distance the silence with which it rages has a subtle terror to us who know all too well the uproar that is going with it. I know every inch of the road from Silvan to Monbulk, and can well imagine what it's like along there now.

West and south-west it seems to be all over. One side of that range was burned out yesterday, the other today. We can't pick out the familiar undulating crest, but the entire face below Kalorama is dotted with glimmering points of light — smouldering trees — like the camp-fires of a bivouacked army.

A lot of people are around the hall as we walk up, including more strangers than ever I've seen in Dogwood before. One animated group is clustered around the tall figure of Vic Chubb, the local policeman. He's in regulation trousers and peaked cap, but no tunic, and is every bit as grimy and red-eyed as the rest of us. Jim stops to speak to a mate, and I hear a woman's hysterical voice. 'How do you know? You didn't see — you told me so! Did you *see* her get picked up?'

I recognize her as Mrs Moran, wife of a postal telegraph

worker who lives down behind the store, and whose home was saved. She's being controlled and comforted by two other women.

'Elsie dear, she's all right, she's all right. Somebody must have taken her out.'

'Nobody got burned . . .'

'You're only saying that — nobody saw where she went!' She lurches forward. 'Mr Chubb — oh, Mr Chubb — get them to ask over the wireless. She's only three. She's got a pink frock on — white shoes — she'll be carrying her bride doll . . .'

Chubb's been doing a good job. He has an advantage over many other police in that he's bush bred. Jim said he saw him in the thick of it along Ridge Road last night. He looks all-in now, ready to weep from exhaustion — and pity. His articulation, usually crisp and officious, is like that of a man in the early stages of intoxication.

'I've told 'em, I've told 'em. You got nothing to worry about. She's a'right. Somebody's stuffing her with ice-cream, somewhere . . .'

'Ice-cream!' The woman bursts into renewed tears, and her friends drag her away.

Jim's mate curses. 'She isn't the only one. If these panic merchants only knew when to leave alone! They whisk kids off and never think of letting somebody know.'

Two men are looking northwards and arguing whether a distant flash was lightning or a speeding car taking a turn in the road. The wind is still in that quarter, but all the violence has gone from it. The long trumpet flowers of a datura growing in the angle of porch and wall give off a sweet smell, overcoming in their immediate vicinity the prevailing odour of smoke. It makes me feel sleepy again, but as we go in we're caught up in a confusion of voices. The dry old hall is buzzing like a beehive.

Some men in the porch are wrangling a familiar bone of contention:

'. . . can't fight fire on this scale with water.'

'Might as well . . .' the speaker glances around, grins with relief when he sees we aren't women, but still doesn't finish the sentence.

'Then what the hell are we going to fight it with?'

'Fire! In twenty-six . . .'

We push through, and out of earshot.

'Twenty-six me Aunt Fanny!' mutters Jim into my ear. 'We can't burn back in an area like this now.' He has one hand over his eyes. 'Get me into a corner, Bob. Find somebody with a first-aid kit.'

How strange it all looks! Candles and hurricane lamps and one pressure lamp. The Mechanics' Hall, traditional social centre of the Australian bush township. Dances, church bazaars, election polling days. Protest meetings: against the Shire Council over a rise in rates, against the Country Roads Board over the state of the highway, against the Board of Works for not laying water on to us. Picture nights, when nothing was quite real except the Little White Hand resting in one's own in the secret darkness.

Relics and familiar features are all here, but they seem fiddling and meaningless on this night of fire. The stack of card tables against the back wall. The Christmas decorations still festooning the dusty rafters. The out-dated billboards, informing us, cajoling us, threatening us. The faithful old piano below the stage.

Tonight it's a refuge, and local headquarters of operations. Some of the trestle tables have been set up, and the forms around all but two of them are full of people, many of them known to me. All are dirty and dishevelled. Some eating and drinking, some quietly talking, some sleeping with heads resting on folded arms. A few, those who have lost their homes, just stare at nothing in particular. They're so used to reading about other people's misfortunes — *has this really happened to me?*

Two tables have been reserved for work only, one for the preparation of food and drinks, the other as a first-aid post. Several men are seated at this latter, with their heads resting on an improvised heightened backboard. All have damp cloths over the upper parts of their faces. Along the nearest wall are a few prone figures, the utterly collapsed and the more seriously burned. All the helpers are women and girls.

I take Jim by the arm and steer him over. A Mrs Shields takes him from me and settles him on the form. She knows both of us.

'You can lie on the floor if you like,' she tells Jim, 'but we're out of pillows. All right like that? Slide down a bit — what d'you think you're going to get, a haircut? Get your head on that board.'

Funny, she seems different tonight . . .

Jim's too lanky to be comfortable, but doesn't want to be fussed over. 'I'm apples,' he assures her. 'It's only me eyes. Got anything to put in 'em?'

I stand by while she puts the drops in and lays a cloth over his eyes.

Jim doesn't want anything else, but I accept a mug of coffee, roll a couple of cigarettes, take a few puffs of Jim's before placing it between his lips, and sit down alongside him.

Some men on the other side of the table are discussing the latest news. I gather that several more lives have been lost during the day, making a total of eight since the fires began. One voice gloomily forecasts a 'crown' fire tomorrow if the north wind works up again.

'Sherbrooke Forest hasn't been burned out in living memory. If it gets in there it's good night, nurse . . .'

Two women are kneeling beside a man on the floor who is retching violently into a hand basin. Mrs Shields, now dabbing the blistered foot of a youth sitting beyond Jim, looks at them over her shoulder.

'He's poisoned, that's what I think,' she informs them. 'Better get him down to hospital. There's plenty of cars running around.'

Yes, she's different. I've only known her as a woman who lives somewhere up the road, one of the store gossips, and not usually involved in local activities. Tonight she's taken on quite an air of authority. Perhaps she was a nurse once.

One of the women immediately gets up and goes out. The youth, his hair damp with perspiration, groans and clutches his stomach. Another one who's been drinking from a knapsack pump. Rural brigades' equipment is all right, but most of the others pressed into service have been used by the orchardists for insecticides.

Up on the small stage several families are bedding down as best they can for the night. The children, well aware that stern matters are in hand, are well behaved. Some men have just

come in carrying mattresses and pillows. They look new, probably part of a donation from some furnishing store. All kinds
of stuff is being rushed up from the city.

Somebody comes in from the front and says that a lot of
soldiers have just gone up the road. 'Six trucks, full to the
gills . . .'

We need equipment far more than we do men, but the news
sinks into me. Perhaps we won't have to go out again. Perhaps
the rain will come. Jim is fast asleep, the dead cigarette fallen
from his slackened lips.

The coffee has brought the sweat out on me again, but it's
pleasant sitting here. And full of interest. I keep thinking: this
is how people behave in a crisis. Voices come at me from all
sides. One that I recognize is telling the story of the big aviation
tanker that was sent up to the Christmas Hills outbreak:

'. . . and lined it up on a row of fowl houses that was just
beginning to burn. Bloke in charge told us it could pump four
thousand gallons in eight minutes. 'Give it a burst!' somebody
yells. Stone the crows, you should have seen them sheds go!
Flattened 'em like a tack. Chooks streaking in all directions —
burn or drown . . .'

Chuckles, and more voices . . .

'According to the newspapers every bloody township in the
Dandenongs has been evacuated.'

'They like that word — evacuated.'

'Like they talk about houses exploding.'

'Fibro-plaster houses *do* explode. The walls don't burn
through. The heat keeps building up inside, then off they go
— poof!'

'You're talking about balloons! What about doors and windows? I saw a couple . . .'

'It's things in the houses, and round about, that explode. Like
cylinders of porta-gas and drums of petrol.'

'Bill Renton got trapped . . .'

'Old Ma Stevens — coming up the track with that useless
little foxy bitch under one arm and a clucky hen under the
other . . .'

The wagging tongues are beginning to run together, to lose
sense and individuality and merge into all the other noises —

shuffling feet, clattering dishes, scraping forms, and rumbling wheels out on the road. It's been a long day.

There was the hard-bitten Board of Works man. Two of us had been left behind to keep watch after the fire had been beaten back at a point where the aqueduct emerges into the open to cross a small depression. He pointed to the blackened and still-smoking concrete pipe-line, hung with stalactites of melted bitumen. 'We bloody nearly gave 'em a hot-water service in Melbourne, mate!'

It amused me at the time. I begin to shake again now. Somebody standing in front of me puts a hand on my shoulder as I lurch forward, and I look up into the face of Mrs Shields.

'What's up with you? You're sitting there with a grin on you like a half-stunned duck.'

I'm saying something, but I don't know what. She keeps on looking at me, curiously.

'Evacuated? What the heck are you talking about?'

'We're still here, aren't we?'

'If I knew where you was getting it from I'd say you was drunk.'

True, Mrs Shields, I'm not drunk. And you're too busy to guess what it is that's tickling me. And that's the whole point of it.

· The Prophet of Pandaloop ·

The new groom was the beginning.

Oliphant waited half an hour at the Wanganella Hotel for the station car to come in for him. When Jimmy Rankin, licensee, parted the bead curtains of the bar parlour to announce its arrival, Oliphant stood up and folded his newspaper with the satisfied air of a man sure of every move in a perfectly organized society. A telephone call had informed the homestead, twenty miles away, of his arrival at the township, and for thirty minutes he had sat before Rankin's big fire, luxuriating in a good cigar, neat whisky, and visions of the highly trained automatons of Pandaloop going smoothly into action. His young wife was, it appeared, out riding somewhere, but the voice of old Mrs Telson had trembled happily over the wires. Things would be moving out there now.

'Arthur, Mr Oliphant's back! He's in Wanganella.'

'Helen, do try and find out which way Mrs Oliphant went!'

'Hi, Jim! You gotta take the Lancia in for the boss. He's at Wanganella.'

'Where's Mr Dennis? Better let him know Mr Oliphant's back.'

'Helen, did you put fresh flowers in the smoke-room?'

Geoffrey Oliphant smiled contentedly. Discipline and efficiency! Wasn't it only right that such qualities characterize the entire establishment of a man who was himself both disciplined and efficient ... 'I am the master of my life; I am the captain of my soul.'

Then Rankin had to go and throw the first spanner into the well-oiled works.

'Are you leaving right away, Mr Oliphant?' he asked between the curtains.

'Yes. Tell Veale to put the bags in.'

'He's putting 'em in. But it ain't Veale.'

'What?' Oliphant swung round with his overcoat half on.

'It's the new man, Calder. Didn't you know Veale's gone?'

Oliphant would hardly have been more shocked if Rankin had said the orange trees were gone, or the new swimming pool. Fifteen years of faithful service had made Veale an intrinsic part of Pandaloop.

'Left a week ago,' added Rankin placidly. 'I thought you'd have known.'

Oliphant gave his head a slight shake and finished pulling on his overcoat. It mortified him to have such a vital piece of news broken by the hotel-keeper. Rankin must think it funny he didn't know. Why the devil hadn't Louise told him over the telephone? She'd chattered over a dozen things much less important.

Even the smart appearance of the new groom failed to lighten his frown as he came out to the car. Veale, part of The Structure, was gone. Things were not, after all, precisely as he had left them. His proprietorial pride was injured. He felt a new hurt that Louise, his wife, had not been at hand herself to drive in for him. Louise, for whose pleasure, in the final analysis, the whole precision-built machinery of Pandaloop was but an instrument.

'Good afternoon, Mr Oliphant.' The new groom, a young man neatly dressed in town clothes, opened the car door and stood respectfully at one side.

'Good afternoon,' replied Oliphant with a cold stare. 'Got all the bags?'

'Yes, Mr Oliphant, they're all in. Mr Rankin said you'd sit in the front. Do you want to drive?'

'Yes, I'll drive.' Oliphant paused with one foot on the running-board. 'My men usually address me as "sir",' he said softly.

The new man coloured slightly. 'I beg your pardon, Mr Oliphant. I'll remember.'

Oliphant let that go. Probably the fellow had never been in real gentleman's service before. He'd learn.

There was little conversation on the way out. Even the smooth efficiency with which the new groom slipped out to

open the many gates did not improve the squatter's ill-
humour. He spoke only twice; once to ask Calder if he was married, and once to ask him what his last job was. For the rest
he drove in sullen silence, brooding stubbornly over the irri-
tating hitch in his clock-like organization. A quiet little talk
with Veale was to have been the first of the many pleasures of
his homecoming, all of which had been laid out in nice
sequence in his well-ordered mind. Veale knew his place so
well ... his place in society. The perfect confidential servant.
With Veale at his side Oliphant would, in the short journey
to the homestead, have learned of everything that had happened during his absence.

As it was he sat moodily pondering the reason for Veale's
departure. Perhaps Louise had committed some innocent
indiscretion. Louise, the new, youthful, and very English, mistress of Pandaloop. Louise, with her childish ignorance of the
subtleties of staff management, and her wild infatuation with
station life. Louise, who said and did such odd things, getting
away with them all on the strength of an irresistible charm and
friendliness. Everybody on Pandaloop was at her feet, but perhaps for once ...

As the miles and the minutes passed, Oliphant's bad temper
kept finding fresh grievances. Seated in the hotel he'd been as
happy as a perfect egoist can be, exulting in the swollen rivers
as he had seen them at Deniliquin and Echuca, and completely
satisfied with Louise's explanation over the telephone, two evenings ago, that the condition of the roads would prevent her
from meeting him at the rail-head.

Now the great clouds, emptied of rain and rolling away to
the east, depressed him immeasurably. Visions of good feed
and heavy lambing no longer brightened the puddled and
grassless plains which reached monotonously to every horizon. And it came to him suddenly that the roads hadn't been
so very bad after all. The mail-car hadn't bogged once between
Deniliquin and Wanganella.

Louise wasn't even at home.

Suddenly they were at the homestead. The afternoon was
getting late. Newly-released horses with the sweaty outlines of
saddles still fresh on their backs, edged into the scrub and
turned curiously to watch the car pass. And in the very moment

that the twisted mallee gums thinned away from the wide drive leading to the house, the western edge of the great cloudbank lifted. A moist sun, like an immense orange, beamed over the drenched plains.

Oliphant's spirits lifted too. The imp of loneliness that had pestered him since leaving Wanganella fled away. One keen glance took in the whole scene. Veale was gone, but everything else, thank God, was as it should be. Familiar with every detail of the station routine, he looked at his watch. Four-thirty. And there was Jackson, the houseboy, coming away from the fowl yards after locking up for the night. And the bowed head of Pu Yin, the vegetable gardener, moving slowly along the top of the saltbush hedge. And Joe McGrath, the blacksmith, going up the track to his shop with a big box on his shoulder ... no doubt lamb-marking equipment to be sharpened up for tomorrow. And Nesbitt and Timms, two of the boundary riders, unsaddling their horses in the stockyards.

This was better. Veale or no Veale, *it* still remained. The Machine, ticking over as surely and sweetly as the engine of the Lancia. Every man just where he ought to be, fulfilling his own little duty as if it were a matter of personal intimate concern.

Oliphant's pride in his workmen was hardly less than his pride in his stock. Pandaloop stud merinos had taken fifteen firsts at Sydney and Melbourne shows. But other breeders had done as well, and Oliphant knew it wasn't so much his sheep that evoked their envy as the team of loyal and capable servants with which he had surrounded himself. Over cigars and liqueurs his guests waxed less enthusiastic over Pandaloop Bonnet and Pandaloop Pasha than over the constancy of his boundary riders, the skill of his blacksmith, the abundant vegetables of Pu Yin, the delicious white bread of German Karl, and the impeccable housekeeping of Mrs Telson and the two maids. Aicheson in particular, owner of neighbouring Maboodah, never ceased to wonder.

'Geoffrey my boy,' he said once, 'if I could get together a crowd like yours I'd turn up managing and go off and puddle in the fleshpots of Egypt for the rest of my life. How in the name of creation do you keep 'em?'

And Oliphant had given an appreciative chuckle and replied,

'Treat them fair and keep your dig, Bob. There's nothing else to it.'

That, however, was very far from the truth, whether he was aware of it or not. Probably he'd never consciously worked out a formula. Had he done so it would have run something like this: Sow a little discord, cultivate petty rivalries, stimulate private conceits. Aim, in short, at a staff which has nothing in common except an anxiety to win your good graces. Cherish a dignified aloofness, unbending only when there is a definite end to serve, and so rarely that the occasion never ceases to excite wonder and gratitude. Grant few favours, but let them be big ones, big enough to create a legend of generosity. Keep remunerations at an absolute minimum, the better to emphasize the favours. Above all be eternally vigilant against precedents and the intrusion of disturbing outside elements.

To workmen on neighbouring stations Pandaloop was a carefully insulated nest of efficiency, servility, and treachery.

To Geoffrey Oliphant it was the sublimation of a colossal conceit ... that rewards go only to the just and the diligent. Since his marriage it was also something else.

'You'll have to show me where to take the bags, sir.' The car had come to a standstill in front of the house. Calder's pleasant voice broke a fifteen minutes' silence. 'I haven't had time to find my way about yet.'

'Bring the two small ones along,' said Oliphant. 'I'll show you where to put the others as we go.'

They set off along a spacious verandah, Oliphant carrying only a briefcase. Annoyance was on the upgrade again. An hour had passed since the telephone call from Wanganella, and he had been dwelling hungrily on a hope that in the meantime Louise might have returned. All his irritation would have dissolved immediately at sight of her gay figure waving to him from the top of the steps.

But Louise had not returned, and in the very moment of certain disappointment Oliphant received another blow.

Mrs Telson did not wave to him.

She was crossing from the dairy to the kitchen as he reached the side porch. Perhaps thirty yards separated them across the garden, and Oliphant spontaneously raised his hand in greeting. It was a salute he gave to no one else on Pandaloop, a graceful little tribute to twenty years of irreproachable service, and fully consistent with his every precept. He'd offered it a hundred times before, on similar select occasions, and invariably the old lady had responded with a jolly flourish of her fingers.

Not until Oliphant was alone in the smoke-room did he fully comprehend what she had done this time.

Mrs Telson had raised her hand. That was all. She had raised it with ostentatious diffidence, and without any flourish whatever had let it fall to her side again. She hadn't even smiled, although she'd looked straight at him.

Oliphant could misinterpret neither the gesture nor the look which had accompanied it. In twenty years he had never once known Mrs Telson to be seriously angry, yet today the whole bearing and expression of the old lady, passing clear against the white wall of the laundry, had been one of smouldering hostility.

Veale gone. Louise out when she knew he was coming home. Mrs Telson angry.

When Helen the housemaid came in ten minutes later with a tea-tray her master sat brooding in evening shadows. Peering into the corner where his surly voice had come from, she made out the white dome of his bald head against the mahogany bookcase.

'Ah, thank you Helen.' He did not move as she set the tray on a little antique table.

'It's nice to see you back again, sir.'

'Thank you, Helen. I understand Mrs Oliphant is not at home?'

'No, sir. She went out to Dolman's. The baby's sick —'

'All right, Helen.'

He wasn't interested in Dolman's baby. Dolman was only the boundary rider on the out-station. Oliphant's mind was on other things. Hurriedly he searched for a way of putting a few discreet questions. Helen was one of the lesser lights he made a practice of keeping at a particularly frigid distance.

'Is there anything else I can do for you, sir?'

'No, thank you, Helen. Is everything — er — all right?'

What little light was left in the room fell full on the girl's face, and he lost nothing of the quick smile nor of the effort which instantly suppressed it.

'Well, Helen?'

She began to fidget, and lost control of the smile. 'You didn't hear about it, sir?'

'About what?'

'About me.'

'About you? Come, Helen, if you have anything to tell me —'

'We're getting married, sir! Bob Camm and me.'

The pale head moved forward a foot. 'Getting married? You and Camm?'

'Yes, sir.'

Oliphant heard the announcement only as it affected the functioning of Pandaloop. Camm was a key man, leading teamster, expert fencer, and a wizard with an axe. His five years' courtship of Helen was a joke in the district. On Pandaloop they said Camm hadn't the guts to shoulder the responsibility of married life. On other stations they said he hadn't the guts to give Oliphant the necessary week's notice.

'This is rather sudden, isn't it?' said Oliphant sourly.

'We've been going together five years, sir. Bob said —'

'I assume this means he will be leaving me?'

No longer smiling, the girl was observing her employer with growing anxiety.

'Come, you must have made some plans?'

'Perhaps I shouldn't have said anything yet, sir.'

'What does Camm propose doing?'

'He's — taking over a farm down in Gippsland.'

'All right, Helen.'

Oliphant's voice was weary. The abashed maid turned to go.

'Helen.'

'Yes, sir?'

'What's wrong with Mrs Telson?'

'Nothing that I know of, sir.'

'Mrs Telson is angry over something. What is it?'

'Really, sir, I don't know. Unless —' Helen stopped, nervously twisting the hem of her pinafore.

'Unless what? Come, girl, there's something here —'

'It might be the lighting, sir.'

'The what?'

'Oh, sir, I don't want to make trouble —'

'Stop beating about the bush! What do you mean? — the lighting —'

'Mrs Telson says we should have better lighting over there in the wing.'

'Better lighting? What in the name of God has come over the place? Those lamps are the best —'

'I know, sir. But Mrs Telson says we should have a Gloria system, the same as you have here. I've got no complaints myself —'

Oliphant relaxed, 'No, you're only getting married —'

'Mr Oliphant, sir, you won't —'

'That will do —'

'If you please —'

'You can go, Helen.'

Hastily, and without the slightest enjoyment, the squatter sipped a cup of tea and munched a biscuit. Then he went out to the garden. His orderly and fastidious soul revolted at secrets — secrets that were not his. Four times within an hour a hole had been blown in the beautifully assembled pattern of his life. Something had happened in his absence. Some new and malignant force was operating on Pandaloop. And, as befitted a man master of his affairs, he went out to seek it.

Like many egoists, Oliphant was keenly sensitive to the beautiful, but his anger only increased now as he encountered the rich scents and colours and sounds of the winter evening. Over the stockyards a shower of gold flashed as a flock of galahs wheeled against the setting sun. Beyond silver saltbush hedges the dogs howled for their supper. In the garden mynas chattered excitedly around the last bursting pomegranates. Ripe fruits glowed in the deepening gloom of the orange trees. On the breathless air hung a fine smell of rain-soaked dead leaves. Oliphant observed all these things, and fumed because events were robbing him of his customary epicurean enjoyment of them.

He found McDuff, the gardener in charge of fruit and flowers, raking up leaves under the fig trees.

'Evenin', sir!' McDuff's deferential salute was encouraging.

'Good evening, McDuff. Everything in order?'

'Aye, sir, everything in guid order. 'Cept maybe the weether. The rain washed oot a' ma winter seed.'

Oliphant nodded sympathetically, but without any real interest. 'We can't have it all ways, McDuff. They were good rains.'

'Och, far be it frae me tae complain, sir. They were a godsend for the run. An' I'll be a' richt. I'll bring a bit o' stuff alang under glass.'

'You'll be all right, McDuff.'

Oliphant's senses must have been finely tuned, for in the very act of turning away he became aware of a peculiar alertness in the old Scotsman's eyes. He wasn't a bit surprised when McDuff's voice arrested him.

'If ye dinna mind, sir, there was a sma' matter I had a wish tae ask ye aboot.'

'Yes, McDuff?'

Uncomfortably the gardener shifted his bamboo rake from one hand to the other and noisily wiped the stubble of his chin. 'It just came tae ma mind the ither day, sir. I've bin with ye nigh on ten years, an' I'm no gettin' a bawbee more than the day I came.'

Oliphant's expression hardened. A rise in pay this time. Always a serious request on Pandaloop, it possessed today a new and ominous significance.

'Make yourself a bit clearer, McDuff,' he said coldly.

'Weel, sir, I'm won'ering if it wad be verra much oot o' order for me tae ask ye tae consider a sma' rise in ma pay. I ken fine —'

'McDuff, why do you ask me this today?'

The gardener again shuffled uneasily. 'That's no an easy question, sir. Ye micht ask me that ony time. I just seemed tae decide in ma ain mind that the moment was opportune.'

'Why did you think this particular moment opportune?'

'Ye maun excuse me, sir, I'm no insinuatin' —'

Oliphant had an inspiration. 'McDuff, have you had a union official here while I was away?'

'God forgive ye, sir!' McDuff's reply was swift and emphatic. 'Whatever micht a put sich an idea intae your heed? I need no man tae —'

'Has anybody been here while I was away?'

'Not a soul, sir. That's exceptin' Mr Aicheson frae Maboodah, an' that owld swaggie.'

'What swagman?'

'Didn't ye ken, sir? I keep forgettin' ye're jist hame. Mr Dennis put a swagman on for a bit o' work. But he's awa' noo.'

Oliphant began to scent elucidation. *Beware of disturbing outside elements!*

'Just what was this man doing?'

'Weel, sir, Mr Dennis seemed tae be a bit shorthanded for the lamb-markin', an' there was naebody tae spare for a bit o' fencin' aboot the place.'

'Did you say he's gone now?'

'He went off only this mornin', sir. Took it into his heed tae ask Mr Dennis for his cheque last nicht. Y'ken what these swaggies are —'

'Who did this man hut with?'

'Wi' Veale and young Camm, sir. There was only the one empty bunk on the place. Ye'll hae heerd aboot Veale?'

'Yes. Why did Veale leave?'

McDuff ventured a quaint smile. 'Since ye ask me, sir, I'd say it was just a case o' itchy feet!'

'Itchy feet? At Veale's age!'

'The rovin' instinct must ha' been in him, sir. He seemed tae tak it into his heed a' of a sudden he'd like tae have a look aroond. He said he was awa' tae Queensland. Maybe that auld swaggie had been blawin' doon his ear aboot the big money on the canefields.'

'What was this man like, McDuff? The swagman.'

McDuff was eyeing his employer with increasing curiosity. 'He's no done onything wrang, sir, has he?'

'I asked you a question, McDuff!'

'I beg pardon, sir. What sort o' man was he? That's no sae easy tae say. He seemed tae me tae be an erudite sort o' person.'

'Erudite?'

'Learrr-nid, sir. Mind ye, I micht a been mistaken, for I make nae pretensions tae scholarship masel'.'

'What made you think he was learned?'

'Sir, he just talkit. But he talkit sae weel.'

'Talked — what about?'

'Everythin' under the sun, sir. There wasna a thing in heaven or earth that he didna seem tae ken a' aboot.'

'What was his name?'

'Och, sir, wi' his whiskers an' a', he just seemed tae answer nat'rally tae Pop. But we a' called him the Prophet behind his back.'

'The Prophet?'

'He was sae dignified, sir. An' seemed tae have sich a great heart, for a' his dirty face. A grand faith in humanity. He was aye sayin' that we were livin' in great days. That michty forces were bein' loosened and workin' oot a new way o' life. Some o' his ideas micht a been far-fechit, but I maun say —'

'All right, McDuff.' Oliphant wanted no more. Not instinct, but all the solid experiences of a lifetime, screamed that this was it.

Beware of the intrusion of disturbing outside elements!

He passed on, satisfied that he had laid the ghost, but still troubled. What else was to come?

McDuff's voice, low and infinitely humble, followed after him. 'An ye'll gie that wee matter a bit o' thocht, will ye, sir?'

Oliphant waved his arm non-committedly. Yes, he'd give it thought, more thought than McDuff ever dreamed of. He was glad to get outside the garden gate, away from the encroaching trees. Enough light still remained to reveal the magnificent Riverina distances, always food for his self-esteem. Everything, far as the eye could see, was all his own. It was in vain, however, that he searched the cold plain for the only thing he really wanted — a woman riding in on a grey horse. Instead of Louise there was a spectre — the receding figure of a tall bearded man.

A swagman! Oliphant had learned, even before becoming master of Pandaloop, of the demoralizing effect of people who went around 'just talking'. He'd mistrusted sundowners all his life, and the last caution he had administered to Dennis, the overseer, before leaving was to keep strangers off the place. Lamb-marking always presented its labour problems, but this was the first time he had been away at such a season. His practice every year was to use Veale and McDuff, sometimes even Pu Yin and the houseboy in the catching pens. Now, in his absence, a stranger had come by, stayed a little while, and passed on — leaving Pandaloop disintegrating like an ant-eaten house. And the stranger had 'just talked.'

Just talked.

Oliphant's anger began to focus itself on Dennis. Dennis, who should have known better, who had betrayed a trust. Who, considered simply as a man, held so many advantages over his employer, and who — like Louise — was out now somewhere on the run. Old jealousies and anxieties began to stir. Talk was powerful. It released forces. It lifted inhibitions. It had put the idea of a Gloria lighting system into Mrs Telson's contented old head. It had moved the servile McDuff to ask for a rise in pay. It had uprooted Veale. It had filled Camm with a courage he had been groping after for five years. And it had all worked so insidiously that probably not one of them even suspected where the real driving force came from. What else had it done? What had it done to Louise? To Dennis?

Love and marriage had come late in Geoffrey Oliphant's ascetic life. Even now he was still a little suspicious of his good fortune in winning the charming young Englishwoman who, only eighteen months ago, had come as a visitor to Maboodah. Keenly sensitive of the considerable difference in their ages, his bald head, and the shortness of breath that denied so many extravagances, he had never been able to rid himself of a conviction that for Louise it had been a marriage of convenience. That Pandaloop, and not himself, had been the attraction. The short, incredible, but triumphant courtship had, therefore, given a fresh impetus and a new twist to his peculiar egoism. Where the model station had been an end in itself, it became now the means to an end — the pleasure of Louise. By Pandaloop she had been won, and by Pandaloop she would be held. Pride in achievements became conditioned by the gratitude and enthusiasms called up in Louise. Pandaloop was no longer the song; it was the instrument. He who injured it, therefore, laid hands on the inmost nerves of Geoffrey Oliphant's emotional existence.

That was what the stranger had done. And it was Dennis who had made it possible. Dennis, with his straight limbs, his dense curls, and his merry laugh. With defections following fast one upon another in the ranks of the faithful, Oliphant's hand strayed uneasily over his own barren head, and the hunger which had possessed him for two months became a raging torment. He wanted Louise as never before, and she was —

Half-way between the garden and the men's huts he caught sight of the houseboy going across from the dam, and, struck by a sudden thought, he called him over. Jackson was only seventeen but had been on Pandaloop long enough to imbibe its stultifying breezes.

'Leslie,' said Oliphant, 'do you think you can find Mr Dennis for me?'

'Mr Dennis isn't in yet, sir,' replied the boy.

Oliphant looked at him searchingly. Why had he been hurrying so? Why had he approached with such a guilty air? Why, now, was he so obviously relieved at the innocence of the question? What had he been expecting?

Oliphant glanced across at a point in the creek just below the windmill, where the punt was kept moored. He remembered painfully the reason why six times in five years he had had to sack his houseboy. The boat provided an irresistible temptation to otherwise excellent youths. True enough, Jackson was at the fowl pens only half an hour ago, but had he seen the car arrive?

'You haven't been using the boat, have you?' demanded the squatter sternly.

'Oh no, sir.'

'Then what were you doing over there?'

'I was looking for eggs, sir. Karl said some of his chooks must be laying out, so I . . .'

'All right, I'll take your word for it. You know the rules regarding the boat, don't you?' Oliphant wasn't convinced, but knew that this was a matter in which the culprit had to be caught in the very act. Besides, he'd had another reason for stopping Jackson and would only defeat himself if he upset the boy.

'Have you any idea where Mr Dennis went?' he asked with engaging friendliness.

'Yes, sir. He went out to have a look at the overflow. The creek came down yesterday.'

'Ah!'

'Did you want me, sir?'

'No, Leslie, that was all.'

The overflow was in a direct line with the out-station, where Louise had gone.

Jackson was only a few yards away when his master's voice brought him back. 'One moment, Leslie!'

'Yes, sir?'

'You had a swagman here while I was away?'

'Yes, sir.'

'What sort of a man was he?'

'He was a nice kind of a bloke, sir. He's gone now.'

'So I understand. Rather a studious fellow, wasn't he?'

'Studious, sir?' Jackson's incredulity was almost scorn. 'Oh no, sir. I don't know who could have told you that. There was nothing quiet about him.'

'What was wrong with him?'

'Nothing, sir. He was a bonzer bloke. Everybody liked him. He used to sing and recite ...'

'Sing and recite?'

Oliphant knew of stations where the men amused themselves with impromptu concerts, but nothing like that ever happened on Pandaloop. Here again, on the impressionable mind of the houseboy, the stranger had left his mark. Oliphant had not missed the inner significance of the suspected boat stealing. And there was a new and subtle self-assertiveness about the boy tonight which was right out of harmony with the traditions of Pandaloop.

'Yes, sir. He knew every line of "The Man from Snowy River".'

'Quite a talented fellow!'

'Oh, he was clever all right, sir. He used to get us all going. Everybody had to do something. Sing a song, recite a poem.'

'What, everybody?'

'Yes, sir. He even had old Karl going last night. Something in German.'

Visions of 'Rabbity' Karl, the cook, singing in his native tongue made Oliphant smile for the first time since his return. But it wasn't a happy smile.

'You've had quite a time, Leslie!'

'Yes, sir. We all called him the Prophet. He had a long ziff ...'

'All right, boy. Tell Mr Dennis I'd like to see him after dinner.'

So. In the gathering dusk Oliphant continued on to the men's quarters. He wanted to be done with all this, to know everything — the very worst — now. It was like a survey of damage after a storm. Ghosts of all the swagmen he had ever known moved tantalizingly before him. What was this one like? McDuff's evidence indicated a dirty but dignified patriarch of the roads. But that didn't at all fit in with Jackson's convivial troubadour. Where was he now? What was he doing? Somewhere along the track to Wanganella — to Booligal — to Moulamein — an agent of destruction tramped. A man who sang songs, recited poetry, and — just talked. And wherever he passed nothing remained quite the same.

To Geoffrey Oliphant there was an uncanny falseness in the familiar sights and sounds of this Pandaloop evening. Boots thumped on wooden floors. Washing basins rattled. A broken voice sang the silly refrain, 'Lal-lal to Geelong.' Someone came out and cracked a whip to hush the yelping dogs. And every sound agitated the squatter by its very mundaneness. These were the sounds of every night, and this night was like no other night. He had a fantastic impulse to walk out over the plain calling Louise home. He wanted to get her in a good light, place his hands on her shoulders, and look down into the adorable oval face. To see if contamination had reached even here, into the brown eyes of Louise. To hear her speak, so that he could examine every inflexion of the beloved voice. The stranger had torn down his defences. What had Louise seen?

Old Karl, standing in the doorway of the cookhouse, beckoned him over. Beyond any surprise now, he hardly noticed that Karl omitted to give him 'good-evening'. The cook's lips were tightly closed. His lower jaw kept up a ceaseless trembling, like a rabbit's. Rabbity Karl.

Silently he stood to one side, motioning Oliphant in with an expressive gesture of his rheumy thumb. As if he had a great secret to communicate. Oliphant was right inside before he quite realized what he was doing. Suddenly the last of the daylight was gone and it was night. All the paraphernalia of cooking wavered vaguely in the light of a hurricane lamp hanging from a rafter. Scrubbed pine benches, pots and pans on the smoke-blackened walls, shelves stuffed with bottles and canisters. A heap of wood alongside the glowing range.

Immobile but for his quivering jaw, the old German remained just inside the doorway, watching his employer much as a father would watch a child he had caught in some particularly exasperating prank.

'Well, Karl,' said Oliphant, 'it smells good. What are you giving them tonight?'

'I cook in here,' said Karl heavily.

'You do a good job. That light isn't too good, is it?' Perhaps Karl also wanted a Gloria.

Karl nodded without returning the smile. 'Eight years I cook here. Und I say noddings.'

'What's the matter, Karl? You speak as though —'

'Vat iss not de matter! How you tink I kip on cooking tings in dis place?'

'You want a better light?'

'In summer I sweat to death. In vinter I freeze to death — und get blown out. Alvays I squint lak a damn mouse.'

Oliphant convulsively stiffened. Here, it seemed, the stranger had left him nothing. Not once had Karl addressed him as 'sir'.

'Is this any way to make a complaint, Karl?' he blustered. 'You're forgetting yourself.'

Karl's hand slashed impatiently. 'I forget noddings. You tink because I say noddings, I tink noddings. I tink always. Und alvays I tink vat a damn fool —'

'Karl!'

'Dese men vant foods —'

'Karl, what is it you require of me?'

'Gott damn it, sir, I vant a new kitchen!'

'I beg your pardon!'

'Mr Oliphant, for why should I beat about de bush? Eight years I say noddings, und vat do I get? I get noddings? Of vat matter iss it to you if I poison de mens so long as I giff de goot vite breads? I cook better in a ship's galley. Here I am not a cook — I am a bloody gypsy! You giff me no milk. For my puddinks I mix powders, so your hens haf milk in dere mash. Ven I get no eggs from my chooks, I get none from you — you giff eggs to your dogs. For vegetables I get vat you don't want, vat you haf too much of. Vunce I vas Rabbity Karl. Now I am Carroty Karl — Pumpkin Karl — Onions Karl. Ven am I going to be Cabbage Karl? Iss it any vonder dese men say I am not a cook's arse?'

'Karl!'

'I tell you now, vunce and vunce only —'

'You'll tell me not another word! I'm not prepared to listen to this.' Oliphant moved towards the door, but Karl blocked the way. The harassed squatter was keenly aware of the hush which had fallen upon the immediate neighborhood. Everybody was listening.

'Mister Oliphant —'

'You can get off the place first thing in the morning!'

'Good! In dis place I stay not anudder day. But before I go I tell you —'

'You're like the rest of them — you've been listening to that damned bagman!'

'Bagman?' Karl's voice fell. 'De man who shust go avay?'

'Yes, I know all about him. That whispering blackguard —'

'Blackguard?'

Oliphant divined a fresh storm gathering, but rage carried him on. 'You pack a weak idiots! You're working on the finest station in the Riverina, and when an infernal waster —'

'Vaster?'

'Yes, waster. He didn't even have the guts to face me himself. He just filled all your witless heads —'

'Mr Oliphant, you do great wrongs.' Karl's voice trembled with indignation. 'Dat vas de finest gentlemans who ever stepped foot on Pandaloops.'

'Why, you old fool —'

'Don' you dare call me an ol' fools! Vat do you know of bad mens? All your life you stay here und see noddings. I tell you dat man vas a — a saint. He vas too good ever for to stay here. He love everybody, und everybody love him. To me he vas a friend. He cut my vood, he vash my dishes. Vun night ven my bones ache he rode all de vay to Vanganella for to bring me brandy. He was a very vise and good man —'

'And he told you you needed a new kitchen! And the men needed more vegetables!'

'Und vat if he did? Iss it not true?'

'The men have been satisfied here for years —'

'Und now dey all vakes up!'

'I had a man cook in this kitchen for fourteen years!'

'I vunce knew a man who cook between two stones, but he did not call it a kitchen!'

Karl jumped to the stove as a pot boiled over, and Oliphant seized the opportunity to retreat outside. Around him closed an atmosphere of breathless suspense. In all the huts not a man moved. But shadows were deep, and the tormented squatter felt all eyes on him as he stumbled away up the track to the house. Stars winked frostily in the velvet dome of the sky. Out on the plain a boobook called. Louise always said that the little owl reminded her of the English cuckoo.

Louise — if she were not yet home!

What had he done to Louise, this awakener of men's conceits, gratitudes, and aspirations? What ambitions had he stirred in the brave head of Dennis? The fact that the man was gone quite unnerved Oliphant, giving him a sense of contending against remote and intangible forces. On every side in the unfathomable night there hovered a Shape, the spectre of a big bearded man with flowing overcoat, netted hat, blanket-roll, and billy can — going away — going away —

Through the open doorway of the storehouse Lessington, the jackaroo, called a respectful greeting, but Oliphant didn't hear him. He wanted Louise, only Louise —

A minute later she was in his arms. She was waiting for him at the top of the verandah steps, still in riding costume. She began to speak, but not a word really reached him. Life, which had been suspended, suddenly pulsed again as he silently took her in his arms and pressed her small head against his breast. So they stood for some seconds. Once she moved as if to disengage herself, but he only held tighter. He felt her hand come up and begin to caress the back of his head, and knew that, in her woman's way, she had sensed something here more than the natural joy of seeing her again and the physical pleasure of embracing her.

'What's the matter, dear?' she whispered.

Placing his hands under her arms he held her off and looked at her long and searchingly. He could make out little more than the flash of her eyes. 'Darling, why weren't you here?'

'But Geoffrey, didn't anyone tell you?'

'Helen said you'd gone to Dolman's.'

'The baby's terribly sick. I shouldn't have come away even now.'

'Isn't Mrs Dolman there?'

'Dear, there are four other children, and she's not well herself. You wouldn't grudge me —'

'I so wanted you to be here.'

'Poor Geoffrey! But it's pneumonia. And Mr Dolman has been away all day with Mr Dennis.'

'Ah! And where is Dennis now?'

'Isn't he back yet? He was at the Two-mile all day, getting the sheep out. The creek came down —'

'Did you see him?'

'No. He'd been to Dolman's before I got there. He'd left word for Mr Dolman to follow him out if he came in. Dolman came in for lunch. He was worried about the baby.'

It was impossible to doubt her. Greedily Oliphant seized on the tremendous fact that, after all, the worst had not happened. All the black background of collapse remained, but here, thank God, was still a foundation. Louise, warm and intimate, just as he'd left her, asking nothing except himself, her every gesture breathing welcome and devotion. How simple and plausible was her explanation of Dennis's movements! In the circumstances where else should Dennis have been but at the overflow and the Two-mile? Where else should Louise have been sought but with the sick baby?

Filled with gratitude and a new hope, he tilted up her chin and kissed her on the lips for the first time, a slow deliberate kiss in which his immense mental relief melted into physical longing.

'Let us go in,' she whispered, 'anybody could see us here.'

Arm in arm they went into the drawing room. Louise began to say something about dinner, but Oliphant drew her over to the table, seated himself on the edge of it, and taking her by the hands looked at her very seriously.

'Louise, darling, it's wonderful to find you just the same. Whatever has been happening?'

'And how,' she asked with a provocative smile, 'did you

expect to find me? What did you suppose had been happening?'

'The whole place has been turned upside down. Everybody is at my throat. There's a rot set in. Veale's gone, Camm and Helen are going, Mrs Telson —'

'Oh, that swagman!' Her spontaneous chuckle made him wonder if, after all, the whole business wasn't a huge misunderstanding. Sheer delight flooded her face. 'Geoffrey, we've had the most remarkable old man! I do wish you could have met him. He only went this morning —'

'Louise, do you realize what that man has done here?'

'H'm, he did rather set the place on fire, didn't he?'

'Then you saw it?'

'I couldn't help seeing it. Why, everybody perked up the very day he came. It was funny. They're such a fusty lot we have here!'

'Fusty? My dear, I prided myself on this staff. Don't you understand yet how hard it is to get a crowd of the right sort of people together on these up-country places? Station hands are notoriously birds of passage. It took me years to get this team together. Ask Aicheson. He's going abroad next month. It's the first time he's ever been able to trust —'

'Geoffrey,' Louise was no longer smiling, 'is that why you're so angry about it?'

'What do you mean?'

'Well, you've always enjoyed scoring over Aicheson, haven't you?'

'Louise!'

'There, don't look so outraged. You know perfectly well you don't like him to have something you haven't got.' Flicking his nose playfully with her forefinger, she added, 'Sometimes I think you're just the tiniest little bit selfish.'

'Louise, darling —'

'Confess, you're thinking of how Aicheson will chuckle when he hears of this? Whereas — are you aware that you did something very unkind tonight?'

'Unkind?'

'Mrs Telson asked me to go in and comfort Helen. The child was in her room crying. Whatever did you say to her?'

'Good Heavens! Did that girl —'

'She would tell me nothing. She was on her bed, sobbing her heart out. Mrs Telson said you were very angry about Camm and her getting married.'

'I was nothing of the sort. The girl's a fool. I'll admit I'm angry, but not necessarily with her. There's a conspiracy. They were all waiting to pick me the minute I came home. Mrs Telson, Helen, McDuff —'

'McDuff?'

'He asked me for a rise in pay. Karl merely wants a new kitchen. I sacked him.'

'For that?'

'Certainly not! He was most insolent. He swore at me.'

Louise's face twitched. Oliphant was shocked to recognize that she was struggling to suppress a smile.

A short silence fell. His confidence of only a few minutes ago was already dissolving. Louise had a thoughtful air, as if she were groping for something.

'Geoffrey?' she said in a doubtful little voice.

'Yes, dear.'

'I'm going to say something not very nice.'

'Say it — if you think it!'

'I believe it's your — your vanity that's hurt.'

'My vanity?'

'Geoffrey, don't you see? — none of these people have really injured you. Yet you're furious with them. Just because they've presumed to ask you for something. That's all —'

'That is not all! I'm furious with none of them. I'm furious with that — that renegade —'

'Sssh! Don't raise your voice, darling. At least admit that you're visiting your fury on them. Wait — listen to me. I'm trying to help you. Tell me this: did you congratulate Helen when she told you she was going to be married?'

'Louise, I was too full —'

'See? You didn't. How hurt she must have been! She's such a pet, and the minute she ceases to be useful you turn on her. The others, too. Yes, I know — they're only servants. But it disturbs me. Supposing they were friends? Or even — nearer? You make me wonder —'

Oliphant winced. All his worst fears returned in a rush.

Louise's slight body, within his arms, became strangely immaterial. An abyss was yawning.

'Louise,' he said with a heavy stare, 'were you talking to that man?'

'The swagman? Yes, I met him. The men called him the Prophet.'

'How did you come to speak to him?'

'Why, Mr Dennis sent him to mend the garden fence one Saturday morning.' In a deliberate effort to give the discussion a lighter turn, Louise cheekily wrinkled her face. 'And you needn't be jealous! He was as old as Methuselah and as dirty as Paddy's pigs!'

'I'm also informed that he was very erudite!'

'Erudite? Oh, how delicious! I'll bet that was McDuff!'

'It was. You might take note that immediately afterwards McDuff asked me for a rise in wages.'

Louise whistled.

'Now,' said Oliphant, 'will you please tell me what this — this Prophet had to say to you?'

'But why? What on earth could that matter?'

'Just tell me, dear. Let us say for academical reasons.'

'All right. Academically — quite academically — he remarked that every man made a home in his own image. I'd happened to say that you were very fussy about the fences, and he replied that few things expressed the personality of a certain type of man as clearly as the nature and condition of the fences with which he marked off his chosen bit of God's earth. I couldn't quite make him out at the time. He had the loveliest smile, and he looked so terribly wise. I had the funniest feeling that he was secretly laughing at me. But tonight I'm beginning to see what he meant. You once — why, whatever's the matter?'

Oliphant had gasped. And even as he felt the first cold premonition of final calamity the telephone bell rang. It was in the same room, but instead of answering it he suddenly clasped Louise to him and snuggled his lips into her hair.

'Louise, darling, if I were to lose you — your respect —'

'Whatever are you saying?'

'That man poisoned everything.'

'Geoffrey, don't be silly! You're upset. The telephone —'

'Never mind the telephone —'

'But Helen will come —'

She remained by the table, watching him curiously as he went over to take the call.

'It's Bob Aicheson,' he said, putting his hand over the mouthpiece. His expression suddenly became alert.

'What is it?' she whispered.

'Your Prophet has turned up on Maboodah. Asking for work. Bob wants to know the strength of him.'

'Geoffrey — how extraordinary!'

It was Oliphant's crowning misfortune that he didn't look at his wife just then. His eyes were riveted on the floor, and slowly he began to smile, a smile ever so gentle and ironic. Louise uttered a little warning cry, but even that did not save him. Quite involuntarily he raised his hand, hushing her to silence. And in a voice deliberately affable and composed she heard him say:

'No, Bob, I'm just back. I didn't see him myself, but I've no doubt he's all right. I'll get Dennis to ring you later if you like. What? Well, please yourself. I've heard no complaints about him. On the contrary, they're all in tears here because he's gone. Eh? Yes, I know, but that's the form of these gentry — they never stop more than a week or two anywhere. Busy? Yes, I know, but he'll tide you over. No, he hardly needs a diploma for catching lambs! Mind, don't blame me if — eh? — well, I'm just warning you — no responsibility attached! I didn't see him. I'm just telling you — all right. What's that? Yes, any time you like. Make it lunch? Good. We'll be at home. 'Bye, Bob.'

Oliphant was still smiling when Louise reached him.

'Geoffrey, you recommended that man to Maboodah?'

'My dear —'

'You deliberately — oh, Geoffrey! Then he was right after all!'

And only then did it come to Geoffrey Oliphant that, all unwittingly, he himself had set the final seal of righteousness and infallibility on the Prophet of Pandaloop. Louise also was lost, and nothing, absolutely nothing, would ever be the same again.

· Appointment at Princess Gate ·

There was a seat at the far end of the garden where he was in the habit of going when there was a problem to be solved. At such a time most men go for a long walk or take to pacing up and down a room. George Mace preferred absolute stillness and isolation. The seat was set in a bower of clipped cypress which lay at the end of a short path sheltered on both sides by other evergreens. An ideal spot for a reflective man to get away from it all. Even Eunice, his late wife, of mixed memory, had never bothered him there. Nor had June, his daughter, since she'd learned better as a child.

He took out from his pocket the letter and began to read it again, the umpteenth time since picking it up from his friend yesterday. He knew now what was in it, and after the first few lines he skipped a whole page and came to rest on that one passage which lay at the very heart of his present agitation, which had put him off his breakfast, which had made him forget to put out the garbage bin, and which had precipitated one more altercation with the neighbour whose rioting convolvulus was still prising apart the palings of the dividing fence:

So you must agree to meet me immediately, on Friday morning. Otherwise please regard this as my last letter. I want no more of this exchange of confidences with a man who, however much he interests me . . . and you do interest me . . . I have not yet seen, and even whose real name and address I do not know. Mutual anonymity was all right to begin with . . .

On Friday. That was tomorrow . . . He let the hand holding the letter fall to his knees, and for several minutes sat very still, his eyes fixed on a blackbird which was noisily scratching

193

among the dead leaves on the path. He heard the bang of the fly-door at the back of the house thirty yards away, and knew that June had come out to water the pot-plants that stood at either side, perhaps also to glance over the garden just to see what he was up to. She knew he hated daffodils, and yet had planted a dozen of them in a corner of the bed he had specially prepared for early poppies.

Tomorrow. Well, it had been going on for four months now, and he supposed this mystery 'Alice' was entitled to expect him to bring matters to a head one way or another. She'd raised the question of a meeting in her last three letters, but this was an ultimatum. Tomorrow, or else. The old familiar doubts began to grip him again. Fifty-five years old, but at least he *was* free. He still had what he'd wanted and dreamed of for so many years. And a sly smile came over his face as he recollected the grim little story of that other man, the story with which Eunice had once convulsed a birthday party, which he had lived to experience himself, and of which he had ultimately learned the bitter inner irony. The story of the man who wouldn't be consoled at the funeral of the wife with whom he had lived in discord for thirty years, who wept real tears, who responded to every word of sympathy with a heart-rending moan 'Alone! Alone! Alone!', and who, when all was over and the last mourner departed, suddenly threw up his arms and did a dance of joy around the silent and deserted house, crying over and over again in a new voice filled with delirious laughter, 'Alone! Alone! Alone!'

He'd thought it funny at the time, just a funny story, the kind of story that men delight in telling about women, and which women accept with the same resignation that they accept stories about mothers-in-law. He'd laughed with the rest of the party, for reasons of his own, and because Eunice had made the most of taking the floor, as she always did, rolling her eyes, clapping her hands, and jumping up and down in a delightfully simulated ecstasy, 'Alone! Alone! Alone!' She'd had quite a talent for mimicry.

He frowned now, closed his eyes, and gave a little shudder. It hadn't taken long for some disillusionment to set in, and when it did the shock was devastating. The real trouble was that it hadn't stayed that way. Of mixed memory . . .

He lifted the letter and began to read again:

It's true that when I replied to your advertisement I did so only partly in earnest, but your first letter did impress me, and I've liked you more and more as the weeks have gone by. Just as you say you've liked ME more and more as you read MY letters. But what do we really know about each other, for certain? Yes, of course I've kept a few things back. Haven't you? And who now is putting off a meeting? I'm the woman, isn't it up to you to make the advances? What do I know about you except that you are in my age group; that you have, like me, been married before, but not happily; that you are a retired civil servant and in good health; that you are interested in gardening and music; and that you have a spinster daughter who lives with you, who teaches violin, and with whom apparently you don't get along very well. I believe you are a good man, but I want to satisfy myself that you are telling me the truth. I want to see what you look like. I give you my word that I really am one of the two women in the photograph I sent you, and you seemed content in your last letter to leave it at that for the present. But I'm not so sure about the photograph of the two men that you sent me. The time for any further joking and mystery between us is past. I must see you, and I must see what your reaction is when you see me.

My family is off my hands, as the saying goes, but I want to meet this daughter of yours. I'm experienced enough to understand that what you say is true, that she will probably move out if anything comes of all this, but if it has to be so I want it to happen in a civilized way, without making enemies of us. I would want her to visit us, as I know my married son and his family will. They would miss me, because I have lived in harmony with them since my husband died, and the children are attached to me. You would come first once we were married, but you must see that it would be important for all of us to remain on good terms. They also I want you to meet before any decisions are made.

There is nothing more I can say now that has not already been said. I want to meet you on Friday. At ten o'clock in the morning I expect to find you waiting for me on the new plaza at Princess Gate. There are seats facing the steps leading up from Flinders Street opposite St Paul's. You will wait for me there. At ten o'clock I will come up those steps. You should recognize me immediately as one of the two women in the photograph, but to put me beyond any doubt I will be wearing a two-piece brown suit with hat and shoes in contrasting browns, and beige accessories, gloves, handbag and umbrella. I will walk straight across from the Flinders Street steps to the St Kilda Road steps. If no man gets up from those seats to greet me as I pass I will not wait, and you will not hear from me again. And that would be something I would not like. I hope with all my heart that I WILL be writing to you again, and that next time I will not need to sign myself just . . . Alice.

Tomorrow . . . or else.

He was still looking at the final warning sentences when, a few minutes later, June came out and called him in for morning coffee.

'Are you there, Dad?' She did, of course, know exactly where he was. 'Smoke-oh!'

He immediately got up and went into the house, wondering on the way if Alice would call it smoke-oh, or if she would come out and find him and tell him coffee was ready. Perhaps, on a nice day, she would bring out a tray and sit with him in the garden. The idea pleased him, as did so many others which were passing through his mind these days. No doubt June would bring out a tray if he suggested it, but there was no point in starting new habits now. He didn't want it anyway, because conversation never had flowed easily between them.

It didn't now, as he entered the kitchen and sat down at the little table already laid out with embroidered cloth (Eunice's work), fine china, and his favourite biscuits. He never could dispute that June took after her mother in a talent for running a home.

She was standing at the stove watching the coffee-pot, and, knowing from experience that it was usually left to him to break the silence, he remarked, in a voice which expressed only half of what he felt.

'I've just had another go at old Skelton.'

'About the fence?' He noticed that she was dressed for going out, and remembered that Thursday was one of the days when she had an outside pupil. Not that dressing up helped her much; one thing she had not inherited was her mother's flair for clothes. Nor would it have mattered much; he ran his eyes distastefully over the broad shoulders and short neck, the too-heavy legs. There was a time, before music took over completely, when she had shown promise as a swimmer.

'Yes, about the fence.' He was rapidly making up his mind to drop the bombshell, but would wait until she settled down. 'I don't think he has any intention of doing anything about it.'

She poured the coffee and took the chair facing him. 'I still think it doesn't matter that much. The fence will have to be renewed soon anyway.'

'Because of his damned convolvulus! I told him years ago that nothing should be grown on a paling fence. It needs circulation of air to keep it dried out. And convolvulus runners get in between the boards and prise them apart.'

'Is it worth falling out with Mr Skelton over? He isn't a bad neighbour.'

'I never did like him.'

'Yes, I know you didn't.'

A distinct challenge there. All this had been gone into before, but it was giving him time to steel himself and get rid of final inhibitions. She was sipping her coffee, but her eyes met his over the rim of her cup. The cold poker-faced expression she'd been in the habit of turning on him when he said something unpleasant to her mother. Well, he'd see how she stood up to this one.

He waited, for perhaps ten seconds, just long enough to establish an understanding that the subject of Mr Skelton was closed. He wouldn't turn back now, but it wasn't going to be easy. He set down his cup, and only as it clattered a little in the saucer did he realize that his hand was shaking.

'June,' he said, in a voice he tried to make as gentle as possible, 'I have something to tell you.'

'Something important?'

'Yes. I'm thinking of getting married again.'

So, it was out.

She kept on looking at him, but her eyebrows had come down, and he thought she flinched. She gave him a faltering, disbelieving smile. 'You wouldn't joke about a thing like that, would you?'

'Hardly.' The smile, however uncertain, had helped a little, and he managed one in return. It was a matter now of getting around to the point at issue, but he wanted her to make the running, if possible. 'Surprised?'

'Well, only because you sprang it on me.'

'Pleased?'

'Of course I'm pleased, for your sake. You aren't really old.' She was relaxing. Her smile had warmed. 'How long has this been going on? You kept it very dark.'

'Just a few months. She . . .'

'Tell me about her.'

'Well, she's about my own age. She's a retired school teacher, and has a lot of good tastes, books, theatre, garden. She does some work for Red Cross and the Adult Education Council. And I believe . . .'

'A widow?'

'Yes, for a long time. Her husband died in the war. She —'

'Family?'

'Two daughters and a son. But they're all well up, of course, and only the son is in Victoria. He's married, and she lives with him. There are two grandchildren.'

'What is she like, to look at?'

A woman's question. The interrogation was taking place quite amiably. She hadn't taken her eyes off him for a second, but there was still puzzlement in them, as if she hadn't yet accepted that what he was telling her was indeed true, and not just a crude joke.

'I think she's rather nice looking. For her age, anyway. None of us are beauties once we get into the late fifties. And she does enjoy excellent health. But you'll meet her soon. I'll probably bring her to dinner one night next week.'

'What's her name?'

He was prepared for that. 'I want to leave that one until I introduce you,' he smiled. 'You know how it is with some people. They have two names, one for . . .'

'Yes, I understand that. It isn't important.'

A short silence fell. When she did speak again he knew they were going to reach the crisis sooner than he'd anticipated, sooner than he really wanted to.

'You say she lives with her son. She doesn't have her own home?'

'No, not really. Her son continued to live with her after his marriage. It worked so well that it became a settled arrangement. I believe she's already made over the deeds of the house to him. That's a good sign, you know. She must be an easy woman to live with. Not many women can live peaceably under the same roof as a daughter-in-law.'

'Nor a step-daughter! She will be coming to live here?'

'Well, obviously. But that shouldn't present any problems. Apparently her daughter-in-law ...'

'That's different. There's a son and grandchildren as well. Perhaps she'll find *me* difficult ... as you do!'

The last bit was too deliberate for him to ignore the dry smile that went with it. He fidgeted in his chair as if about to get up, settled down again, and pushed away his cup and saucer. 'Look, June, don't let's start going into that. You'll be reminding me next that I didn't find your mother easy to get along with ...'

'Well, you didn't, did you? Anyway, there is no problem. Aunt Helen still has my room, just as I left it. She'll be quite happy to have me back.' As if to spare him the embarrassment of labouring the point any further, she went on quickly. 'When is the wedding?'

'Nothing is finally decided yet.' He stopped himself just in time from telling her that there was no need to rush her fences. Better to have done with it now, once and for all. 'We'll see how things work out, but, as you say, Aunt Helen does simplify matters.'

She got to her feet and picked up her cup and saucer, but halfway to the sink she turned and fixed him with a stare the cold penetration of which shocked him.

'Look, Dad, you don't have to beat about the bush. What you're telling me is that you're going to get married again soon, that your new wife will be moving in here, and that I must move out. That's how it is, isn't it?'

'June ...'

'You can put your mind at rest. Whether there's another woman or not, I would be going. And whether there's another woman or not, you don't want me to stay. I'm going to live with Aunt Helen.'

Nothing more was said. Torn with doubts about how he had

handled the situation, and shaking from tension, he sat in silence while she cleared the table, washed and put away the cups and saucers, and wiped down the draining board. There was a deliberation about her movements which worried him, but each time he got a glimpse of her face it told him nothing.

'June . . .' he began again as she hung up the tea-towel and walked towards the door, but she went out as if she hadn't heard him.

He remained seated, listening to the movements in her room at the far end of the passage. They went on for a long time, perhaps twenty minutes, rustlings, the pulling open and pushing in of dressing-table drawers, the creaking of that noisy door of her wardrobe, and it dawned on him that she was going now. Once she went into the lounge to make a telephone call, a very brief one. To order a taxi?

A little later she opened the front door and set something down outside on the verandah. A suitcase?

He still had not moved when she appeared again in the kitchen. She was wearing hat and overcoat, and had her violin case under her arm. 'I just want to say goodbye, Dad,' she said in a tired voice. 'I'm going now.'

He got up to go to her without any clear idea of what he wanted to say, but she motioned him to keep still.

'It's what you wanted, isn't it? I hope you'll be all right.'

'June, please . . .'

At the doorway she turned and looked back at him. 'She won't be there, you know,' she said, as if stating something of which he should already be well aware.

'She won't be there?'

'Your Alice. Tomorrow.' She smiled. A long, mocking, malicious smile such as he had never seen on her face before. 'Don't fool yourself; she won't be there.'

She went out then, closing the door quietly behind her. And as he heard her footfalls recede down the passage, and the opening and closing of that other door, the last door, the meaning of that smile fell on him like a clap of thunder, like a ton of bricks, and he knew that he really was alone, alone, alone.

STORIES OF THE WATERFRONT
John Morrison

'John was born in England, but no native-born
reflects the spirit of Australia more than he does. This
country, of which he is so much a part, has absorbed
and recreated him as one of its most significant
voices.'

Alan Marshall

These imaginative and sensitive stories begin at a time
when wharfies turned up at the docks to be picked
like cattle, and often went home without work or pay.
The events range from personal dilemmas like
sharing lottery winnings to coping with pig-headed
bosses and the tragedy of sudden death.

John Morrison worked for ten years on the
Melbourne waterfront in the 1930s and '40s. His
Stories of the Waterfront, collected here for the first
time, give a realistic yet unusually sympathetic
account of the much-maligned wharfie.

Set in the years after the turbulent times depicted in
the television film, *Waterfront*, the book provides a
narrative of improvement of conditions and the
constant struggle to maintain them by a group of
warm and down-to-earth people.